A Win - Win

The Story That Follows
A Miracle or Two for Christmas

Trish Titus

A Win – Win

The Story That Follows A Miracle or Two for Christmas

Write to the author at <u>TrishTitus.dyd@gmail.com</u>

Book Cover:
>Evening Colors, John Sfondilias/Dreamstime.com
>Late Evening from Kerry Park, Chris Labasco/Dreamstime.com (Insert back cover)

Editing: PWA-GR

Proofreading: Proofreading Pamela

Graphic Designer: Rebecca Shaw, BrockleyDesigns.com

Library of Congress Control Number: 2021925337

ISBN (978-1-7323352-7-1) (Paperback)
ISBN (978-1-7323352-8-8) (EBook-EPUB)
ISBN (978-1-7323552-9-5) (EBook–Mobi)

Also written by Trish Titus

A Miracle or Two for Christmas
Published December 2019
TrishTitus.dyd@gmail.com

DELILAH and Others Like Her
Published March 2019
Tmtpetstories18@gmail.com

Table of Contents

Chapter 1

Christmas Morning

Jason woke up early, with an enormous smile as he turned to face her. He had received the best and most beautiful gift last night. He learned he was going to be a dad, and his heart was bubbling over with so much love and joy at having this beautiful woman in his life. And now his second miracle had moved and was safe in its mommy's tummy. In June, there would be another celebration, if all went well. Everything had aligned and come full circle. For the first time in a long time, Jason was going to enjoy Christmas morning. He loved it, experiencing this with his new wife, Talia.

As it got lighter outside Jason looked at his wedding ring, and felt such peace. Picking her left hand up, he felt and looked at her wedding rings, feeling like the luckiest man alive. Bringing her hand to his lips, he kissed it and then laid it down.

Jason slid his hand under the sheets, resting it on top of her stomach, feeling the warmth of her skin. He knew that tiny baby bump would grow, and he had fun imagining what it would look like under her clothes. Of course, he also didn't have to worry about his body changing and the different emotions going through pregnancy. His mind wandered, and he hadn't felt Talia place her hand on top of his. She looked at him with a loving smile.

"Merry Christmas, my love," Jason said as he focused on her eyes and then her lips, kissing her.

Talia echoed back softly with, "Merry Christmas, my love." Looking into his eyes, she took a moment and then said, "I wonder if Santa Claus has been here." She grinned at him with eyes wide like a child and then giggled. "Should we go see?"

"I received the most precious Christmas gift last night that you could have ever given me, telling me that our baby moved and that I'm going to be a dad," as he stroked her stomach, giving her another kiss. Too many Christmases had come and gone because of his work as a paramedic/firefighter. He had worked those holidays or was on call so the married guys could spend it with their families. The station would be decorated, and the catering company would carry in the food. He'd heard from the married ones about how excited their children were on Christmas morning, opening presents, and all the festivities and food.

There were moments he had felt envious of them having that Christmas Eve and Christmas Day. His family would celebrate the week before or well after Christmas had passed. Before his grandfather died, his parents and grandparents would have a nice big dinner at home, and sometimes they would go out to eat at a charming restaurant. After his grandfather passed, they would always head over to Grandma Jean Porter's, enjoying dinner and conversation. Gift-giving was minimal. Everyone had what they needed. Grandma Jean watched Jason over the years and could see the sadness and longing in his eyes, wanting to share that special holiday as well as his life with someone he has loved for a long time.

Talia kissed him back, saying, "I think there is something special you might do for our little one, even before he or she gets here."

He looked at her with raised eyebrows, wondering what she meant by that. "Something special I might do."

"Yup. I think you would be very good at it." She could see the curiosity in his eyes. They agreed not to do anything too big for each other, to save money for a late honeymoon and hopefully return overseas before the baby was born.

"OK then, why don't we see if Santa stopped by," Jason said, smiling at her. Walking toward the Christmas tree, they could smell the scent of the evergreen and bayberry candles that sat on the coffee table, and then looked at each other after seeing a few other gifts sitting around the tree, trying to figure out when the other might have placed them there. "So, we don't have a chimney; I wonder how Santa snuck in?" He looked at Talia, who grinned and shrugged her shoulders.

They sat down on the floor, looking at one another like, *who's going to start.* Jason reached over for a present and handed it to Talia, saying, "I knew what I wanted to give you, but I needed a little help picking some things out." Jason watched as she unwrapped her gift. The smile on her face told him she loved it. It was a set of 48 designer colored pencils. The ones she'd been using were wearing down, and she didn't have this many. She opened the container and looked at all the beautiful colors. Then lifted the top tray to see the second set of pencils underneath. She looked at him, leaned over, and kissed him, telling him thank you and that she loved them.

He handed her a smaller, elongated present. In the small box were three very nice graphite pencils, again, giving him that same beautiful smile. She hadn't gotten around to buying any new ones, and figured she'd make do with what she had. Jason was going to give her another gift, but she beat him to it. Talia reached over for two medium-sized presents and handed the first one to him.

"I had a little help picking some pieces out," she said.

Jason carefully unwrapped the box and opened it. With a grin on his face, he took out a beautiful woodcarver's mallet. He gripped the handle, tapping it in his other hand. "Thank you. I think I know where this might be going," he smiled. Talia handed him the next gift. Seeing two Bevel Edge Chisels by Two Cherries (German made), he knew these were well-crafted. And he also saw two sanding pads. He definitely liked where this was heading, and some ideas already popped into his head.

"Me next," Jason said, as he reached around the back of the tree bringing out a larger, flatter present, giving it to Talia. She was pretty sure she knew what it was. She took the ribbon and paper off, and there were two different-sized sketch pads. One of the sketch pads had an envelope paper-clipped to it. Talia looked at him, tilting her head, and then opened the envelope, pulling out a sturdy stock card with a picture of an adjustable dressmaker's dummy. With a questioning glance, "Jason, I don't understand."

"I learned these are a 'must-have' item when a designer needs to see how things will look on a human. And I found out that you could use another 'body' in your shop, one where if you stick them with pins, they don't shriek." He grinned at her. "So, when you head to your shop next time, you'll find this greeting you at the door or looking at you through the window." Talia knew they could be expensive.

"Thank you. You didn't have to do that." It took very little to make her happy. She leaned over, taking Jason's face in her hands, and kissed him.

"I wanted to. You've brought me so much joy, and I love watching you work on your designs. So, maybe next time I stop in, you'll have some amazing piece of clothing on this non-human," he said, looking into her eyes and watching her smile.

Talia leaned back and pulled a larger box from behind the tree, sliding it toward him. This one he decided to just rip the paper off, which he had never done before. Jason learned to be careful when opening presents at a young age, as you could reuse the paper. He had a big smile on his face, feeling like a kid. Opening the top of the box and then getting on his knees, Jason pulled out a red and black Craftsman Versastack System Tool Box. He could feel the weight of it and whatever was inside, making it heavier. After opening it up, he found a 10-piece woodworker's spring clamp set and a few other tools.

"Someone else wanted you to have a few starter items of your own. The toolbox and clamps are from me. The other items are from—" Talia wasn't able to finish her sentence.

"Jéan-Paul," Jason said with a big grin. She nodded.

"He wanted you to have a few other things, and then you could add to your tools. Perhaps a baby project might be on your list?" she asked with a smile.

"Thank you, my love. Is that what you would like me to do?" Although he was a step ahead of her with a design for a crib.

Talia looked at him. "I know we don't have any room here, but hopefully, we'll find a place you can call your own. I remember you sanding the bench at the cabin." She had learned that besides hiking, woodworking was something else he loved. He scooted closer to Talia, giving her a hug, and a kiss. They each leaned around their side of the tree, bringing around another gift and giving it to the other. They were the same size, and both started laughing after unwrapping them. They now had two new beautiful photo albums to fill with pictures from last September and other events.

Jason thought, *This is how Christmas should look and feel, being with the one I love so much. I get to share a home with her and see all the decorations, the white lights around the windows, the Christmas tree with its colored lights and ornaments, and the gifts, plus the wonderful smells of baked goods, and candles.*

Several small presents were still under the tree, but those were for the rest of the family when they got together later for Christmas dinner. They would head over to Grandma Jean's, where Jason's parents, Mary Ann and Jeff, would arrive. And Talia's mom, Elizabeth Rose, was also invited. Talia's brother, Kurt, would spend Christmas Day with his sweetheart, Caren, and her family up North.

Jason stood up, pulling Talia to her feet, giving her a hug and a long kiss. "Thank you for making this the best Christmas I've had in a very long time," he said.

Chapter 2

Christmas Day with both families was so much better with Talia by his side. They enjoyed good food, holiday music, and engaging conversation about the new year and what everybody wished to do. Of course, another major topic was the impending birth, even though it was still six months away. Talia's next doctor's appointment would be toward the end of January, unless any other medical changes occurred sooner.

Jason decided to educate himself better about what Talia was and would be going through, and would attend as many birth classes as he could. He had training as a paramedic but wanted to be prepared, especially when planning a late honeymoon. He felt better about traveling overseas, knowing his good friend, and mentor, Dr. Jéan-Paul Lemaitre, would be there to help, just in case.

Jéan-Paul helped with the work abroad program when the paramedic/firefighters had gone over for their week or two in Germany, since he also speaks German and Italian.

☓

The next couple of weeks after New Year's Day were busy for Jason's fire station. Several small house fires due to neglect in watering Christmas trees, which people hadn't wanted to let go of yet, and some small grease fires. Even though it's not Spring yet, there were several car accidents because people weren't slowing down when driving on slick roads. There were a few heavy snows that blanketed everything, so other injuries occurred because of shoveling snow, strokes, and heart attacks. For Talia, some good things were in the works for her small business; she just didn't know it yet.

It was Tuesday, January 14th, and along with the other mail was a large envelope. It caught Chloe's attention, and she wanted to show Jana. Both girls knew from past experience that Talia still felt she wasn't good enough yet for something like this, even though she has gained several new clients that have been more than happy with her designs. Since Talia's car accident, she has spent more time at home working than going to her office since she doesn't have a newer car yet. So, between the girls and Jason, they would get her to work and then bring her home. Opening the envelope, Chloe showed the contents to Jana.

"When are you going to show Talia this? The deadline is Friday," Jana said.

Chloe replied, "I know. I know she can do this. You and I have seen the designs out there by other designers, and I'm not impressed. There's a website here on the back side. We need to go online and check out all the information so we show her this."

"When WE show her this?" Jana asked, looking at Chloe with a raised eyebrow. "I think this is something you should handle. You're so much closer to her than I am. I mean, you two went through college together. You just know her better."

"Maybe. I can hear her tell me with a big fat, NO, that she wouldn't be interested. Doesn't think she'd have a chance against all those other designers. So maybe I need to show this to Jason first, explain this to him, and he can help convince her to do this if she won't listen to me," Chloe said, looking at Jana.

"Well, if you're going to show Jason, then we'd better get the information gathered. Oh, and maybe have him stop by here, like tomorrow, since time is running out," Jana replied.

"Then I better call him and see if he can stop by tomorrow without Talia knowing. She'll be coming on Thursday afternoon. I'll call the fire department since I don't have his cell phone number."

◌

"Hello, is Jason Porter there, please?" Chloe asked, then waited for him to come to the phone.

"Hello, this is Jason Porter."

"Hi, Jason, it's Chloe Chang."

"Chloe, how are you doing? What's going on?"

"I wondered if you might have some time tomorrow to stop by the shop after you get off work. There's something I want to run by you."

"Me? If it has to do with the shop, why not talk with Talia? She's coming on Thursday. I don't know anything about the design business, except what I see her working on at home."

"Well, this is something that could easily change things for her in a big way. But I have a feeling she'll tell me no when I show her. I'd like to have you in my corner to help me get her to agree with this," Chloe said, while looking at Jana.

"Chloe, I don't understand. It can't be that awful that she would say no to something that would help her and the shop."

"I think I would feel better running this by you. I've gone over it with Jana, and she agrees with me in getting your thoughts. What do you say?"

Jason sighed, and then said, "OK. I don't get off until three-thirty. We have a meeting at the station, a new volunteer firefighter is coming in. I can probably stop by after that, which will be after four-fifteen. I'm supposed to pick up Talia around five for dinner."

"That works for us; it won't take that long, and thank you, Jason. We'll see you tomorrow. And remember, not a word to Talia."

ℬ   ℭ

The time was edging closer to four-fifteen. Chloe and Jana spoke earlier that morning with Talia about her first design. She was getting close to finishing it and would bring it when she came. They were pretty sure that Jason had said nothing to Talia, otherwise she would have been quite vocal about it, wanting to know what was going on.

Jana tapped Chloe on the shoulder and pointed toward the window. They saw Jason park and then head their way. It was show time for Chloe. She felt nervous, but hopeful that he was on their side in telling his wife that this is a good thing, that she's a very talented designer, and to remember what her grandfather told her. Chloe took a slow, deep breath and glanced over her shoulder, seeing Jana standing off to the side. The front door opened, and Jason walked in toward the counter, looking at both girls.

"Good afternoon, ladies. OK, so I'm here. Why all the secrecy in not talking with Talia?"

Jana moved and now stood beside Chloe who looked at Jason. Turning the brochure and entrant form around for him to see and then said, "A similar brochure came in the mail the last two years, and Talia dumped them in the trash. I don't want her to pass up another opportunity to show case herself and what she's capable of doing. She's talented and has an eye for design. You've seen what she can do."

"I know. So, talk to me." Jason continued looking at the material in front of him.

"We, or I, plan on showing this to Talia tomorrow when she comes in. I know she'll throw it in the trash. She won't even look at it. I want your help to convince her she is good enough to show her designs at this year's fashion show," Chloe looked at Jason.

"So, when is the deadline for this show?"

Chloe looked at Jana, then back to Jason. "Deadline is this Friday at midnight. We just got this in the mail. They don't like to give anyone too much time to think about it. You're either in or not, depending on how good you think or feel you are and want to show what you're made of as a fashion designer."

"What do you want me to do here, Chloe?" raising his eyebrows.

"Well, Talia's coming in tomorrow afternoon to bring in her first design. And I was hoping you might find your way to the shop and be here when I show this to her so that she won't toss it," looking at Jason apologetically.

Jason continued to look at the brochure and then at both girls with a half-smile. "Alright, I'll see what I can do about stopping by. I also think this would be a great opportunity for my lovely wife to put herself out there. But, right now, I have a dinner date with her, and I best get moving."

☙

Thursday arrived. Talia called the girls and said she'd be late. Jason would pick her up after getting off work and take her to the fire station first. He was going to introduce her to the new volunteer firefighter starting next week, and some of the other wives were going to be there as well.

As they headed into the fire station, they heard voices and laughter. Walking into the kitchen, the voices became a little softer. Nadine Peters, wife of Jim Peters, and Ally Daily, wife of Paul Daily, both stood up and walked over to Talia, hugging her.

Nadine piped up with, "*Ciao.*"

Talia repeated it back to her, "*Ciao.*"

Jim looked at Jason, saying, "She's been practicing ever since the two of them had that little intervention. She's used a few simple phrases on me, and I have no idea what she's saying."

"*Non è colpa nostra,*" Talia said.

"Are you going to translate this time?" Jason saw Cole look at him, then at Talia.

"I simply said, 'it's not our fault,'" she said with a half-grin.

Jason introduced Talia to Cole. "Sweetheart, I'd like you to meet our new volunteer firefighter, Cole Thomas. Cole, this is my wife, Talia."

"Cole, it's nice to meet you," She reached out to shake his hand.

"It's nice to meet you, Mrs. Porter. So you speak Italian?"

"Yes, I do. And, I've hyphenated my last name, it's Rose-Porter. So, Cole, where did you move from?"

"As I was telling the others, I've just moved from Marietta, Ohio."

"Well, welcome to Iowa. I'm sure, over time, we'll all get to know you better."

"No goodies this time, Talia?" Paul asked.

"No. I think that's something we wives are going to have to discuss, bringing in food or any other goodies like the German's wives," Talia said, looking at Paul, then Jason.

Cole asked, "Your wives bring in food?"

"It's kind of a long story. We'll fill you in later," Jason said.

"I have to get going to my shop. I have a design to drop off," Talia said, looking at Nadine and Ally.

"How exciting," Nadine said.

"Yes. So, I best get this one to my shop." She turned toward Cole saying, "We'll have a get-together soon, and I hope you'll join us. And please, call me Talia." He smiled at her, and then she turned and headed out the kitchen door with Jason following.

Chapter 3

Arriving at the shop, Jason parked his jeep, coming around to open Talia's door and the back door, taking out her canvas bag. Talia took it from him, leaned up for a kiss, then turned and walked to her shop's front door. She saw Jason's reflection in the shop window and saw that he was following her. She turned with a smile and said, "Thank you for bringing me and making sure I'm safe. I love you, but I think I can get inside with no help."

"Oh, I know you can. But I'm going in with you," Jason said, looking at her with a slight grin.

Both Chloe and Jana came from the back room and looked at Talia and Jason. Jana perked up with, "Hi, Talia. Hi, Jason." Jason nodded his head.

"Hi, Jana," Talia said, laying the canvas bag down on the counter, then saying, "Hi, Chloe." She unzipped it as she was looking at the mail on the counter. Taking out the first design, she handed it to Jana and then reached over, sliding the mail closer to her. A few pieces went in the trash. Talia came to the larger envelope looking at its front and saw that it was already open. She looked at Chloe, picked up the envelope, and started to drop it in the trash.

Remembering what Chloe told him, Jason stepped quickly behind her, taking her hand before she released it in the garbage can. She turned to look at him with a glare, then turned and looked at Chloe and Jana, who were watching them. "What's going on here?"

Chloe took a step closer to the counter, and before she could say anything, Jason said to his wife, "Why don't you open the envelope and see what's inside." He then took the envelope from her, looking at the return address on the outside. "Meydenbauer Convention Center, Bellevue, Washington. So, what exactly is this? Can I see?"

"If you don't mind, I don't need to look at the contents. I know what's inside, and I'm not entering," she responded quickly, trying to take the envelope from her husband's hands.

Moving his hand, he looked her square in the eye. "Why don't you want to enter?"

Talia turned to look at the girls, now feeling on the defense and with a raised voice. "I asked before, what's going on?"

Chloe spoke up. "It came in the mail on Tuesday. Do you remember when these came before, taking one look and dumping them? You wouldn't even open them. Talia, you are so talented. I think this would be an amazing opportunity for you to show people how good you are."

"I don't want to talk about it," Talia said. She turned back to Jason. "You knew about this and said nothing to me."

"The girls asked me to stop by yesterday, showing this to me. Chloe explained what happened before, that you wouldn't even look at them." Talia didn't say anything. "What are you afraid of?" Jason asked, softly.

"I'm not afraid," Talia said. She didn't want to admit that she was scared and still felt she wasn't good enough for something like this.

"You're a creative designer. I've seen you think outside the box. Where did the ideas come from for some of your winter designs?" Jason asked. "I watched you work on this first design. You were so happy, sketching away." He took hold of her shoulders, looking into her eyes, "I love you. Why not show off your talent," he stated.

Chloe opened the envelope, taking out the brochure and other information. Talia looked at her, then picked up her canvas bag and headed toward the door, not saying a word. Chloe and Jana look at Jason with sad faces. "Never give up, girls."

"The deadline is midnight tomorrow, Jason," Chloe said softly. "She's going to put up a wall here. I feel she's missing out and being stubborn about it. I truly think she could place in the top five."

"I see how important this is, and the boost it could give her. Give me some time," he said and headed toward the door. The girls just looked at one another, not saying a word.

The ride home was quiet. Once home, Talia hung up her coat and walked over to her draft table. Jason hung his coat up and went to change out of his uniform. After coming out of the bedroom, he looked across the room and watched Talia. He wondered what was going through her mind, and wanted to get to the bottom of it and understand why she didn't want to enter the contest.

"Could we finish the conversation from earlier, please?" Talia stopped and looked at him; it was not a happy face. She didn't say a word. "Please talk to me. I want to understand why you don't want to enter the contest."

She laid down her pencil and sat back in her draft chair, looking at the rough design in front of her. Jason walked toward her and waited for her to respond. Talia turned, and he saw the sadness in her eyes. After a moment, she said, "There's still this tiny little part of me that doubts myself, that I'm still not good enough. And that's because of my former employer's voice and his cohorts, which replays itself over and over. They would remind us young designers that we would never be good enough. Most of us will just get by with mediocre designs."

"You remember on the train when I asked you what made you want to go into fashion design?" taking her back to that moment. "I want you to remember what your grandfather told you. He believed in you with all of his heart. I think he would look you in the eye and tell you to go for it. He said for you to design your dream. And I'm asking you now, what are you waiting for?"

Jason moved closer and hugged her. "You deserve this just as much as any designer. I want to be there with you. This is a journey you need to continue for yourself. Your grandfather believed in you, and I believe in you. I'm going to fix dinner while you work. Think about what I said. I love you with all my heart. And then, tomorrow, I think you need to fill out that application and submit it. What's the worst that can happen? You deserve this chance, and I want you to go for it, OK?"

軙   軃

After dinner, Talia said little, but worked on her design. She knew Jason was right as she grinned to herself, that her grandfather would have told her to go for it. She could see his face clear as day, with an eyebrow raised and the corner of his lip turned up, looking at her in a loving but stern fashion. Maybe it was seeing his face that gave her the push she needed. He had always supported, loved, and believed in her.

Looking out the window, she thought she better not let this opportunity slip through her fingers, again. *It wouldn't hurt to fill out the entry form. I have nothing to lose, but maybe some things to gain, like confidence and courage. And if nothing else, it would be a lovely, long weekend getaway with the love of my life.* She just needed to take that leap of faith, do it, and enjoy.

Jason watched her work while also trying to read, but it wasn't working. He laid his book down, picked up the digital picture frame, and started going through all the photos they had taken during their time in Europe. These included him proposing to her on the Rhine River and their winter wedding at the Des Moines Botanical Garden just before Christmas.

He forgot about the photos he'd taken in Germany during his time there working with the German paramedics and firefighters, and wanted to add those. Picking up his cell phone and the cord to the digital frame, he loaded them. He hadn't gotten around to showing Talia, because he forgot, and wanted to share them, so why not now?

"My love, would you like to take a break?"

She stopped what she was doing and turned to look at him sitting on the sofa as he looked back at her with those puppy dog eyes. *How can a grown man have such beautiful eyes, and how can I say no.* "I guess I could. My concentration at the moment is lacking." Sitting down next to him, she kissed him, and he put his arm around her, letting her hold the device as he told her what he and Jim and Paul did.

The three Americans went out on many calls with their German comrades, but Jason still got some picture-taking done, including the guys they worked with at the fire station, the Porsche Museum, and sometimes Jéan-Paul. He wanted to share these with her because it was important to him.

After finishing up with the photos, Talia leaned back on Jason's shoulder. A moment or two passed, and she said, "I'm ready to go back. There are so many things I still want to see and do with you before this baby comes." Turning her head toward Jason, she looked into his eyes. He then kissed her forehead.

"I know. I want the same. It seemed magical, being there and seeing things through your eyes. I'd love to show you things I saw in Germany. One day soon, I promise. We'll go back for the honeymoon we didn't take, and maybe go back to the cabin like we said," lightly laying his hand on her stomach, then looking at her soft lips, kissing them.

She returned his kisses. He whispered into her ear and then leaned back, looking at her with a sultry look. Standing up, he took hold of her hands while looking into her eyes, giving her another tender kiss, and led her to the bedroom.

⚜

The sun would be up soon. Thank god it was Friday. It had been a long week as Jason lay there, letting his mind wander. He took a slow, deep breath, thinking about his next night shift, tonight, with Jim and the newest volunteer, Cole. He didn't remember Cole saying whether he ever worked any night shifts back in Ohio. Jason thought back to the last long, three-day shift he worked and how he could have lost his wife-to-be and unborn baby.

Looking toward the window his thoughts went back to the conversation with Talia before dinner. She never answered him, perhaps still having some doubts and afraid to show what she's made of and shine. He so wanted her to fill out that application and get it submitted before midnight tonight. He wanted to be there with her in Seattle to support her and encourage her. And having never seen anything like a fashion show contest, it intrigued him, also wondering how she would handle it. And, since it would be Valentine's weekend, discovering a few extra adventurous things to do with her was going to be fun. He just had to talk her into it.

He also thought about the baby crib he wanted to build, but where? They'd have to have a baby's room. Do they stay put? Should they move? What's that going to involve? And then Cole; Jason was appointed to take him under his wing.

He turned toward his beautiful wife, who's about four months pregnant and very sexy-looking, wanting to hold her close and make love to her again. He turned to draw her close to him, and instead of Talia, it was her pillow. She wasn't sleeping beside him. "Talia?" Jason sat up in bed, seeing a soft light from under the bedroom door. He got up, putting on his light sweats, opened the door, and saw her across the room in her robe, sitting at her drafting table. Jason stood near the kitchen counter, looking at her before walking toward her. "Talia is everything alright?"

She turned to look at him and said, "Yes, I'm fine. I didn't want to wake you. Did I?"

"It's pretty early. Why don't you come back to bed."

"I woke up early because I had to go to the bathroom. My light was still on, and then I had an idea I wanted to get down on paper, so I've been working on it. Why are you up? You don't have to go to work until this afternoon."

Jason grinned at her. "I woke up with thoughts running through my head, and then I turned toward you so I could hold you and make love to you again, but it was your pillow instead. And I called your name, with no response. That's when I got up and saw you sitting at your table." Looking at her, "Maybe now is as good a time as any, while you're working on your design." Again, he went on about why she should enter the contest, telling her it would be an amazing opportunity. That she shouldn't pass this up, and to think about what her grandfather would say to her. All the while, Talia just looked at him, nodding and agreeing. He stopped talking, looked at her, and gave a sigh. "You need to do this for you and your grandfather."

"I'm going to," she said, looking at him and turning back to her table.

"Wait. What? You're going to do what?"

"I'm going to submit my application for the Valentine's contest," Talia said clearly.

"You are?" Jason replied with a tilt of his head.

"Yes. I already decided before you asked me to take that break last night. It was after you pleaded your case as to why I should enter. I knew my grandfather would have wanted me to go for it. He was in my head talking to me."

"Why didn't you tell me this last night?" he asked staring at her.

"I was going to, but I got caught up looking at your photos. And then we were kissing and heading to bed, my favorite, with you," she said, beaming at him.

With a slight frown, "So, you let me ramble on this morning trying to convince you to do this, and you'd already decided you would last night."

"Yup. You were very convincing, too. I would have said yes," she said with a teasing smile.

Jason took hold of her waist, bringing her to him, gently shaking his head and looking into her eyes. "I think we need to go back to bed for a bit. I'd rather be holding you than your pillow."

Chapter 4

It was 9:15 a.m. when they got up a second time. Jason fixed the two of them breakfast. Talia wanted to head to her shop, hand over her design to Jana and see what was needed to enter the contest.

Jason said, "What if we left shortly after eleven, I could go in with you. I wouldn't mind seeing this invitation a bit more closely, and we can take the girls out for lunch. I have to be at work early. Captain wants to have a meeting with Cole, Jim, and me."

"OK, I think that would work. I can get this design finished up before we go. The girls can drive separately and bring me back to the shop and home later, and you can leave when you need to."

He smiled, giving her a kiss. "I'll let you get back to your drawing. I have a project of my own to work on."

❧

Jason changed into his uniform and was ready to go when Talia was. She also changed her clothes, and then she put her design into her black canvas bag. With coats, gloves and scarves on, they headed out the door. There were lots of gray clouds. The weather people said there was a seventy percent chance of snow that evening into tomorrow afternoon. You could feel it and smell it in the air.

Arriving at her shop, they headed inside where it was warm. Jana and Chloe looked up simultaneously when the door opened and then felt the frigid air.

"Morning, girls," Talia said as she unwrapped the scarf from around her collar and then took off her gloves, keeping her coat on. She opened the canvas bag and took out the design, giving it to Jana. Then, Talia walked around the back side of the counter, sifting through the mail. She picked up the envelope from the Meydenbauer Center, seeing that one of the girls put the card stock back inside of it. Jason looked on as both girls watched to see what Talia was going to do with it. She pulled the card out along with the information that was printed off, looking over the invitation.

Seattle's 10th Annual Valentine's
Fashion Designer Show
February 14th - 1:00 P.M.
Meydenbauer Convention Center
Bellevue, Washington

For more details, follow the instructions on the back side of this invitation. To enter, fill out your online application. Submit your entry fee of $125.00 where indicated by January 17th, before midnight. Each fashion designer will go through an interview. Four winners will be awarded cash and other prizes.

Talia turned the card over, and saw the instructions to help fill out the online form that was required. She looked at Jason with a grin, and he grinned back at her giving her a wink. She turned toward the girls who had "deer in the headlights" looks.

"Well, it looks like I'll be entering this contest. And Jason and I would like to take you both to lunch. He has to leave early then, but I'll have to come back with you and get this filled out and submitted this afternoon."

"So you're going to enter?" Chloe asked with a questioning look.

"Yup. And, Chloe, thank you for printing off the information."

Both Chloe and Jana walked up to Talia and hugged her. Chloe walked around and hugged Jason as well.

"Ladies, if you are ready for lunch, we should head out," he said. The girls grabbed their coats, gloves and scarves, and were ready to go. They would follow Jason and Talia to the restaurant.

﬐   ﬑

Even though Jason would have loved to stay longer, it was time for him to leave. He and Jim were meeting with Captain Robins and Cole. They'd be learning more about him and vice versa. It will be the first night shift Cole would be on with the guys, even though he's only a volunteer firefighter, a way to break him in as a fill-in when someone is gone.

After paying the bill, Jason leaned over, kissing Talia. "I'll see you tomorrow afternoon. I'll be eager to hear about this application," looking at her with a big grin.

"I'll fill you in on all the details. Just looking at what is needed, I have my work cut out for me. Tell Jim, Captain Robins, and Cole hello for me."

"I will." Jason put his coat on, and bent down giving Talia another kiss. "I love you." He looked at Chloe and Jana, telling them to have a good afternoon, and then left. It was only another twenty minutes, and the girls headed back to the shop so Talia could get started on the application. There wasn't a lot of time left.

ભ

Jason arrived at the fire station. He didn't see Jim's car yet but saw several of the other guys' vehicles. Then he spotted an unfamiliar truck with Ohio plates on it. Walking inside, Jason saw Mike and David talking with Cole and walked toward them. "Afternoon, Jason," David said.

"Afternoon, David, Mike. Cole, how are you?" Jason asked, reaching out to shake his hand.

"I'm good. Nice to see you again," Cole replied.

It was getting close to two o'clock. The side door opened, and in walked Jim. Then Paul and Ted came walking out from the kitchen, followed by Lonnie and Jackson. Their shift would end around three. Both Lonnie and Jackson were firefighters who were also working towards becoming paramedics.

"Ok, I'm here. Jason, Cole, why don't we head to the captain's office."

Jason knocked on the door before opening it. Captain Robins motioned for them to come in and take a seat at the conference table. Captain started by thanking them for coming in early and getting Cole acquainted with their station rules, and to let Cole know he would be partnered with Jim and Jason. When the captain finished and sat back, he let the three of them talk, getting better acquainted with Cole and his work in Ohio.

"I didn't have a lot of time to talk with you yesterday. What did you do in Ohio?" Jason asked, sitting back in his chair.

"Besides being a volunteer firefighter, I worked in a small travel agency as an agent. It was owned and operated by the Daye family. Mr. D, as he preferred to be called, passed away less than a year ago, and his wife, Emma, didn't want to continue without him. She felt it was best to sell the business and retire. They were both in their early seventies. Neither of their daughters wanted the business. Emma wanted to be closer to one of her daughters in Tennessee, so she moved down there a couple of months ago. She provided me with a very nice severance to keep me going until something else came about."

"So how did you end up coming to Iowa?" Jim asked.

Cole smiled and said, "There were a lot of things that made me decide to move here. As a kid growing up, my family and I went on vacation every year before school started. We traveled to a lot of states. That's how I got the travel bug. Every other year, we headed west, which sometimes took us through some part of Iowa, and there was something about the state as we passed through that felt good, and safe. I liked what I saw, and felt something pulling me here. I can't explain it."

Captain Robins sat listening and watched the interaction between the three men, having a good feeling that they would work well together. They would form a bond of trust and friendship that would stay with them for a long time.

"How long have you been a volunteer firefighter?" Jason asked.

"A little over four years," Cole answered. "If I hadn't volunteered and worked in the travel business, I would have been working with my dad. He'd been an electrician for a very long time. He passed away just over a year ago. Growing up, he had me go along with him on jobs, teaching me the 'ropes' and hoping that I'd take an interest in it, go to school for it, and then join him in his business. But it wasn't what I wanted to do for the rest of my life. I wanted to travel wherever and whenever I could and see what's out there and meet people."

"I'm sorry about your dad," Jason said, and Jim also told him sorry.

"How did he feel about you getting into the travel business?" Jim asked.

"He was not happy about it, didn't think it was a good idea or a way to make money. He called it a 'glamourous' job, and said, 'being an electrician is a better way of earning a salary. It's solid, and people need electricity,'" Cole replied with a grin. "I went to travel agent school to learn everything possible, and there was a lot to learn concerning domestic and international travel. Lots of rules and codes and laws. But I enjoy it, and I'm good at it."

"What about your mom?" Jason asked.

"My mom was a fourth grade schoolteacher. She retired just before my dad passed."

"So, Jason, what do your parents do?" Cole asked, and then he thought, *It's only fair that I also get to interrogate them, like I was once upon a time. Just not as nicely.*

"My mom is a critical care nurse at Mercy Hospital, has been ever since I was young. You'll probably get to meet her at some point. And my dad's been a mason close to twenty-eight years. He was also in the Air Force. They both still do their current jobs. My grandmother, Jean Porter, was a junior high schoolteacher for many years. It looks like we have something in common there," Jason replied.

"Jim, are your parents still living?" Cole asked.

"They are. My mom worked as a server and loved it, and still helps in a pinch for some of the other gals, and my dad's a CPA," Jim replied.

"Any siblings to annoy either of you?" Cole asked.

"No, I'm an only child," Jim answered with a smile.

Jason looked at Cole, and was a little annoyed that he asked, but Cole wouldn't know. "I had a sister, Amy; she was killed when she was five years old."

"I'm sorry," Cole said with a sad look on his face.

"What about you? Someone you could get rough and tumble with?" Jason asked.

Cole thought for a moment before answering. "I have one older brother, Carl, and a younger sister, Lisa; both married with kids." There was a pause before he continued. "We lost my second older brother, Staff Sergeant Jake Thomas, in a roadside bomb two years ago. It was his third tour. Before enlisting in the Army, he worked with my uncle Ryan, a firefighter, as I did. I think it was because of Jake's death that my dad, whose health wasn't the best, deteriorated so rapidly. He became very distraught and heartbroken over Jake's death."

Both Jason and Jim looked at Cole and then at the captain. "Did you know he lost a brother?" Jason asked the captain.

"We spoke briefly about it, kind of like when Jim and I talked about his combat days. It wasn't for me to discuss with anyone," Captain said.

Looking at Jim, Cole asked, "You served?"

"I did, for nearly fifteen years as a sergeant and served several tours, those last five years as an Army medic. I'd seen my fair share, and it was time to take care of my family here at home," Jim said.

"Gentlemen, I think your shift starts in a few minutes. Cole, welcome aboard," Captain said.

Chapter 5

The girls arrived back at the shop, excited for Talia to get the application started. Pulling it up online, Talia said, "Wow, look at this." Chloe and Jana looked on with eyes wide. She started filling out the obvious, her name, the business name, address and so on. And then had Jana pull the photos of the designs she finished before Christmas, showing different views of each of them, the last one almost not getting finished. It was created by someone who did a little designing and sewing. This garment would be a pleasant addition for those in a different age group. Talia helped fine-tune this lovely piece.

It was time to type out the descriptions with the four choices made and who would wear which outfit. Photos were not allowed to be uploaded. Chloe was to check on the hotels that the convention center listed. Once she found them, she bookmarked each, showing the cost, amenities, and location to the convention center. Reservations needed to be made very soon.

Another section said: Please answer the following questions. This is a way for us to get a sense of who you are before we meet.

1. What was your inspiration for your designs?
2. Who helped you with each piece?
3. Why did you pick these four?
4. Where did you go to school for fashion design, and why?
5. Anyone else in your family a designer?

The questions weren't as tough to answer as she first thought. Talia enjoyed the process, and it stirred up good memories. She wondered how the interviews would be set up, if questions were being asked now or if there might be other questions not on the application. She knew nothing about the other designers' work or where they were from or even how many were submitting an application, *So it's anybody's guess,* Talia thought. She hadn't kept up on anyone else, but maybe she should have, and it was too late to think about it now.

The afternoon slipped into evening as Talia completed the entire application. But before uploading it, she wanted the three of them to take a short breather. It was nearing 6:00 p.m. They had eaten nothing since lunch, and they were getting hungry. Talia told the girls she needed to make a phone call, if they could hold on just a few minutes longer, and then they'd go out for a nice meal.

After the phone call, Talia was excited for her to join them in Seattle. It would be an experience, and this fifth person was very excited. Talia said she would give more information soon. So, going over the entire application one last time, she hit the submit button, and off it went. It was about 6:15 p.m. She would check both her email and the website later this evening.

ೂ

Before heading to bed, Talia texted Jason: *The application is completed, uploaded, and I've received confirmation. The next thing will be to make hotel reservations for five of us and purchase airline tickets. I love you.* Talia wanted to wait until Jason got home to reveal who the fifth person would be. She knew he would wonder and surely be thrilled with who would join them on this trip.

Jason didn't respond until a few hours later, knowing she was asleep, but wanted her to receive his text when she woke the next morning: *I'm excited to hear all about it. So, this is a mystery. Who are the five? I love you.*

⁚ ⁜

Late that night, it started snowing heavily. The temperature had fallen, causing overpasses and roads to become slippery. Throughout Jason's overnight shift, he and his two partners received many calls, most all related to auto accidents, but thankfully no serious injuries or deaths. It seemed like they just got back to the station and in their bunks when another call came in, and then out the door they went again.

After getting off work and heading home, Jason was tired. Talia had made a big pot of chili earlier that afternoon, and it was ready to go whenever he got home.

He could smell the chili powder and the tomato juice mixed with the chili beans and hamburger even before he got in the door, making his mouth drool. It's delicious, just as it is, but adding sharp shredded cheese, a dollop of sour cream, and oyster crackers were the best, along with a mug of yummy, smooth hot chocolate. Jason's favorite was Amaretto, and Talia's was Snickerdoodle. Although they were finding that Caramel and Cinnamon were becoming favorites as well.

After changing his clothes, he came out and walked over to Talia, giving her a big hug and a kiss, and patted her stomach.

"I want to hear about this application process, but I'm so hungry. You ready for some chili?" Jason asked.

"I might have a little with you," looking at him sheepishly.

"Just a little? You love chili, unless you've been taking bites here and there. You probably couldn't resist, could you." He commented filling his bowl and smiling at her.

After dinner was over, he helped with the dishes and put things away. "Tell me about this application. Did it take you a long time? What designs did you choose? Who is this fifth person?" His questions came quickly.

Talia smiled at his curiosity. "Well, it wasn't as bad as I thought. There was the basic information, then answering the interview questions. I just wrote from my heart. Then it was choosing which four designs and who would wear them on the runway. That was a bit harder. Two of the designs were ones I sketched out in Europe, and then I thought hard about the third one, which I hope could be a top contender. At first, I didn't want to put it in, but I'd love to see it on someone else. And I'm OK with it. And the fourth one wasn't designed by me, but I helped with the finishing details on it."

Jason wondered and asked. "I remember someone who enjoyed doodling and sewing. Is that fourth design, by chance, Grandma Jean's design?"

Smiling, Talia said, "Yes, it is. I think women in her age range wouldn't mind wearing something like it for a special occasion. It's bold and would be comfortable and has a feeling of grace. Grandma Jean looks wonderful in it. I'm not sure what the judges may think, but I decided it should be entered. And that brings us to who our fifth person is."

He looked at her with uncertainty, and said, "Really? Are you going to talk to her about this? I don't know if she'll agree. Talia, she's in her late eighties, and then to travel to the west coast on an airplane and the time—"

"She already said yes." Jason looked at her in disbelief. "After talking with Chloe and Jana about all the outfits, and then about Grandma Jean's, they thought it was a wonderful idea. They thought their grandmothers would love to wear it. Then I told them I needed to make a call. Jason, she was totally on board with it. She loved it. And I think, given her age, to have something like this take place and then to tell her friends would be so wonderful, to let them all know that they are never too old to shine."

Wrapping his arms around Talia and looking into her eyes, he said, "You continue to amaze me, over and over, with how giving and caring you are of other people."

"She's important to you and me. This will be an amazing experience for her, and I wanted her to share in it." Jason smiled, giving her a long kiss.

⁂☘   ☙

Later that evening, Talia checked for the follow-up email, which gave more information. They would have to tell Jason's parents that Grandma Jean would travel with them and be in the show. He thought they would flip hearing this, especially his mom, but he would call them in the morning. In the meantime, Talia called her mom and brother, Kurt, and told them about the contest. They were super excited for her and supportive. After lunch tomorrow, they would meet the girls at the shop to go over the hotels that Chloe found and get plane reservations made for the five of them.

The email suggested that all contestants and their people arrive well before 4:00 p.m., Wednesday evening, the 12th, at their hotels. Check-in at the convention center would be at 5:00 p.m., a brief gathering at 5:30 p.m. for the contestants, and at 6:00 p.m., a banquet. Coordinators would provide information packets upon sign-in for each contestant for the next two days.

"Talia, what if I were to ask Cole to meet us tomorrow at your shop? He's a travel agent besides a volunteer firefighter."

"Oh, that would be wonderful. Can you call him yet this evening? Do you have his number?" wanting Jason to call right now.

"Yes, I have his number. If he can meet, what's a good time?"

"The girls will be there at 1:00 p.m. Maybe Cole could come at that time." She got up and headed for the bathroom. Jason called Cole to explain about the upcoming trip, and he was more than happy to oblige. He would be there at 1:00 p.m. Talia was ready for bed, tired, but happy with how things were going so far.

Jason was off tomorrow, Sunday. Talia's next doctor's appointment will be that following Tuesday at 4:00 p.m. That worked well for Jason, and he was hoping to attend as many appointments and birth classes as possible. And they'll also have to let her doctor know about the upcoming trip.

☙

Sunday morning, Talia continued working on another design while Jason made the phone call to his parents about the contest and that they would be gone with a few other people. Listening to his mom, Mary Ann asked, "How long will you be gone, and who all will be going to this fashion show? Has Talia ever been through one of these before?"

Jason took a moment to respond. "This is her first contest. And, there will be five of us flying out on the 12th. Talia and I will be coming back the following Tuesday. There's some sightseeing we'd all like to do before three of them fly back on Sunday. You remember Chloe and Jana? They'll be wearing three of Talia's designs, and the fourth design will be worn by, um, Grandma Jean. They're all pretty excited and—" Jason wasn't able to finish his sentence.

"WHAT? What do you mean Grandma Jean will be wearing one of the outfits? You mean to tell me that Grandma Jean is your fifth person? You can't be serious. Jason, what are you guys thinking? How did this come about? She can't be for going out to Seattle with you. And just what is it she's going to be wearing? You know she is in her late eighties. That is crazy—"

"Mom, just hold on a minute. Before Talia's accident, she was helping work on one of the last designs. It was Grandma Jean's. Look, let me put Talia on the phone." Jason walked over to her, handed over his phone, and said, "Please explain to my mom why Grandma Jean is going to Seattle with us."

With that, Jason walked away and let Talia do the talking. He sat down on the sofa, listening to her tell his mom all about the contest, how it came about, and why Grandma Jean was going. And then heard her say goodbye. Looking at her, she turned back to her work. "So, what did she say? How'd she sound to you?"

Talia turned toward Jason and, with a smile, said, "Well, she's still not totally happy about it, but I think she somewhat understands that this is a big deal for Grandma Jean. You heard me tell her we would look out for her, that she's excited about the whole fashion process, getting to wear her outfit on a runway. And we'd all do some sightseeing and that everything would be fine. And that they'll have to pick her up at the airport when she returns."

Chapter 6

The girls arrived at the shop well before 1:00 p.m., with Chloe booting up the computer. She had the information about the hotels laid out so they could all see. Soon, Talia and Jason arrived, as did Cole, and introductions were made. Cole had his laptop set up on the counter so he could go over their flights, but first, it was going to be making hotel reservations. Looking at the short list provided by the Meydenbauer Center, they all decided on the—

Just then, Jason's phone rang. It was Grandma Jean checking in. She wanted to be a part of this meeting and hear what was going on. Jason put her on speakerphone, telling her they were looking over the four hotels listed and that the best one would be the Silver Cloud Inn - Downtown Bellevue. It was half a mile from the convention center, and a shuttle would be provided.

Grandma Jean was getting excited hearing about it and now could hardly wait for the day to arrive. She asked about flights, telling them she had flown only once in her life with William, several years after they were married. But knowing she was with family made it less scary.

Jason told Grandma Jean to hold her horses; Cole was going to tell them about that next. They needed to make the reservations for the hotel first. They would arrive on the 12th, and have four nights, except for Talia and Jason, who would be staying for two more nights. They all agreed to this, and it would also give them a little time to do some sightseeing. Once the reservations were made and confirmed, now it was time for the flights.

Before arriving that morning, Cole had already checked out flights and some things for them to see while in Seattle. It would be on the chilly side with the probability of rain every day. Jason told Cole the evening before that they would need to be at their hotel by 4:00 p.m. That helped Cole with departure times.

He went over the flights he found, giving them a few options departing from Des Moines International Airport (DSM). They agreed on a United Airlines flight leaving at 9:00 a.m. with a stopover in Denver, then arriving at Seattle-Tacoma International Airport (SEA) around 1:15 p.m. They would have plenty of time to get settled in and relax before any evening's events started. Cole would also book all return flights. He made everything easy for them.

Talia looked at Jason with a tilt of her head, and hoped he was thinking what she was thinking for a trip overseas. Cole would be an asset with those travel arrangements. The girls headed out after the final reservations were made. Jason asked Cole if he could stay for just a few minutes.

"Cole, Talia and I are thinking about a return trip overseas for a late honeymoon before this baby is born. Would you be willing to help us when we get ready for that trip?"

"I would be more than happy to help with flights and hotels. Whatever you need, just let me know when you're ready," Cole said. "Where did you two meet?"

"Well, that's kind of a long story. What are you doing this evening?" Talia asked.

"No plans, just thought I'd put something in the microwave and watch some TV."

Jason said with a smile, "No microwave dinner. Why don't you come over to our place and have dinner with us, and we can tell you how we met."

"I'd like that a lot, especially since I don't know anyone here yet."

"How about you come over around 4:30-ish. We can have some dinner and visit," Talia said. Jason gave him their address and said they lived about a mile from the fire station.

ك

With the big pot of chili on the stove warming up, Talia made up a salad while Jason straightened up the living room. He laid out the photo albums and the digital picture frame. With Cole in the travel industry, he'll enjoy these photos. There was a knock at the door. Cole had arrived.

"Cole, are you ready for a big bowl of chili?" Talia asked.

"I could smell it at your door. I haven't had chili in a long time."

"Well, take your coat off and make yourself at home. Here are some bowls, some grated sharp cheddar cheese, sour cream if you like, and oyster crackers. And I've made a salad," Talia said. As they prepared their bowls, they sat down at their new dinette table, a wedding gift from both of their parents and Talia's brother, Kurt.

While they ate, Cole asked the question he'd asked earlier that day. "How and where did the two of you meet?"

Talia and Jason looked at one another with grins. Jason started, "We were quite young when we first met. It was in Switzerland at the Basel Zoo, and it was love at first sight. Well, it was for me."

"Really? OK, you've got me intrigued here," Cole said.

Between Jason and Talia, they told Cole about their family's first meeting and the various vacations they had together.

"So, I feel like there is more here," Cole stated with a grin.

"Well, we'd like to share our photos with you, along with the rest of our story. We thought you'd like to see where our adventure picked up," Talia said.

"Cole, why don't we head to the living room," Jason said. "Being a travel agent, we think you'll enjoy seeing these." Throughout the rest of the evening, Talia and Jason shared their photos and how they got to this point in their lives. Cole thought to himself, *What if I finally had the woman of my dreams come into my life that I could love like this, and be loved back just as I am, past and all. Would I be good enough for her, and could I keep her safe from...* It was time for Cole to head out. It was getting late.

Tuesday afternoon arrived, and it was time to head out for Talia's next doctor appointment. Jason had just gotten off work and was taking her. After checking in at the birth center, they waited their turn before heading into an exam room. Dr. Shera's nurse, Cassie, started the pre-exam on Talia, and then shortly after, Dr. Shera entered the room. She had combined her OB practice with her many years as a midwife making sure her patients had the best of both worlds. "Good afternoon, Talia, Jason. Talia, how have you felt since I last saw you?"

"Well, the nausea has lightened up considerably, and we're preparing healthier meals. I'm taking my prenatal vitamins, so overall, I'm feeling pretty good." Talia had several questions, and Dr. Shera answered them. Jason even had a few of his own. Being a paramedic, he and his partner, Jim, have come across many pregnant females at different stages, and even a different country.

All the paramedics had taken classes or were continuing classes to help with pregnant women. They told Dr. Shera about the upcoming trip to Seattle. She was excited for them and didn't see any reason Talia couldn't fly, although she warned her about going through the body scanners. And if Talia had any other concerns before they left, she wanted to know about them. Talia and Jason agreed. They were given a list for flying during pregnancy.

Dr. Shera then said, "So, we're not done just yet. We're going to check your baby's fundal height."

Thinking she didn't hear right, Talia asked, "You're going to check the what?"

Dr. Shera smiled and said, "Fundal height is another term for measuring a baby's growth and development, and another way to check your pregnancy health." Once the measurement on Talia's abdomen was complete, it was recorded in her file. Then Dr. Shera asked, "OK, who wants to hear the baby's heartbeat?"

"As if you have to ask," Talia said, grinning. Dr. Shera placed the gel on Talia's stomach. This would be the first time they would hear the baby's heartbeat. As they waited for that sound, Dr. Shera moved the wand around. There were various noises, and then it was loud and clear. Talia closed her eyes and just listened as she held Jason's hand.

"What you're hearing are the sound waves of the baby's heartbeat. Baby's heart rate right now is about 115 beats per minute. That heart rate will steadily go up as your baby develops inside of you," Dr. Shera said.

Neither Talia nor Jason said anything. They just listened. It made it even more real that she was carrying a baby inside of her, and that this baby bump would continue to grow. They weren't sure if they wanted to know the sex of the baby at her next appointment. When the exam was over, they headed home with smiles on their faces.

☙

The rest of January came and went. Talia was busy working on another design or two, and Jason was busy at the fire station. Cole was put on the on-call list, getting called in several times, and worked a night shift or two with Jason and Jim.

Now into February, they have ten days to go. They were all feeling pretty excited about it, especially Grandma Jean. She had done nothing fun and rewarding in a very long time. Some of her friends thought she was nuts and too old, while a few others were envious of her that not only did she design an outfit, but she was going to wear it on a runway. Grandma Jean told them she would tell them all about it upon her return. Knowing four other people with cell phones would be with her, lots of photos would be taken on this trip. Who knows if she might get to take any other trips. After all, she was in her late eighties. She told them she wasn't dead yet.

☙

Jason and Cole talked about him filling in with Jim while Jason was gone. Some of the guys teased Jason about going to a Valentine's fashion show. Jason said he was looking forward to it, and would be surrounded by LOTS of women. The look on some of the guys' faces was priceless.

The first Wednesday in February was another overnight shift for Jason, Jim, and Cole. There were a couple calls that evening, and one throughout the middle of the night. The following morning and lunchtime, it was quiet. So this allowed them to wash and take care of their vehicle and restock supplies. It was getting close to quitting time now, less than twenty minutes before the next shift would start. Well, no such luck; a call came in, and the alarm went off. Jason, Jim, and Cole had to respond.

A neighbor had checked on an elderly female and couldn't find her. It was thought the woman walked away from her home and got lost. Unknown to anyone, the woman slipped on some snow and ice and tumbled down a little ditch. The report said she had no coat on, just slacks, a shirt and sweater, and shoes, with a scarf around her neck. The temperature was in the middle thirties. They would have to drive slowly and watch both sides of the road as they neared the address given, which was very near Grandma Jean's house, and for a moment, that worried Jason. They neared the road to turn and go past her house. Jason saw a black SUV in the driveway with US Government plates on.

"Holy crap, what?" Jason said as they passed her house.

"Jason, you OK?" Jim asked as he continued to drive, not knowing it was Jason's Grandmother's house.

Jason replied, "We just went past my grandmother's house, and there was a government vehicle in her driveway. I'm going to stop after work and see what's going on."

An ambulance was dispatched. Finding the woman on the ground, they put a blanket around her, and checked her over. They learned her name and who to call, and then the ambulance took her to the hospital. The three of them returned to the station, with Jason eager to get over to his grandmother's and see what the hell was going on.

Chapter 7

Jason texted Talia, letting her know he wouldn't be home right away and where he would be for a while. He neared the end of the road to turn toward Grandma Jean's house, and he saw the black SUV was still there. Jason hoped he would have the chance to speak with whoever was talking to his grandmother, wanting to know what was going on, and to make sure she was safe and not agreeing to anything.

Walking up to the door, he gave a brief knock and then opened the door. "Grandma Jean," Jason said loudly.

"I'm in here with these nice gentlemen," Grandma Jean called out.

Walking into the living room, the two servicemen stood up. One reached out his hand to Jason, stating his name as Captain Luke Radner of the United States Army. He introduced the other military man as Sergeant Bryan Green.

"I'm Jean Porter's grandson, Jason Porter." Then, looking at her, Jason asked if she was alright.

"Yes, Jason, I'm fine. Don't you ever check your texts?" Grandma Jean asked in a light, scolding tone.

"When did you text me?" Jason asked as he walked toward her, taking out his phone to check. The servicemen looked at her, probably thinking she wouldn't know how to text at her age.

"About an hour ago. It was just after these two showed up. I told them I was going to text you."

"Sorry, I was fairly busy with a call that came in, and we had to drive by the house when I saw their vehicle sitting in the driveway." Jason then sat down near her on the end of the sofa. He gestured for the two servicemen to sit.

"I thought that was your rescue squad going by. I was telling them you're a paramedic and a firefighter, and that I'm very proud of you." She smiled.

"Thank you, Grandma." He looked at the two servicemen and told them, "thank you" for their service. "So, Captain Radner, what brings you to my grandmother's house?"

"It has to do with your grandfather, PFC William Lee Porter. We started to explain to your grandmother, but she stopped us and told us we had to wait until you arrived. She made us sit here and chatted to us, and then told us about an upcoming trip to Seattle and that she gets to wear an outfit she designed in a fashion show." The captain grinned as he spoke, probably thinking this woman was off her rocker, while looking at his comrade.

"So, you've just been sitting here, talking, and waiting for me?" Looking at the two of them, and then he turned and asked, "Grandma, why didn't you call Dad and have him come over?"

"I had my reasons, and I don't get to spend enough time with you. Your dad was in the service, but I had a feeling that this would be good for you." Jason just looked at her, knowing it was best not to say anything.

"Well, we'll be spending time together next week," Jason said, looking at her. Then he looked at the servicemen and said, "And gentlemen, she told you the truth. She designed an outfit for women of her age and will be wearing it as she walks down the runway. My wife is a fashion designer and has a few other outfits for the upcoming show." That seemed to take the smirks off their faces. "So, what is this about my grandfather? Why are you here?"

The captain placed a briefcase on his lap, taking out several documents, and then started to explain as the sergeant handed them to Jean. She gave them to Jason.

Captain Radner said, "Because of clerical errors back in the fifties, many soldiers were not compensated correctly, and there were some who were never awarded medals they earned and deserved. Paperwork got shuffled and misplaced. Between then and now, a lot has gone on, which we know is no excuse. It has taken time tracking down the whereabouts of these veterans, many who have sadly passed away, and William Lee Porter was one of them."

The amount indicated on the form was not huge by any means, but it meant that Grandma Jean would be more than alright for the rest of her life. Her house was paid for. William left her with a comfortable life insurance policy. She had her IPERS and social security, so this military settlement was like the icing on the cake.

Captain Radner asked if Jean would check the box for restitution and then sign and date the original document, which would be filed back at headquarters. She would have a copy for her file, and a short letter from the general apologizing for the Army's failure to act and get this resolved promptly.

Jason read through the form and general's letter, with Jean listening. Once her decision was made, she signed and dated the form, giving it back to the captain.

Captain Radner then opened up his briefcase and pulled out a small black box. Before telling her about it, he had a document and said, "If you would allow me to read this, a report the Army received back in the fifties:

"PFC William L. Porter, of Company K, 10th infantry division, second platoon, arrived in Tokyo, Japan, June 9, 1951. Porter, a rifleman, has been in Korea since June 12, 1951 fighting on the frontline. After being seriously wounded in action by a missile he was transported from the frontline to an aid station and then flown by chopper to the 121st Evac. in Seoul for surgery and then to Tokyo General for recovery.

"He wears the Korean Service Ribbon with one campaign star. Porter is also awarded the Combat Infantryman Badge while serving as an infantryman. This badge, which is only awarded frontline combat infantrymen, distinguishes the actual fighting man from the rear area and service troops in a combat zone. A soldier must be a member of an infantry regiment to be eligible to receive it. He's also received the Purple Heart, and a medal for bravery in action." Captain Radner then handed the document to Jason.

"There is one other badge many soldiers missed receiving, and I present it to you now," he said, giving it to the sergeant to give to Grandma Jean. She opened it, and her eyes misted over, as did Jason's, seeing this beautiful badge. Captain Radner continued, "It is the United Nations Medal, which was to be awarded to military personnel serving in Korea. As you can see, it is of bronze alloy suspended on a ribbon of vertical blue and white stripes. On the other side, it's inscribed with, "For service in Defense of the Principles of the Charter of the United Nations."

After a moment, the captain said, "Our sincere condolences for your loss and apologies that your husband did not receive this when he should have."

Jean just held it close to her heart and let the tears fall. Jason held her other hand in his and was quiet.

"Back in 2007, there were students from this city that had to interview and write a memoir for their Western Civics class about someone they knew that pertained to history. Copies of some of those chosen memoirs were sent to Fort Des Moines Army Base, where they were put in the Army base's library for others to read.

"Over the last five years, the decision was made that these memoirs go back to the soldiers if still alive." Captain Radner then said, "There is one last thing we'd like to give to you. If that soldier had passed on, it was to be given to their next of kin, which, Mrs. Porter, is you." The captain brought out an 8x11-inch sealed envelope and handed it to her.

Jean looked at it with her husband's name on the front: Private First Class William Lee Porter (2007). Jason looked at her, then turned toward the captain and the sergeant. "Gentlemen, thank you for bringing these items to us. It is greatly appreciated." Both the captain and the sergeant stood, as did Jason. They shook hands, and Jason walked them out.

Walking back to the living room, he sat down next to her. Jason waited for her to talk. After a few moments, she looked at him and asked, "Can you come tomorrow and go over this with me? I don't want to this evening. It's been a long afternoon."

"I can come over tomorrow. It's my day off. I'll bring Talia with me. And afterward, we can have lunch?"

"I love Talia. You know that. But I want it to be just you and me." Looking at her only grandson.

He looked back at her with a smile and nodded his head. "Are you going to be OK this evening?"

"Yes. I have Esther and Lily stopping by for tea and munchies. I'll be alright, Jason. I'm grateful you were here with me this afternoon." She paused. "You know how I can sense things?" He smiled, nodding. "With your grandfather, I never could. Not like I have with you and your mom and dad. I didn't know what he would be doing or where he was, if he was gone too long, or if something was about to happen. I couldn't sense or feel anything when he was in Korea, except being scared for him. It's getting late now, and you need to go home to your beautiful wife."

"When would you like me to come over?"

"Maybe around ten in the morning?"

"I'll be here. Then afterward, we can still have lunch with Talia?" Grandma Jean smiled. Jason stood up and kissed her on the cheek, and then left.

⁗ ⁖

It was almost 10:00 a.m. when Jason arrived at Grandma Jean's. He came through the door, and smelled the coffee and her cinnamon streusel. "Good morning, Grandma," Jason called out.

"Good morning. Come into the dining room." She had laid out some small plates, silverware, coffee cups and napkins. The coffee pot and streusel were sitting there, as well as the envelope that was given to her.

"So did you have a nice evening with Esther and Lily?" Jason asked as he sat down at the table.

"Yes, I did. We chatted and gossiped a bit. I told the girls about our upcoming trip, and my great-grandbaby. Talia's feeling so much better, isn't she, and the baby's heartbeat is strong," Grandma Jean stated.

"She's doing well. I went with her two weeks ago, and everything's looking good. It was the first time we heard the baby's heartbeat. I don't know if I can explain how I felt hearing it, except I felt such joy and relief. I know Talia certainly did. It made it more real that she's carrying my child, and she's showing more. I think she wants to go shop for some maternity clothes this week so she has something to wear in Seattle." Jason smiled.

As Grandma Jean filled his coffee cup and put a big piece of warm streusel on his plate, they chatted about the upcoming trip. Jason and Talia would pick her up early and head to the airport next Wednesday. Chloe and Jana would meet them at the airport so they'd all be together. Grandma Jean then became quiet, laying her fork across her plate. She looked over at the envelope and then at Jason, and he watched her.

He'd taken another sip of coffee, set his cup down, and asked, "Grandma, are you OK?"

Nodding, she picked up a letter opener. The document was stapled in the upper left-hand corner. Looking at the top sheet of paper, there it was: "Memoirs from Korea" by Emma M. Tilley, Western Civ. 6, dated November 20, 2007.

"I vaguely remember this young schoolgirl. Her family used to live not too far away. She would stop by periodically and chat with us, but your grandfather would tease her. She was a wonderful young girl, and bright. I don't know if they still live in the area or if they moved. I think I remember getting a condolence card from them when Bill died. You know how my eyes get tired. Jason, I want you to read this to me, please," she said, handing it to him. He moved his plate aside.

After looking at the front, Jason asked, "Are you ready?" Grandma Jean nodded. "If there are photos, I'll show you." And so he began reading.

Memoirs from Korea

Emma M. Tilley
Western Civ. 6
November 20, 2007

Saturday, December 16, 1950

Today I received my draft notice stating that I had "volunteered" for the Army. The first thing that ran through my mind was, "oh, shit!" I can't say that I was surprised; part of me knew it was coming, but most of me hoped it wouldn't. To say I'm not scared would be a lie. I'm terrified.

Tuesday, January 9, 1951

At 9:00 a.m. this morning, I was waiting for the train at the depot with my girlfriend, Jean. I couldn't help but wonder aloud how military life would be. She said if this was the last time she was going to be able to talk to me face-to-face for a while, then there was no way we were going to talk about the military. I didn't bring up the subject again; I didn't want to leave her angry. Come to think of it, I didn't want to leave at all.

At 9:45 a.m., I was able to board the train. I said goodbye to Jean, that I loved her and told her I would write soon. At 10:00 a.m., the train started to move out, and I was on my way to Fort Riley, Kansas. At about 2:00 p.m. this afternoon, I was inducted into the military. Part of me was proud, the other part was scared to death. Right after the induction, we were split up into platoons. I was placed in Company K, 10th infantry division, second platoon. After we were placed in our groups, we started orientation. Rules and regulations were the basis of it.

Wednesday, January 10, 1951

Basic training started today. We were up at 5:00 a.m., and we had calisthenics first thing. Calisthenics kicked my butt, and the drill sergeants were yelling at us like there was no tomorrow. This lasted for two hours, just a bunch of pointless exercises. But finally, thankfully, it was over, and it was time for breakfast. I can't say I was really hungry. To be honest, I felt a little sick, and the food did nothing for my appetite. But I ate it anyway.

The next two hours, we had a seminar about weapons. I can't say it was the most interesting thing in the world, but it was much better than calisthenics, and definitely more interesting than breakfast. The main weapons we were trained in were .30 caliber rifles, .30 caliber carbines, .45 caliber revolvers, the machine gun and hand grenades.

We got into the hands-on training. This sounds much more fun than it actually is. We learned how to take the machine gun apart, learn the parts, and put it back together. By the time lunch came around, my head was so full of weapon information it felt like there wasn't much room for anything else.

Thursday, February 15, 1951

I've been here in Fort Riley for about six weeks now. In a way, camp is kind of repetitive.

The hands-on seminars are getting more interesting and more precise, and our marches are getting longer. I haven't had time to write because they've been pushing us so hard, and by the time day is done, most of us just want to sleep. On the bright side, there's only ten weeks left of camp, but after that, it's off to the real thing. I can't say that I'm excited.

Saturday, April 28, 1951

Time has gone so fast. In two days, I'll be on the train going home for two weeks, and then I ship out for Japan. It's hard to imagine that I learned so much in such a short amount of time.

Monday, May 20, 1951

I've been on the U.S. Naval Ship James O'Hara for about six days now. We shipped out the 15th, and it's supposed to take us twelve to fourteen days to get to Japan. I've never been much of a water person, so it took me a few days for me to get used to the constant rocking of the ship. I'll just be glad to be on the ground again.

When I first got on the ship, I didn't understand why the tables in the mess hall had rails on the sides. I understand now. You see, when the ship sways from side to side, your tray tends to go with the rocking motion, so you're never quite sure which tray is yours.

A couple of nights ago, I met this fellow named LeRoy. He recognized something I was wearing and asked me about it. I came to find out later that he was from Ida Grove. Ironically, his wife's maiden name is the same as Jean's last name. Talk about your coincidences, but since then, he's been my best friend here.

Tuesday, June 12, 1951

We arrived in Tokyo, Japan today. Most of us GI's were amazed at the bustling city; people everywhere, and most of them were quite friendly. We didn't get to see very much of the city. Once everyone was off  the ship, they loaded us on buses and took us right to the base where we were assigned divisions. They told us we'd be here about a week before we have to get on the ship for Korea.

Wednesday, June 20, 1951

We boarded the ship for Seoul, Korea this morning at about 8:30 a.m. We got to the harbor a little after noon. It was one of the most amazing things I've ever seen. When we arrived in the harbor, there were little Korean kids swimming. When they saw us GIs, they would reach out their hands, hoping for treats.

We didn't stay in Seoul very long. From the ship, we got on a train, which was cattle cart-like and had wooden benches. We were headed toward the 38th Parallel. The train only went part way, where we then got on convoy trucks which brought us here to the base.

Once we got here, they said what they needed, and if you were good at it, you raised your hand. If you were quick enough, you might get to stay behind the front line. I am now a rifleman, assigned to Hill 403.

Tuesday, July 23, 1951

The last couple of weeks have been crazy. During the day, we sit in these fox holes, watching for the enemy. At night, we go back to the base. And when we get back to the foxhole in the morning, we see the enemy's bean cans lying around. It's terrifying to think that they're so close.

A couple of days ago, our C.O. decided to take Hill 403, even though it belonged to the enemy. The tanks were in front, with us riflemen trailing. Thank God the Koreans don't have tanks and that they're scared to death of them.

Wednesday, August 15, 1951

I've been here at Tokyo General Hospital the past couple of weeks, because I was wounded in the leg by a missile. I went from the front line to an aid station, was flown by chopper to the 121st Evac. in Seoul, where they did the main surgery, and then I was sent here.

I've never felt anything more painful in my life. My whole leg felt as if it was on fire, and I thought I was going to die right there.

Monday, September 16, 1951

I'm still here at Tokyo General. I thought I would have been out of here long before now, but I came down with malaria. I have no idea where I got it from; it could be from a million and one different things. All I really remember is that I was shaking so bad that I was shaking the cot. I think they put me on Primaquine, I'm not sure. Between the Primaquine and the malaria, it changed my blood type, and the doctors don't know how or why.

Sunday, September 30, 1951

Recently, the cavalry units all got transferred here to Japan. HQ was undecided whether they wanted to send me back to my original unit or to a new unit. They decided to send me to one of the cavalry units that is newly-stationed here in Japan, since I was already in the cavalry. The first couple of days, we've just been setting up camp, which isn't as easy as it sounds.

Tuesday, November 20, 1951

It started to snow a few days ago, and they get just as much snow here as we do back in Iowa. There's about three and a half feet of snow now.

I'm on the right.

I never thought I would learn to use snowshoes in the Army. Yesterday was our first day of snowshoe training, and we all fell down quite a bit. Today was better, but most of us were still pretty clumsy.

Friday, January 18, 1952

For about the past two months, we've been doing mountain training. Mountain training is different, to say the least, going on marches up and down the mountain in snowshoes.

We also have sled training, and that's with about six or eight of us guys on snowshoes pulling a sled, kind of like a dogsled. We've been pulling supplies and ammo, not to any particular place, it's just training.

I'm pushing the sled

Monday, May 19, 1952

For the past two months, we've been doing tank and weasel training off and on. I don't have much to do with the tanks; I drive a weasel, which is kind of like a mini tank except it's less intimidating and

is amphibious. The weasel, like the tank, is on treads, which makes it easy to maneuver on this terrain.

Tuesday, July 22, 1952

Photo lightened for you, we were in total darkness

Last month, we started blackout training. I don't think I've ever done anything that hard. We followed one vehicle in a line, in the pitch blackness, and all you could see of the vehicle in front of you were the tail lights. They had a special type of tail light; instead of being normal sized, they were made to look like cat eyes in the dark.

This month, we also started ship climbing. This is another thing I never thought I would learn to do in the Army. We started out taking Higgins boats out to a ship. The ship had rope ladders hanging down the sides. We had to climb up the ladder from the little boat with our full packs on. Once we got on the ship, we had to cross it and climb down the other side, and back into one of the little boats. A few unlucky fellows, while climbing back down to the boats, got their ankles caught between the side of the ship and the boat.

Wednesday, October 15, 1952

Not much has been going on the last couple of months because discharge notices are starting to come out. While waiting for my name to come up on the list for discharge, my duty was to drive a

jeep and give officers rides to where they wanted to go. Sometimes, I would have to drive for a bug-out and had to drive three or four different officers to the new location.

Monday, December 1, 1952

My name finally came up on the notice board. I'm going home! I am so extremely happy. I'm to leave Japan on the third of this month, and it'll take about 12-14 days to get back to the States.

Saturday, December 20, 1952

I was discharged yesterday at the base in Colorado. I was discharged a Private First Class. No more military time or food; back to real food. Ironically, the ship that I came back on was the same ship that I went over on. I'm happy to say that today I am a civilian. By tomorrow, I'll be home with my family.

Works Cited

Porter, William L. Personal Interview. 13, 20 Nov. 2007.

<u>1951 Calendar</u>. 17 Nov. 2007.

<u>1952 Calendar</u>. 17 Nov. 2007.

1951

	January					
S	M	T	W	T	F	S
	1	2	3	4	5	6
7	8	9	10	11	12	13
14	15	16	17	18	19	20
21	22	23	24	25	26	27
28	29	30	31			

	February					
S	M	T	W	T	F	S
				1	2	3
4	5	6	7	8	9	10
11	12	13	14	15	16	17
18	19	20	21	22	23	24
25	26	27	28			

	March					
S	M	T	W	T	F	S
				1	2	3
4	5	6	7	8	9	10
11	12	13	14	15	16	17
18	19	20	21	22	23	24
25	26	27	28	29	30	31

	April					
S	M	T	W	T	F	S
1	2	3	4	5	6	7
8	9	10	11	12	13	14
15	16	17	18	19	20	21
22	23	24	25	26	27	28
29	30					

	May					
S	M	T	W	T	F	S
		1	2	3	4	5
6	7	8	9	10	11	12
13	14	15	16	17	18	19
20	21	22	23	24	25	26
27	28	29	30	31		

	June					
S	M	T	W	T	F	S
					1	2
3	4	5	6	7	8	9
10	11	12	13	14	15	16
17	18	19	20	21	22	23
24	25	26	27	28	29	30

	July					
S	M	T	W	T	F	S
1	2	3	4	5	6	7
8	9	10	11	12	13	14
15	16	17	18	19	20	21
22	23	24	25	26	27	28
29	30	31				

	August					
S	M	T	W	T	F	S
			1	2	3	4
5	6	7	8	9	10	11
12	13	14	15	16	17	18
19	20	21	22	23	24	25
26	27	28	29	30	31	

	September					
S	M	T	W	T	F	S
						1
2	3	4	5	6	7	8
9	10	11	12	13	14	15
16	17	18	19	20	21	22
23	24	25	26	27	28	29
30						

	October					
S	M	T	W	T	F	S
	1	2	3	4	5	6
7	8	9	10	11	12	13
14	15	16	17	18	19	20
21	22	23	24	25	26	27
28	29	30	31			

	November					
S	M	T	W	T	F	S
				1	2	3
4	5	6	7	8	9	10
11	12	13	14	15	16	17
18	19	20	21	22	23	24
25	26	27	28	29	30	

	December					
S	M	T	W	T	F	S
						1
2	3	4	5	6	7	8
9	10	11	12	13	14	15
16	17	18	19	20	21	22
23	24	25	26	27	28	29

1952

January

S	M	T	W	T	F	S
		1	2	3	4	5
6	7	8	9	10	11	12
13	14	15	16	17	18	19
20	21	22	23	24	25	26
27	28	29	30	31		

February

S	M	T	W	T	F	S
					1	2
3	4	5	6	7	8	9
10	11	12	13	14	15	16
17	18	19	20	21	22	23
24	25	26	27	28	29	

March

S	M	T	W	T	F	S
						1
2	3	4	5	6	7	8
9	10	11	12	13	14	15
16	17	18	19	20	21	22
23	24	25	26	27	28	29
30	31					

April

S	M	T	W	T	F	S
		1	2	3	4	5
6	7	8	9	10	11	12
13	14	15	16	17	18	19
20	21	22	23	24	25	26
27	28	29	30			

May

S	M	T	W	T	F	S
				1	2	3
4	5	6	7	8	9	10
11	12	13	14	15	16	17
18	19	20	21	22	23	24
25	26	27	28	29	30	31

June

S	M	T	W	T	F	S
1	2	3	4	5	6	7
8	9	10	11	12	13	14
15	16	17	18	19	20	21
22	23	24	25	26	27	28
29	30					

July

S	M	T	W	T	F	S
		1	2	3	4	5
6	7	8	9	10	11	12
13	14	15	16	17	18	19
20	21	22	23	24	25	26
27	28	29	30	31		

August

S	M	T	W	T	F	S
					1	2
3	4	5	6	7	8	9
10	11	12	13	14	15	16
17	18	19	20	21	22	23
24	25	26	27	28	29	30
31						

September

S	M	T	W	T	F	S
	1	2	3	4	5	6
7	8	9	10	11	12	13
14	15	16	17	18	19	20
21	22	23	24	25	26	27
28	29	30				

October

S	M	T	W	T	F	S
			1	2	3	4
5	6	7	8	9	10	11
12	13	14	15	16	17	18

November

S	M	T	W	T	F	S
						1
2	3	4	5	6	7	8
9	10	11	12	13	14	15

December

S	M	T	W	T	F	S
	1	2	3	4	5	6
7	8	9	10	11	12	13
14	15	16	17	18	19	20

Chapter 8

When Jason finished reading the memoir, he showed her the last page with Grandpa Porter's photo of him smiling because he was heading home. The tears rolled down her cheeks as she touched his photo. Jason got up, and kneeled beside her and held her. He then leaned back to look into her eyes.

"I remember the day he finally came home, just before Christmas. I cried, he cried. I was so relieved that he was back home and safe. There were so many that lost their lives, and for what? The cost and suffering on both sides were too great. So many wasted lives. It was the same with all the wars before it and those that continued after, even today. I will never ever understand the fighting, the conflicts. And honestly, I'm sorry, Jason, but it's grown men acting and behaving like little children not getting their way, throwing temper tantrums and being bullies. That's what's so sad. When will any of us learn," she stated and then looked into his eyes. "I'm grateful that you didn't have to go fight."

Jason looked toward the memoir as he sat back in his chair and softly said, "I thought about enlisting a few times when I was in my middle twenties as an escape. I had friends that enlisted, and they served, and a few are buried at Arlington Cemetery. Jim, my partner, served for fifteen years. He doesn't talk about it, what happened over there. But I can tell when we've gone out on a call, that sometimes, what we see, and the smell when someone died in a car wreck or a burning building, for that split second, Jim's had a flashback. I see it in his eyes, and then he'll look at me, and we get to work.

I also thought a lot about the young girl I fell in love with. There was just so much to think about. I love my country. I felt torn about what the right thing was for me to do."

"Jason, I can't imagine what anyone goes through in making that kind of decision. And each person has to weigh the pros and cons of whether to serve, compared to not having a choice and getting drafted. Your dad decided to join the Air Force, and he was fortunate that he didn't have to fight overseas anywhere. I am eternally grateful for that, especially after having his dad fight in Korea. He didn't sign up of his own accord. The decision was made for him, being drafted, unless he ran.

"You are serving your country in another way. Men and women in your position also fight a different battle. You save many lives with your knowledge, training and skills, whether it's here at home or overseas. And just like those men and women in the military, you and your comrades have also lost friends and family with the job you do. Don't you ever think that you aren't serving your country in an honorable way. People need you. I need you."

"Thank you, Grandma. That means the world to me," Jason said, getting up and hugging her.

"Well, how about if we NOT talk about this anymore. I'm hungry. Why don't you call Talia and find out where we can go to lunch. I'm buying!" Grandma Jean said with a smile. "I'm rich now, you know, thanks to the military." They both laughed.

❧

After calling Talia, the three of them agreed on a restaurant. Jason and Grandma Jean headed over to pick her up. After arriving at the restaurant, they were seated, and then they ordered their food. Good Italian food was something that Grandma Jean liked, and hadn't had since her husband passed away.

Jeff and Mary Ann would take her out two or three times a month, usually on a Sunday morning, to an IHOP or a Baker's Square or the rare occasion to some other restaurant. Grandma Jean would make a suggestion about what she'd like or where she'd like to go, but seldom did her son and daughter-in-law take her up on it. After being asked today where she would like to go, she was just glad that her grandson and granddaughter-in-law listened to her. But she knew they would.

Talia said, "This is a wonderful restaurant, Grandma Jean. Have you been here before? I don't remember hearing about this place."

"Bill and I enjoyed a variety of places, but this was one of our favorites. And I'm glad it's still here. But since his passing, I haven't been here but once. And it wasn't the same without him. So, today is an absolute treat for me, coming here with the two of you. Thank you."

"May I ask about the memoir?" Talia asked, looking at Grandma Jean.

"I had Jason read it. I just wanted him to be with me."

Jason looked at his grandmother before looking at Talia and said, "I was really glad to have read it. I learned a few things about my grandfather, and I am very proud of him. For Grandpa, getting drafted was terrifying, as well as feeling proud to serve his country. I learned he hated calisthenics and Army food, and that he was right there on the frontline as a rifleman. When he described getting wounded by a missile and how he ended up in a Tokyo hospital, and then contracting malaria—"

"He got malaria? Where'd he get that from?" Talia asked.

"He didn't know. It could have come from many places. It took about a month for him to get well and be released, and then he was assigned to another unit instead of his original unit. But at least he wasn't back on the frontline. After that, there were lots of other things he did, setting up new encampments, driving a weasel and an Army jeep for officers on bug-outs."

"OK, a weasel? I know what a weasel is. It's a little four-legged critter," Talia said, with a grin.

"Well, this weasel is like a miniature tank that goes on land and water. He had a lot more fun driving it than carrying a rifle. I just don't remember him talking much about Korea and how long he was there. The two military men also presented to Grandma a medal that Grandpa, along with a lot of other servicemen, should have received."

"I wish I would have known him," Talia said.

After finishing lunch, they headed back to Grandma Jean's. After pulling into her driveway, she said, "I'd like to discuss something with the both of you, if you have the time. Can you come in for a few minutes?"

"Grandma, is everything OK?" Jason asked with a raised eyebrow.

"Oh, I think everything is going to be fine," she said.

❧

The drive home was quiet. Talia couldn't believe that Grandma Jean wanted to do this, but totally understood why. After arriving home and getting inside where it was warm, Talia took off her coat and hung it up, then headed over to the sofa to sit down. Jason did the same and then sat down next to her, putting his arm around her and hugging her.

Turning toward him, she kissed him, and then asked. "Did you know she was going to do this?"

"No, I didn't." They sat quietly, holding each other.

ജ   ഇ

Grandma Jean knew the last few years she didn't care to drive as much, as she was unsure of herself, and response time was unreliable. Some of her friends who were younger would pick her up to shop or get groceries, if Jason, or his parents couldn't, and then bring her home. And she'd have a friend or two come to her home for visits of tea and gossip.

Being in her late eighties, and by herself, she felt alone, especially when winter came around. The house was too big, more than she could or wanted to handle anymore. She knew there were some things in store for her, some good changes, and everything was going to be fine and work out the way they were supposed to; especially with this first simple change.

After thinking about this for several months, she knew it was the right thing to do, and someone else could use it. She didn't want that responsibility anymore, or to pay the insurance, saving her money each month. It was only five years old, her silver four-door Ford Fiesta. It was paid for, and had low miles. Grandma Jean wanted to give her car to Talia, who hadn't had one since her car accident, which, of course, totaled her car, the one she loved.

So that was why, after Talia and Jason brought her home from the restaurant, she had them come in so they could talk about it. Talia wanted to make sure that this was what Grandma Jean wanted to do; Grandma Jean didn't want any argument from either of them. They said they wanted to pay for it. After all three did their best to negotiate, it worked out to everybody's satisfaction.

☳

Two days to go before they leave. It seemed like there was still a lot to do. Jason had to work Monday and Tuesday. Talia still wanted to find at least one or two new maternity outfits, plus visit with her mom before leaving.

It would be too early for Talia to head over to Grandma Jean's Monday morning to pick up the title and car, so either Chloe or Jana would have to pick her up and take her over. Talia's mom could have done it, but she was working days at the hospital and had to be there by 6:30 a.m. So, Chloe agreed to come pick her up around eight. The car would stay at Grandma Jean's inside the attached two-car garage until they returned home from Seattle. Driving to Grandma Jean's was only a few miles from Talia and Jason's place.

Chloe and Talia walked to the front door, with Talia ringing the doorbell. Several moments later, Grandma Jean opened the door with a big smile, hugging her granddaughter-in-law, and motioned for the girls to come in.

"Grandma Jean, this is Chloe Chang, my good friend and full-time employee."

Chloe reached out her hand to shake Grandma Jean's hand gently, saying, "It's so nice to meet you. Talia talks about you, and I'm looking forward to going on this trip with you. It should be a lot of fun. I've never done anything like this." Chloe had to be careful what she said, so as not to give away a secret.

"Well, I haven't either. This is on my bucket list," Grandma Jean said, grinning. The girls laughed.

"Talia, do you need me to stick around?" Chloe asked.

"No, you go on to the shop. I'm going to stay here a bit, and then I'll head to the courthouse, and then the shop," Talia said.

"Mrs. Porter, I'll see you at the airport Wednesday morning," Chloe said.

Grandma Jean replied, "Oh, please, call me Grandma Jean." Chloe nodded her head, then gave Talia a quick hug and left.

Talia sat down, and the two chatted about what needed to happen in the next two days before flying out Wednesday morning.

"So, my dear, how was your mother-in-law when she found out I was also going to Seattle?" she asked, looking at Talia with a slight grin. "I'm sure she was concerned, either thinking that I was too old and feeble or would get lost somewhere, or that you wouldn't want an old woman along. No doubt, thinking I would be no fun. Am I correct?"

Talia just looked at her, then figured Jason told her about the phone conversation and said, "It was something like that. Jason must have told you he handed his phone over to me. She wouldn't let him get a word in."

"No. Jason didn't say anything to me."

"But... how did you know?" Talia asked, looking at Grandma Jean. She sat back, and with a grin, said, "Oh, never mind. Jason's told me how you seem to know things." Talia took a moment. "Mary Ann felt it was a bad idea because of your age, traveling by airplane and spending those days with us. You'd get tired. She thought you were nuts, as well as us, for even thinking about taking you along or that you would go and possibly look like a fool on the runway.

"I told her I didn't feel that way at all. You designed a lovely outfit for women of your age, and you should be the one to wear it whether or not the judges like it. It's your outfit. I said you should go and be proud of yourself. That's quite an accomplishment. And I said you'll be in good hands; look who she has as a grandson. And I'm proud of you for having the guts to want to do this. Like you said, jokingly, it was on your bucket list." Talia took hold of Grandma Jean's hands, smiling at her.

"I knew there was something special about you a very long time ago, pretty much when the two of you met in Europe as youngsters," Grandma Jean grinned.

Chapter 9

As a volunteer firefighter, Cole came in at 9:00 a.m. and would work until about 2:00 p.m. He would do the same tomorrow, and then work Jason's hours while he was gone to Seattle. Jim was in the captain's office, while Jason and Cole were in the break room with a little free time.

Cole said to Jason, "I wanted to tell you, I spoke with Anisha Moten at the Mélaton Travel Agency in Madison Valley. I told her that your wife was a fashion designer in this upcoming show Friday afternoon, and how many of you were coming. She inquired about ages for sightseeing tours. I mentioned you were also traveling with your grandmother, who was to be in the show. She thought that was very interesting."

Jason replied, "Well, this is Talia's first show. And I'm pretty sure Chloe and Jana haven't ever been a part of one. It will be my first to watch in person and help my wife in any way I can. Of course, that's why she has the girls, so I can probably sit back and enjoy. It will be a wonderful experience for my grandmother, getting to show off her design. She's thrilled."

Cole continued, "Anisha was excited to help find places to visit, and what costs might be involved for tours. She also lives in Madison Valley, which is across the bay from where you're staying. She works with a Sky Chandler who may be helping. One of them will get back to me."

"Good. Sky's a different name. You don't hear someone being called that very often," Jason said, smiling. "I'm looking forward to this trip with my beautiful wife, and having her all to myself for those extra days. And I'll have to repack my medic bag."

"I can tell you really love her, the way you look at her," Cole said, looking at Jason.

"I do. Like I told you, it was love at first sight when we were young. And each time we were together, that love grew. I just knew she was the one. What about you, Cole?"

Cole sat there, looking at his cup of coffee quietly. "I, um, prefer not to talk about it."

Jason asked, wondering, "Cole, is everything alright?" Just then, Jim started to walk into the lounge.

"I'm fine. I just don't care to—" Cole was saying as the alarm and buzzer went off. All three headed out the lounge door with the others.

ↃↃ

Before leaving the fire station after his shift ended, Cole received an email back from Anisha and handed Jason a list of sites with stars next to various ones around Seattle. Jason looked at the list, and smiled. "These are great." He read down the list. "The Space Needle, Chihuly Garden and Glass. Sounds amazing." Then a quirky grin as he said, "Oh boy, I'll have four females that are definitely going to want to go on this one."

"Which one is that?" Cole asked with a curious look.

"Theo Chocolate Factory," Jason said, smiling. "Matter of fact, I think I'm looking forward to that one as well. These all sound great. Thank you, Cole."

"When I find out more information, I'll get it to you before you leave Wednesday." And with that, he left.

When Jason's shift ended, he drove over to Talia's shop. He wanted to show them the list, minus the chocolate factory. That way, they knew what things they wanted to see and could plan accordingly. Some places could be spontaneous, while others required specific tour times. And with Grandma Jean, Chloe, and Jana only having until Sunday morning before flying home, he wanted them to visit a couple different places. He especially wanted Grandma Jean to have her choices as well. Who knows when she might get to do something like this again.

Ⅎ ☓

Arriving at the shop and walking in, he saw all three of them were busy. There were various pieces of clothing on a garment rack, and Talia was speaking with a client. It wasn't long, and the client left. Talia walked over to Jason, giving him a big hug, then quietly said, *"Ti amo tanto"* (I love you so much).

"Ti amo di più" (I love you more), Jason said, giving her a kiss. He had learned a couple simple phrases in Italian from her, but not as much as he would have liked. He was just happy knowing as much as he did.

"OK, you two. We know you love one another," Chloe said, smiling.

"Yes, we do," Jason said, looking at Talia, and then gave her another quick kiss. He pulled out the paper that Cole provided him, laying it on the counter so they could all see.

"These are some of the sightseeing places Cole was provided from the travel agent, Anisha Moten." After looking at the list and choosing which they would enjoy, and which one's Grandma Jean would like, Jason made notes beside them. He would check with Cole about getting the necessary tickets. These would pretty well fill Saturday so that by Sunday morning, Chloe, Jana, and Grandma Jean would have had a nice breakfast, and then would head to the airport for their flight home.

"I think Grandma Jean is going to love this one," Talia said, pointing to the list. "I just feel it because I like it." Talia looked at Chloe and Jana, telling them at no time could they tell Grandma Jean. Talia wanted it to be a surprise if possible. Both looked at Talia and then Jason and did the 'zip the lip' motion.

"Alright then, I'll call Cole, and he can get back with Anisha. Is there anything I can help you with before calling him?" Jason asked Talia.

"Nope. I think we have it covered. We should be finished by closing time. I told the girls that we'd work tomorrow morning, wrapping things up, making sure we have garments packed, along with some extra sewing notions, just in case. And going over some last-minute details, and then they can go home and pack," Talia said.

"I thought you wanted to shop for some maternity clothes before we leave?" Jason asked.

"There is a store or two I'd like to stop at before heading home." She looked at Jason with a pleading look.

"What kind of look is that?" he asked with a grin.

"It's a 'would you please come with me' look," grinning back at him.

"Is that what that is?" giving her a kiss. "I would love to go with you." He hugged her.

"Good, there are two shops just a few blocks from here, and we can walk there."

"Talia, it's after four o'clock. Why don't you two go now. We can finish up those other things in the morning. It won't take long. Jana and I can finish up this project, and we'll close up the shop." Chloe said.

Talia replied, "Then I best make a pit stop. I'll grab my bag, and we can head down the street." Jason called Cole with the choices they made and told him to get the tour times they'd like to have and the prices, and he'd get it settled tomorrow.

Ω

Walking into one of the strip mall maternity stores, there were many mannequins showing the different months of pregnancy. The salesperson asked if she could help, and how far along Talia was. After trying on various outfits at two different stores, Talia found three. She was done shopping, and getting hungry.

There was a small hole-in-the-wall café they went into and ordered dinner and talked about work, the trip and what they would see. It was time they headed back to the shop, and get their cars and head home.

Getting out of their seats, they heard a loud shriek. Looking where the scream came from, Jason immediately headed over as the gentleman slumped to the floor. He told the people he was a paramedic and a firefighter, as they could see by his uniform. He asked them to move back. He then laid the man flat on his back and started checking the man's pulse and breathing. His bag was in his car.

Realizing the man was having a heart attack, he started CPR while telling Talia to call 911. Two women were crying, and Talia was trying her best to console them. Continuing with CPR, in less than ten minutes, they hear a squad and an ambulance.

Two paramedics arrived with their equipment and oxygen tank. They saw Jason, acknowledged him as another paramedic/firefighter they knew, and all three worked together. The ambulance crew had a gurney waiting to transport. Once the man was stabilized, with an NG tube and an IV and oxygen, it took all three paramedics and EMTs to lift the heavy man onto the gurney for transport. One paramedic, Troy, went with the ambulance, while the other, Ian, gathered his equipment with Jason's help.

"Jason, what do you do, walk around looking for people to help?" Ian asked, grinning at him.

"No, just out having dinner with my wife," Jason replied. And then Ian left.

The owner of the café walked over to Jason, grabbed his arm, and asked where the man was being taken. It was his brother. He was most grateful that Jason was there dining, and told Jason and Talia their dinner was on the house for saving his brother's life.

Jason wrapped his arms around Talia, as she was shaking from seeing this firsthand. Another image that might lead to a nightmare, which Jason hoped it wouldn't.

ℜ ℞

After getting home and sitting down, Jason wrapped his arms around Talia. He waited for her to say something.

"It's hard to un-see something you just saw, just like in Switzerland. Do you think he'll be alright?" She looked at Jason.

"I got to him immediately and started CPR. And having you call 911 quickly may have saved his life. Sometimes people freeze, not knowing what to do at that precise moment. Their brains have that fight-or-flight response."

"Will you check and find out before we leave for Seattle?" Talia asked with a look of concern.

"Yes, I'll call and see how he's doing. I want you to know that I will always be there for you. I promise."

Her expression changed, and she said, "You can't make a promise like that, that you'll always be there for me. There will be times when it's not possible. Look what happened when I was assaulted, and my car accident. I could have died in that snowstorm."

She looked into his eyes. "You couldn't be there or do anything for me then." She embraced her little bulging tummy, looking at Jason.

Jason began to speak, "Talia—"

"And now..." She looked down at her stomach.

"My love, I'm sorry. And you're right. There will be circumstances and times when I can't be there for you. Even if you weren't carrying our child, I would do everything in my power to protect you, wherever and whenever. I can't lose you. I love you so much." Talia's eyes got misty. She knew that in his heart, he would die to protect her life. She hoped he would never have to do that. She wanted a lifetime with him.

Jason looked into her eyes. "I'm going to take a shower. Would you care to join me?"

"Why, so you can see how plump I'm getting?" Talia had a little pouty face as she looked at him.

"No, so I can see how beautiful you are with water running down your body, and caress your little bulging tummy that's carrying my child. And then, whatever else might follow." Jason had a teasing look on his face, pulling her close and kissing her.

Chapter 10

The morning moved quickly with plenty to do at the shop. Talia, Chloe, and Jana agreed that each would pack a show garment wrapped carefully in a protective bag, along with extra notions in their luggage. Grandma Jean's would fit in her bag. Jason would have plenty of room in his luggage if anyone wanted to take anything extra for clothes or shoes which Talia was going to, since the garment she would pack took up more space. It was the middle of the afternoon when they had everything done.

"I can't believe we leave in the morning for Seattle," Jana said. "I'm so excited. I've not really been anywhere. And I've only flown once, and that was a long time ago."

Chloe piped in. "Well, the last time I flew, I was, eight or nine years old, coming into this country with my parents to start a new life. There have only been a few vacations with my parents around the Midwest. It would have been nice to travel more."

Talia said, "And I've flown several times, including last fall, to Europe. That was a long flight both ways. Just know, I'll probably have to use the bathroom a time or two, so don't get in my way." The girls giggled. "OK, is there anything else either of you can think of that we should take with us?"

"I think we've done everything on the list and have what we need. I'm feeling good about it," Chloe said. "I'm excited and ready to go. OK, well, not yet. I have to finish packing."

"Me too," Jana said. "What time do we need to be at the airport?"

Talia replied, "Our flight leaves at 9:00 a.m. on United Airlines. We need to be at the airport by 7:30 a.m. I don't know what lines we'll have to go through with check-in and then security. Jason and I will pick up Grandma Jean and meet you both at the airport near the United Airlines entrance. There's airport parking, so you'll have to find a parking lot, unless you have someone drop you off and then pick you up. That's up to you."

"I think we'll be good. My dad is going to drop us off and pick us up when we get back," Chloe said.

"OK, let's lock up, go home and do some packing," Talia said.

ଔ

By the time Talia got home, she debated on fixing something for dinner, and thought she'd wait until Jason got home. Just having had a late lunch, she wasn't hungry. She brought out their luggage, laid them on the bed, and started packing her bag. Jason texted her, they had a late call to go on and would be home after that. Talia could get most of her packing done early, checking things off her list.

By the time Jason got home, it was closer to 6:00 p.m. He smelled of smoke. There had been a fire that took longer to put out, and two rescues. He looked tired. He said he was kind of hungry but wanted to take a shower first. He asked Talia to make him a sandwich. After eating dinner, Talia did the dishes while Jason packed.

"Did you have time to find out about the man with the heart attack?" Talia asked, watching him pack.

"Before our last call came in, I was getting ready to call the hospital, when the brother who owned the café actually stopped at the station and wanted to thank me. He said his brother, Virgil, was doing alright. He'll be in the hospital for a while before being discharged." Jason's phone rang, and he saw it was his dad.

After hanging up with him, Jason just stood there.

"Is everything OK?" Talia asked.

"Ya, he wants to take the three of us to the airport. And said he'd also be willing to pick us up when we return. I said it would be a few days later, since you and I are staying a little longer. He was fine with that. That way, we won't have to pay for parking at the airport."

"You told him what time we needed to be there and still have to pick up Grandma Jean?"

"Yup. He's willing to do that. I know you want to park your car back in Grandma Jean's garage. I told him to meet us at her house."

They hadn't shut off the lights yet, but were getting ready for bed early, when a knock came at the door. It was Cole. He handed Jason an envelope. "It's got all your boarding passes for everybody. And then Anisha emailed me some of the printable tour tickets, which I printed off last night, so you'd have them on you. I had this in my truck and meant to give it to you before you left, but then you were gone. I had a few things to do, but wanted to get over here as quick as I could."

"Thank you, Cole. We wouldn't have gotten very far without these," Jason said.

"You guys enjoy your trip to Seattle, and be safe. And Talia, good luck with the contest," Cole said. And with that, he shook Jason's hand and then left.

੍ ੁ

After calling Grandma Jean, Jason took a last look around to make sure everything was unplugged or shut off, and the thermostat lowered to 60 degrees. Arriving at Grandma Jean's, the garage door was open for Talia to put her car inside, and Jeff had just pulled up behind them. Opening the back of his SUV, Jason put their luggage in and then headed to the front door. Seeing Grandma Jean waiting for them, Talia went in first, hugging her, then Jason, and Jeff.

"So, Mom, are you ready for this adventure?" Jeff asked, smiling at her.

"Yes, I am. I have been looking forward to this trip for weeks. That's what gets me out of bed in the morning, besides going to the bathroom, and then I get hungry and no one is going to feed me but me," she said, looking at her son. "Jeff, grab my luggage. I've already checked that lights and so on are off and the heat turned down. Jason, if you would help me with my coat. Oh, I assume this coat will be fine out there?"

"Yes, your coat will be fine."

They headed out the door, with Jason locking it, and Grandma Jean grabbed onto Talia's arm as they walked to her son's car. It was really cold and dark out, but they should make good time getting to the airport. They talked about this new adventure and all the memories it would bring.

As Jeff was driving, he said, "Mom, I wanted you to know how proud I am of you, designing an outfit and getting to wear it in a fashion show. I wish I could be there to see you on the runway."

"I know." She glanced at her son. "And Mary Ann was having a hissy fit about me doing this. But her doubts were calmed, and she was reminded that I'm traveling with family and in good hands." She glanced over her shoulder at Talia and Jason.

Arriving at the airport, Jeff headed for the United Airlines drop-off. Not a lot of traffic here yet, but other airlines looked a little busier. Once they were at the unloading curb, they all got out. Jason took their luggage out with the help of his dad, moving them onto the sidewalk. Jeff gave his mom a big hug and a kiss on the cheek, then doing the same with Talia, and then gave Jason a big hug. "You take good care of my girls, you hear," Jeff said, with a stern smile.

"I will, I promise. We'll text when we arrive in Denver, and then Seattle."

As Jason turned to head inside, Jeff called to him, saying, "Jason, I know I haven't told you often enough, but I love you, and I'm so proud of you."

"I know. I love you too, Dad."

Once inside, Jason saw that Talia and Grandma Jean had now joined Chloe and Jana. Before going any further, Jason pulled out the envelope Cole gave him with everybody's boarding passes, and then headed for the United Airlines counter. Their luggage was checked in, except for Jason's paramedic bag, which he would carry on the airplane with him.

It was time to head for the security line. Talia and Jason knew the drill of removing coats, sweaters, shoes, belts, handbags and electronic devices, putting them in bins on the conveyor belt, which then go through the x-ray machine. Talia had Chloe and Jana go first, as she wanted to help Grandma Jean, since she never had to do anything like this.

Grandma Jean watched Jason as he went next, putting his items in the bin. His paramedic bag was opened and checked. After he passed through the scanner, he then put his shoes back on and gathered his things. Seeing others remove items and place them in the bins, she looked at Talia and Jason, who told her it was OK, that everyone had to do this. The reason was because of the September 11 attack on the World Trade Center, everything changed about security.

Thank goodness there weren't too many people in line behind them. Watching Grandma Jean was a little comical as she placed her purse, shoes, and coat in the bin and watched it go through the little x-ray machine. She told the TSA agent to be careful with her shoes and handbag because they were new.

Then she walked into the scanner and stood there looking at the TSA agent. He grinned as he asked her to place her feet where she saw the feet on the floor and to lift her arms in the air. It would only take about five seconds. Grandma Jean just stood there with her arms still in the air until Jason told her it was OK that she could now walk toward him and gather her things.

Jason and Talia talked about her going through the scanner. After she placed her belongings in the bin and before she could tell the TSA agent she is very uncomfortable going through it because she is pregnant, Jana blurted out to Talia, looking nervous, "Should you be going through that machine?"

"Supposedly, it's safe. I don't trust them, and I'm not going through it. I have a very reliable source that says, despite what the TSA was told and wants to believe and tells everyone, it is not safe. So, I'm asking them to do a pat-down on me, and Jason will be with me."

The female TSA agent took Talia and Jason to a small designated area with a curtain. Here, the agent proceeded with the pat-down, with Jason watching. They hadn't realized that Grandma Jean had walked over with them to watch, making sure they didn't do anything to her granddaughter-in-law. Jason turned slightly to see her behind him, watching intently, trying to give the TSA agent an evil eye. He grinned at her.

"So, did you find anything? Any contraband?" Grandma Jean asked the agent sternly.

"No, ma'am. But we have to check for any hidden devices. You'd be amazed at how many innocent-looking people are trying to smuggle something through. I'm just doing my job," the agent said, looking at Grandma Jean with respect.

"OK, then. Carry on," Grandma Jean said. She turned and walked toward Chloe and Jana, with Talia and Jason following her, both smiling at her firmness, as did the TSA agent.

Chapter 11

Terminal B was where they needed to walk to and find seats. Chloe and Jana walked on either side of Grandma Jean, chatting to her like they were old friends. Talia looked at Jason as he smiled, watching the girls with his grandmother.

She took hold of Jason's hand, saying, "This is going to be a great trip. I'm glad you prompted me to fill out that application. And here we are, just hours away from landing in Seattle."

"I wondered whether you listened to me. I kept telling you why you should do this, and then your grandfather was in your head, telling you not to pass this up," Jason said, putting his arm around her, kissing her.

After finding some seats close together while waiting to board, Chloe and Jana asked if anyone wanted anything, as they were going to find some bottled water or juice and a few snacks. Jason explained to them that things were a little pricey at airports. Talia got up to go with them. Grandma Jean asked if they could bring her a bottle of water.

While the girls were gone, Jason and Grandma Jean talked. She was excited to be going on this trip, seeing a different part of the country and spending time with Jason, Talia, and the girls. She told him how happy this had made her, and grateful for her family.

They started to talk about the baby. Jason asked if she knew what the sex was, since she seemed to know things. Grandma Jean just kind of looked at him, not saying a word. The girls came back with bottled water and snacks. Talia told them the snacks weren't that impressive on most airlines, so they were glad to have found enough to share. Handing a water bottle to Grandma Jean and Jason, they sat down to people-watch.

☳

Soon, the announcement came they were boarding, starting with First-Class, then Standard Economy Plus and then Standard Economy. Cole had gotten the five of them decent seats in Economy Plus (Row 11–seats A-E). Grandma Jean kind of wanted to sit by the window, but not directly next to one. She didn't know how she'd feel, looking so far down. Jana wasn't too keen the more she thought about it, so Chloe was happy to sit next to the small oval window. Across, Jason had the aisle seat to stretch his legs better, giving Talia the middle seat. She was hoping no other passenger would sit next to her, as she liked looking out the window and having that space.

"I'm going to have to thank Cole for these decent seats. The man knows what he's doing. I thought we'd be seated toward the back of the plane," Jason said as he put his paramedic bag in the overhead bin. He then sat down so other passengers could continue to their seats. The girls helped Grandma Jean with her seat belt.

"Grandma Jean, is your belt tight enough?" Chloe asked.

"Yes, it's quite snug. Thank you."

The passengers settled into their seats, and the flight attendants headed down the aisle, making sure the overhead bin doors were closed and latched, the tray tables were up, and passengers seated upright with their seat belts buckled. Jason looked over at the girls and asked if they were OK. They nodded yes.

Grandma Jean had been looking out the window. She turned and looked at Jason and he asked her if she was OK. She said, "Yes, so far, so good. But we're still sitting on the ground. I'm sure you'll be able to tell by my face when we move, and this thing lifts into the sky, how I'm really feeling."

"Take slow, deep breaths. Close your eyes if you need to or look straight ahead at the seat in front of you," Jason said.

They could hear the engines and then with the aid of a pushback tug to back the plane, their aircraft could now taxi down toward the departure runway.

"Good morning, ladies and gentlemen. This is your captain speaking. On behalf of your flight crew, let me welcome you aboard United Airlines Flight 0119 to Denver, Colorado, our one-stop for the day to drop off and load other passengers, and then we continue on to Seattle, Washington. Our arrival time to Denver is approximately one hour and fifty-eight minutes. Gee whiz, two minutes short of two hours. We'll see if we can ramp up the speed here and make it one hour and fifty-six minutes. We want to get you there on time. And it will probably feel like that when we arrive, and you look at your watches and it's only 9:58 a.m." The passengers laugh.

"The weather in Denver is a balmy 46 degrees, compared to good old Iowa at 31 degrees. You'd think those numbers would be switched, and we don't have any mountains here. What's the deal?

"So sit back as your flight attendants remind you how to put your seat belt on and tighten it, where to find your motion sickness bag and magazines, along with the restrooms, the drop-down oxygen masks, and the exit doors, not that you'll want to leave anytime soon.

Should you decide you don't like my driving, or flying, just know that's a mighty big step down to the ground. We'll be fourth in line for take-off. I always wanted to be first, but I drew the short straw." Several passengers laughed. "So, on behalf of your cockpit and cabin crew, sit back, try to relax, and we'll make this flight as smooth as possible." As the plane was taxiing, the flight attendants went through their safety speech and had the passengers laughing and clapping.

"Flight attendants, please take your seats, as we are cleared for take-off. Hang onto your hats, everyone," the captain said. "Oh, I was told not to say that. Sorry, folks."

೮ঽ

After waiting their turn in line, the plane now accelerated down the runway picking up great speed. Jason looked over at Grandma Jean and the girls. He thought he could have sat next to her and held her hand, but saw the girls put their hands on Grandma Jean's. Jason glanced at Talia, who was looking out the window. Taking hold of her hand, he kissed the back of it and smiled at her.

The plane lifted off the ground with the pressure pushing passengers back in their seats, and then there was a little drop due to the flaps and slats retracting, and the sound of the landing gear retracting and the doors locking. The plane continued to climb, and Jason watched his grandmother. It wasn't long and they were leveling off.

She turned toward him and mouthed the words, "I'm OK."

೮ঽ

"Ladies and gentlemen, this is your captain speaking again. We have reached our cruising altitude of 32,000 feet, a little over six miles straight up. Our cruising speed is 530 mph. Just think, if you were on the ground going that fast, well, you overshot your destination. We have clear skies to Denver. You'll notice that the seat belt sign has been turned off, but please stay in your seat and buckled just in case we do a little dip."

Talia looked over at Chloe, Grandma Jean, and Jana. They were looking out the window, so she took a picture. She figured she'd get quite a few candid shots like these. Jason had closed his eyes and was sleeping. He had to be tired after the last two days. There's another candid photo. Talia looked back over at Grandma Jean, and she was chatting away with Chloe and Jana, she seemed to be doing alright. Talia got up and carefully stepped over Jason to use the restroom. Once back in her seat, she laid her head on his shoulder and closed her eyes.

₧ ₧

"Ladies and gentlemen, as we start our descent, please make sure your seat backs and tray tables are in their full, upright position. Make sure your seat belt is securely fastened, and all carry-on luggage is stowed underneath the seat in front of you or in the overhead bins. Thank you."

Looking out the small oval windows, passengers saw the Rocky Mountains and how majestic they looked, covered in snow. Such a beautiful sight to see from so high up. It was quite breathtaking. "OK, this really makes me want to go back to Switzerland," Talia said, not taking her eyes off the mountains.

"I'm hoping we can plan a late honeymoon," Jason said. "We'll have to get Cole to do some research for us. I still want to take you to Germany. It would be nice to stop in at the fire station where I spent my two weeks. I know you mentioned Austria, and going back to the cabin. Plus, we also have our gift certificate for our favorite hotel in Basel, and we can see our two favorite hotel desk clerks." Jason looked at Talia. "But, let's not worry about that right now."

Jason looked at Grandma Jean as she looked out the window with a wonderful smile on her face, which made him smile too. He hoped she would be around for many years to come, and hoped that he and Talia and their little one might take her on some wonderful day trips or even a short vacation. Jason wondered how many other families did this with their older parents or grandparents.

He thought, *Someday we're all going to be old. I hope our families don't forget about us like so many are, out of sight, out of mind.* The passengers heard the following between the captain and crew:

"Flight attendants, prepare for landing, please," the captain announced. The seat belt lights came on. "Ladies and gentlemen, we have just been cleared to land at Denver International Airport. Please make sure, one last time, your seat belt is securely fastened. The flight attendants are now passing through the cabin to make a final compliance check and pick up any remaining trash. Thank you."

After several minutes passed, the captain announced, "For those of you who will continue with us on the next leg of our journey to Seattle, Washington, we ask that you remain in your seats as the flight attendants will count heads after others have deplaned, and then new passengers will soon board.

"Cabin crew, please take your seats for landing."

The girls remembered Talia telling them about taking off and landing, a new experience for them. The landing gear doors opened and the wheels came down and locked into place. They watched out the window as everything became closer.

Crosswinds were blowing as the plane came down at an angle with a slight up and down motion. Then they saw the nose lift while the back of the plane set down on the tarmac and the nose gear touch down and then straightened following the runway.

The plane turned off the active runway and taxied to the gate, one of the flight attendants announced, "Ladies and gentlemen, welcome to Denver International Airport. Local time is 9:45 am. —Wow. We are early— And the temperature is 47 degrees. That's because we are so much closer to the sun." She smiled at everyone.

"For your safety and comfort, please remain seated with your seat belt fastened until the captain turns off the Fasten Seat Belt sign. This will indicate that we have parked at the gate, and that you may move about safely. At that time, you may use your cell phones if you wish. Please check around your seat for any personal belongings you may have brought on board with you. What you don't take, we'll consider a gift from you and sell on eBay and throw a party for the crew afterward.

"Also, please use care when opening the overhead bins, as heavy items may have shifted during the flight. If you require assistance leaving the aircraft, please remain in your seat until all other passengers have deplaned. That's another term for 'getting off the plane.' This doesn't come from the old TV show, 'Fantasy Island.' One of our crew members will be available to assist you. On behalf of United Airlines and the entire crew, we'd like to thank you for flying with us, and we look forward to seeing you onboard again in the near future. Have a wonderful day!"

There were many passengers getting off the plane. In between passengers, Jason and Talia talked with the girls and Grandma Jean. When the last passengers exited the plane, the flight attendants went back, checking all the seats, overhead bins, and pockets on the back of the seat.

One of the flight attendants was a man. He stopped and acknowledged Jason, saying he saw the paramedic/firefighter backpack and asked about it as Talia, the girls and Grandma Jean listened. He said they've all had basic first aid training.

"I'm Jason Porter, and I am a paramedic and firefighter from Des Moines, Iowa. We've found it's a good thing to have with us whenever we travel." He looked at Talia, and then the girls. "We have enough in our backpacks to help get someone to a hospital or wherever they need to go for help or just on site. It's not quite the same as traveling in our squads and then having an ambulance close."

"I'm Alex Landon. We try to find out what passengers' occupations are, just in case we ever need any medical help, depending on the length of a trip. It's good to know you'll be with us to Seattle. I'm glad I saw you with your bag when you boarded. Thank you for your service." Jason nodded, and Alex continued checking seats.

Chapter 12

Passengers were now boarding. Talia quietly spoke to Jason, "Doesn't it seem rather silly that First Class boards first, instead of allowing passengers who sit in the back of the plane to board first? This would make more sense, so they aren't standing there waiting for people to put their stuff in the overhead bins and then sit down or accidentally bump people's arms and trip over their feet. It just seems really stupid that this is basically ass-end backward." Jason agreed. They noticed the last two people walk past them, a female passenger with a man behind her. She had a lot of extra weight on her.

It was Alex, the flight attendant that walked by Jason and said quietly, "We just learned that she is quite pregnant. She and her husband are heading home to Seattle. Hopefully, she doesn't give birth on this plane." And then kept walking.

Talia looked at Jason with eyes wide and said. "I also hope she doesn't go into labor or anything. That would be scary."

"Well, if something does happen, at least I've had extra training And maybe there is a doctor on board," Jason said.

☙

"Good morning, ladies and gentlemen. This is your captain speaking. On behalf of your flight crew, let me welcome you aboard United Airlines Flight 0119, which now continues on to Seattle, Washington. This is a non-stop flight arriving in Seattle at approximately 1:15 p.m., give or take a minute or two.

"Our total flying time to Seattle is two hours and forty-six minutes. Our actual in-flight time, 'wheels leaving the ground to wheels touching down,' is two hours and twenty-six minutes, which means we goof around backing the plane up, taxiing down the runway, and taking off. Once we arrive at our destination, it's landing the plane and taxiing to the gate so you can get off of this aircraft.

"We have topped off the tank, to give us that edge over the other airlines, giving us better gas mileage, and surely we can shave off some time. We're happy that you chose United Airlines instead of one of those other airlines that might get you to Seattle five minutes sooner, or not. We've also made sure we grabbed plenty of goodies for everyone to pass out to you later. Our flight attendants all took their happy pills this morning, which should last the rest of the day. Just stay on their good side." The passengers laughed.

"Currently, the weather in Seattle is a damp 48 degrees with clouds. It's better than what we left this morning, minus the snow. So sit back as your flight attendants go through their spiel reminding you about important things. And, we're first in line to take off. I'm so excited. So, on behalf of your cockpit and cabin crew, sit back, relax and enjoy the ride and the view."

The plane once again was being pushed back. And it was the flight attendants, Alex and Shelley, going through the entire flight safety procedure. They also said lots of snacks would be served with the choice of beverages.

"Flight attendants, please take your seats, as we are cleared for take-off," the captain said.

The plane accelerated down the runway and then lifted into the air with the same dip as before, and then the sound of the wheels retracting inside the plane and the doors closing. Jason looked over at the girls and Grandma Jean, wondering what she was thinking. Again, the girls each put their hands on Grandma Jean's hands. Talia took hold of Jason's hand while looking out her window. They continued to climb and soon leveled off. Many of the passengers were taking a last look out their window at the Rockies.

"Ladies and gentlemen, this is your captain speaking. We have reached our cruising altitude of 37,000 feet, with a cruising speed of 540 mph. We have clear skies, at least until we get closer to Seattle. You'll notice that the seat belt sign has been turned off, but please stay in your seat and buckled unless you have to get up. Thank you."

About twenty minutes into the flight, Chloe and Jana needed to use the restroom. Grandma Jean said she was fine for now.

"Grandma, what do you think so far of flying?" Jason asked.

"Well, I don't remember anything from the first time I flew. Taking off both times this morning left my stomach feeling queasy, and my heart was beating a little faster. But so far, the flight itself has been alright. When we were getting ready to land, heavens to Betsy, that ground came up awful quick and made me nervous. I'm sure glad those pilots know what they're doing up there," she replied. "But seeing the mountains from up here is pretty spectacular."

"Yes, it is." Jason turned his head toward Talia with a smile and kissed her. He then got up to use the restroom. The girls came back, taking their seats. They continued chatting about the fashion show. Grandma Jean told a story or two from her younger years and what they wore, thinking they were so fashionable back then.

The flight attendants had already gone up and down the aisle with various snacks and beverages. If you wanted lunch, there was a cost to it. You could choose from a couple different things. Knowing they probably wouldn't get to eat until about 6:00 p.m. at the banquet, they thought maybe they would order something. The girls also had goodies in their handbags from the airport this morning. Once they finished eating, along with other passengers, the flight attendants headed down the aisle, picking up cups and some of the trash.

 beta

There was over an hour to go before they would touch down. Grandma Jean now needed to use the restroom. She got out of her seat and made her way toward the nearest one. Then, Talia needed to use the restroom. As she got up to step over Jason, at least four people walked past her, heading for the front restroom. Looking toward the back of the plane, there were only two people waiting. Talia figured by the time she got back there, she would be next in line. Walking past the couple that boarded last, the woman looked very uncomfortable and was rocking back and forth.

Talia had to ask quickly, "Excuse me, are you feeling alright?"

The man looked worried and then answered for her, in broken English, "My wife, she is most pregnant and feeling sick. We need to get to our home in Seattle very soon. We had a family emergency come up, and she is very worried." By his accent, Talia deduced they were likely Mexican.

"OK. I understand. Give me a moment, and I'll get you some help, alright?" Talia said. "I have to use... I'll be out in a moment."

When Talia came out of the restroom, Alex, the flight attendant, was trying to talk to the couple, saying everything would be OK. They were getting closer to Seattle. He told Talia she should go to her seat.

Talia looked at him and said, "I want you to go get my husband, Jason Porter, in seat 11D, the one you talked to earlier, and tell him to bring his medic bag, unless you have a doctor on board." He started to object, but, Talia had this look in her eye and then told him to "move it." He looked at her and then turned and headed up the aisle.

∮ ∯

The captain came on, announcing they might experience a little turbulence soon. That it's just big pockets of air, and think of it as a slight rocking motion, but it shouldn't last too awful long. They have an hour of in-flight time left, and if everyone would please stay in their seats with seat belts on it would be appreciated.

Alex approached Jason, touching him on the shoulder. Jason turned to look up at Alex as he bent over, and quietly told Jason he needed to bring his medic bag to the back.

Jason looked at him and said, "My wife went back to use the restroom." Jason then got up out of his seat, opening up the overhead bin taking out his bag.

The girls asked, "What's going on? Where is Talia?"

Jason said, "I'll be back soon." Several passengers heard this and watched Jason follow Alex as they headed down the aisle.

A couple of them asked Alex what was happening. He said, "We have a passenger not feeling well. Please stay in your seats." Jason saw Talia, along with another flight attendant, standing next to the very pregnant woman.

He looked at Talia with concern and asked, "Are you OK?"

"Yes, I'm fine," Talia answered, wanting to tell Jason what was happening before Alex had the chance to interrupt. "I headed to the restroom and had to wait my turn. This woman looked miserable, so I asked her if she was feeling alright; her husband said she was feeling sick, and I told them I would get some help. Alex here," looking at

Alex, then back to Jason, "tried telling them everything would be OK, that we were almost to Seattle. Jason, we still have over an hour to go. He told me to go sit down. That's when I told him to get you unless he knew there was a doctor on board."

"OK, let's all calm down," Jason said. He knelt beside the woman, speaking softly, as he looked at her and the man next to her. "My name is Jason Porter. I'm a paramedic and a firefighter." He showed them his backpack with the insignia on it and his ID. "I'm going to see if I can help you, OK?" They both nodded, looking a little less fearful.

Jason looked at the female flight attendant and asked her to please get a couple bottles of water. She left, and Alex stood by, watching. Looking at the woman, Jason asked, "Can you tell me what your name is, please?" as he laid down his backpack, partially opening it.

He felt it was warm where they were sitting and could also smell the restroom, which probably didn't help her condition. He reached up and turned the cool air on, moving the little vent toward her.

The husband answered, "Her name is Theresa Hernandez. I am her husband Carlos Hernandez."

"It's nice to meet you both. Theresa, can you tell me how many months pregnant you are?"

"I am just starting my ninth month," Theresa answered, shifting in her seat. She looked very uncomfortable and didn't look well. "And we have a family emergency at home."

"And when is your baby due?" Jason asked.

"The doctor told me it could be the middle of March," she responded.

"Nice, my birthday is in March." Jason smiled as he took out his BP cuff and stethoscope. "I'm going to take your blood pressure and then listen to your heart, OK? This lovely woman standing here is my wife, Talia, and she is almost five months pregnant. So, you have something in common."

"You are pregnant too? You are not very big yet," Theresa said, looking at Talia's stomach.

"No, I'm not. Our baby is due in June," Talia said with a smile. "It won't be long, and you'll have a beautiful baby." She knew that Jason, for the most part, always seemed to stay calm about most situations, that she was learning. She wasn't sure what he could do for Theresa, and didn't know what kind of training he had at all. But, hopefully, no baby decided, of all places and times, to show up now.

After taking her blood pressure, he jotted down the numbers in a small notebook. He then placed a digital thermometer under her tongue, as it gives the best reading. He listened to her heart, then put his stethoscope around his neck and wrote down her heart rate and respiration.

"Theresa, did you eat breakfast this morning?" She nodded yes. "OK, have you been drinking plenty of water to stay hydrated?" She looked at him and then her husband. He held up the one bottle. The female flight attendant had come back holding two bottles of water, giving one to each of them.

"Have you been able to stand up and do some walking in the aisle to keep your circulation moving? It's not good to be sitting on a long flight without getting up and moving. That could lead to some problems."

"Yes. I was walking a little ways in the aisle when I heard people talking about why am I on this plane. I'm too big, and they said I should know better," Theresa said sadly, as her eyes glistened with tears.

"Sometimes, people don't know any better than to be rude," Jason said, looking at her. "I'm sorry about that. Have you been feeling sick to your stomach? Nauseated?"

"Yes. I was feeling hot, and the smell from the bathroom was upsetting my stomach and giving me a headache," Theresa said, and continued, "I was the most worried though because I felt a little crampy. My belly was getting hard, like maybe contractions were starting up? Do you think this is the beginning of labor?"

"It's possible, but you have a good month to go before your due date," Jason said. "So while there may be the sign that you are in early labor, it is also possible, and even probable that all we're seeing is the result of the stress from the flight and needing to get home, which could be making your uterus more irritable and crampy right now. Let's pay attention to what your pattern of cramps looks like for the next little while."

Getting his notepad, Jason said, "We'll write down when you feel a cramp and time how long it lasts and see if it continues consistently. And while we're doing that, let's also do some other things right now that can help calm an irritable uterus that may be telling us it's tired of this flight." Alex left, and then Shelley, a different flight attendant came and stood.

Chapter 13

Jason continued talking directly to Theresa. "I have learned in my added training that, due to higher progesterone levels, a pregnant woman's sense of smell is much more acute, and different odors can really bother her. Odors like gasoline, garbage, wet cardboard boxes, even the smell of bathrooms. And you're sitting pretty close to a bathroom. It's also warm back here, and we know pregnant women tend to run warmer, plus you're flying so close to your due date. That has made you uncomfortable and nervous. Am I correct?" Jason asked, looking at her with a slight grin, wanting to keep her calm. She put her head down and nodded.

There was a slight dip as the plane was going through some turbulence. Talia came around the back side of Jason and took a seat across from Theresa and Carlos, putting her seat belt on. Jason didn't seem phased by the motion of the plane. Shelley held onto the back of the seat, watching and listening. Alex returned and stood by them, whispering to Shelley that the captain was advised of the situation.

"Well, we're going to fix you right up here, OK. Other information most of us paramedics have learned, at least with my fire station, came from a midwife who comes to our station to teach us about pregnant women every other week.

"She told us, all pregnant women have quiet contractions every day, at least the last half of their pregnancy. These contractions are called Braxton-Hicks contractions. It is the uterus contracting and flexing and maintaining muscular strength in preparation for labor. They are usually not painful, and are often not even noticed by the mother.

"However, if the mother is low on basic electrolytes like salt, potassium, calcium, or magnesium, then these contractions become crampier and more noticeable, though they are still not actual labor.

"So, we need to boost your calcium, as well as magnesium, which helps pick up the calcium. Calcium is abundant in dairy (milk), and magnesium is abundant in chocolate. Now, who doesn't love chocolate?" Jason saw her smile.

"We're also going to get you some electrolytes, like salt and potassium. Those also help pick up the calcium. So, I'm going to ask this nice flight attendant if she could bring you a little carton of chocolate milk and a little bag of Lay's potato chips. The salt and potassium come from the chips."

"You're kidding, right?" Shelley asked, looking at Jason like she didn't believe him and thought he was nuts.

"No, I'm not. If you have them, would you please go and get them," Jason said, standing and looking her in the eye. He then looked at Alex and said, "I'd like to get her moved up a few seats away from the bathroom. I see there are plenty of seats available."

"We'll be landing soon. Can't she just stay here?" Alex asked.

"She could, but I want her moved, now," Jason told him firmly. He closed his bag and gave it to Talia to hold. Jason then helped the woman stand and move up about five rows, with her husband following and then he sat next to the window. Jason then helped her get buckled in and adjusted the small air vent for cool air. Shelley came with a small carton of chocolate milk and a small bag of Lays potato chips and handed them to Theresa.

"Theresa, I'm going to sit back by my wife for a bit, and then I'll come and check on you and see how you're doing. We'll see if everything has calmed down in the next twenty to thirty minutes. I'm guessing that will be the case." She nodded and continued with the chips and milk. Jason moved back by Talia, sitting across from her. He took the small notepad out and wrote in it, then put it back in its place.

"Is she going to be alright?" Talia asked. "And what about a midwife coming to the station? You never mentioned that."

"First, Theresa should be fine. I'll check on her in about fifteen minutes or so. The milk and chips should help," Jason said. "And several of the guys brought up this idea a while back because they've noticed a rise in pregnant women that we have to attend to." He looked at Talia with a sensual smile.

"So, we found this midwife that will come teach every other week for about two hours. She has over thirty-five years of experience with moms and babies, and an amazing amount of knowledge in other areas of healing that could be an absolute benefit. I certainly didn't know about some of the simple things that can be done to help someone. And it's all good stuff, especially with you and our baby and our plans to travel overseas. So, next time I see her, I'll have to relay what happened here."

"I wonder if I'll get that big and uncomfortable," Talia said, looking up toward Theresa.

"I honestly couldn't say. Theresa is taller than you and big-boned. Her baby could be eight pounds or so, but then I don't know. The midwife could probably tell us, but she's not here," Jason said. He reached over and took hold of her hand, looking at her. "However big you get, you will look absolutely beautiful to me because I love you so much."

"I love you more with each day that we're together. You truly are my prince, with his shining stethoscope around his neck." She giggled, and he smiled a big smile.

"I know once we land, we were all going to leave together and then head to the baggage carousel, but I'm going to stay with Theresa and her husband getting off the plane until I know she's OK with the people who are going to pick them up. But, I think you should probably go back to your seat now. I'm going to go up and sit across from Theresa."

They both got up, and Talia gave Jason a quick kiss, before heading back to her seat. Jason then headed toward Theresa and Carlos when another flight attendant came to see how things were going and if he would take his regular seat. He told the flight attendant no. He would be sitting across from Theresa to check her vitals, monitor her, and then walk off the plane with her and her husband. The flight attendant left.

Several people were looking back at him. He placed his backpack on the seat he'd be occupying, then kneeled next to Theresa. "Theresa, how are you feeling?"

With a smile, she said, "Better."

"Good. I'm going to check your vitals one last time. You look like you feel better than you did about thirty-some minutes ago." He took her vitals, making a note of them.

"After we land, I'm going to walk with you to the baggage carousel and then walk with you to the car that is coming to pick you up. When you get home, you call your doctor's office and let them know what happened." He reached into his back pocket, took out one of his cards, and gave it to her. "If your doctor wants to talk with me, he or she can call me, alright?"

"*Gracias*," Theresa said (Thank you).

"*De nada,*" Jason replied (You're welcome).

— —

The captain came on and announced, "Ladies and Gentlemen, we have been cleared for landing at Seattle International Airport and are starting our descent. We should be landing in approximately twenty minutes." The seat belt light came on. "Please make sure your seat belts are securely fastened, that your seats and tray tables are in their upright positions, and that all carry-on luggage is stowed underneath the seat in front of you or the overhead bins. Flight attendants, you know what to do." They made their last compliance check, picked up cups and trash, and ensured that everything was secure.

The captain then announced, "Flight attendants, please take your seats for landing."

Once on the ground, the head flight attendant announced, "Ladies and Gentlemen, welcome to Seattle International Airport. Believe it or not, we made fantastic time. Ten minutes early. Local time is currently 1:05 p.m., and the current temperature is now 49 degrees with sunshine. Don't believe me, look out your window.

"For your safety, please remain seated with your seat belt fastened until the captain turns off the Fasten Seat Belt sign. At that time, you may use your cell phone. Please check around your seat for all personal belongings you may have brought on board with you. We couldn't collect anything after landing in Denver, so if you want to leave something behind for the fun of it, we'll still try to sell it on eBay and buy a pizza for the crew's hard work.

"Please use caution when opening the overhead bins, as items may have shifted during the couple little dips we felt in the air earlier. If you require deplaning assistance, please remain in your seat until all the other passengers deplane. As we commented on the last landing, deplaning is another word for 'getting off the plane,' not what Tattoo from Fantasy Island used to say, 'Deplane, Deplane.' He was so cute, wasn't he, folks?" The passengers laughed.

"Anyway, on behalf of United Airlines and the entire crew, we'd like to thank you for joining us on this trip, and look forward to flying with you again in the future.

"We'd also like to take this time to thank the paramedic/firefighter, Jason Porter, for helping one of our passengers. And no baby born today, I won the bet. Have a great day, everyone."

After the plane came to a complete stop, people were up and turned toward Jason, clapping. Jason just waved his hand as he turned to help Theresa out of her seat.

Jason followed Theresa and her husband, Carlos. Several passengers waited until they walked by to thank him. As they approached the exit door, Captain Acer, his co-pilot, and flight engineer were standing there watching everyone. Alex stood close by and pointed out Jason.

"Mr. Porter, thank you for taking care of this woman. We were kept informed of the situation, and we're glad everything turned out alright. And thank you for your service," Captain Acer said.

"Thank you, Captain, and also for your service keeping us in the air," Jason said smiling. They shook hands, and then Jason followed the others off the plane.

Jason, Theresa, and Carlos walked through the passenger boarding bridge, heading toward the departure gate waiting area. Jason then saw Talia with Grandma Jean, Chloe, and Jana, plus a dozen other passengers waiting for them, and they were all clapping. Talia could see him blush a little at being acknowledged by so many people from the plane and possibly watching what he was doing, which was helping someone in need. That was part of his job, whether on duty or off.

Talia walked over to Jason, putting an arm around him as they headed for the baggage carousel. Once they found it, they stood waiting for their luggage to come through.

Theresa spoke to Talia, "You are a very lucky woman to have this man in your life. He made me feel so much better and calmer."

"I am lucky to have him in my life. I'm glad that he could help you when you were feeling so uncomfortable and nervous," they shook hands. "You'll have to let us know when you have your baby. Jason gave you his card, *Si?*"

"*Si*, he did. And we will let you know," Theresa said, smiling.

As the luggage started coming through, Grandma Jean asked Jason how they were getting to the hotel. Jason said that Anisha got a shuttle for them from the hotel to pick them up. As they all grabbed their bags, including Carlos, they found their way to the United Airlines exit doors. Standing just inside the door was a gentleman holding up a sign with 'Jason Porter' on it. Jason was thinking with a smile, *Now that's service.*

As he turned to talk with Theresa and Carlos about going with them outside to find their people, someone came running up to Theresa and hugged her. They began speaking in Spanish. Then a man and a woman came over to Theresa and Carlos, giving them hugs.

Theresa turned toward Jason and said, "This is my brother, Hector, and his wife Carmelita, and daughter, Maria. They are the ones that will take us home now."

"Good, I'm glad they came in and found you." Then he took a step toward Carlos and shook his hand, and then hugged Theresa. "You take good care of yourself. Remember to hydrate and walk." She smiled at them as they all turned and walked away, talking in Spanish.

"Well, since we didn't go back and watch what you were doing, you'll have to tell us while we're heading to the hotel," Grandma Jean said. "I'm interested in hearing. People were wondering what was going on and if we knew you. I told them you were my grandson, and it's your job to help people."

"Yes, it is my job. Why don't we follow this gentleman out to the shuttle so we can get to the hotel, and I'll relay what happened on the way."

Chapter 14

Getting into the shuttle, they were headed for the hotel. The driver was a gentleman who looked to be in his sixties. He said his name was Robert Anders, and he was born and raised in the Seattle area his entire life. Robert asked what they were doing in Seattle in February.

Grandma Jean perked up and said, "We're in a fashion show at a big convention center."

Robert looked in his rearview mirror, looking at Jason, then Talia. Grandma Jean sat upfront with Robert.

Jason looked at Talia to explain. "She's right. I'm Talia Rose-Porter, and this is my husband, Jason Porter, and I'm a fashion designer. I've entered a contest which is at the Meydenbauer Convention Center. And the other two gals behind me, Chloe and Jana, are my assistants." Robert then nodded his head.

"So, who all is in this fashion show?" Robert asked.

"Well, first I'm the grandmother to Jason Porter," she said, looking at Robert. "And there are three of us in the show, which includes me."

"My two assistants will be wearing a couple of outfits, as well as Grandma Jean," Talia said.

"So, Robert, you said you were born and raised here. Is all your family nearby?" Jason asked.

"No. My wife and I still live here, but our three married children live in different states. So, when we can, we enjoy traveling to visit them and our grandkids," Robert said.

"Is this a full-time job for you, Robert?" Talia asked.

"No. I do this a couple days a week to help out and earn a little extra money. I enjoy driving and meeting new people, finding out where they come from and what brings them to Seattle. So, where are you from?" Robert asked.

"We are all from Des Moines, Iowa," Jason said.

"The Midwest. I've heard of Des Moines, Iowa," Robert said. "But I've never been to that part of the country. I'm kind of a history buff. I'll bet you didn't know that we have a Des Moines here as well. If I remember right, a man back in the late 1800s from your Des Moines urged a bunch of friends to help develop a new town in Puget Sound. And they named it Des Moines. Lots of history all around us, but some people don't care."

A few more minutes passed, and then Robert asked, "Jason, are you also in the fashion design world?" glancing at him in the rearview mirror.

"No. I'm a paramedic/firefighter," Jason replied.

"Wow. Well, thank you for your service. So, you're here to support your family and see what all the hoopla is about," Robert said, smiling.

Jason laughed. "Yes, I am. I had several comrades tease me about going to a fashion show until I told them I was going to be surrounded by lots of women." Robert laughed.

"Good for you. I can only imagine what that would look like. Do you have some sightseeing planned while you're here?"

Talia responded with, "Yes. And we're looking forward to them."

"There's a lot to see and do here if given the time," Robert said. They were approaching the Silver Cloud Inn, and soon Robert was pulling toward the front entrance and then stopped. Everyone got out and retrieved their luggage.

"Robert, thank you for picking us up at the airport. We greatly appreciate it," Jason said, shaking Robert's hand.

"Not a problem. If you need transportation while you're here, I can help. Like I said, I was born and raised here. And Talia, good luck with the fashion design contest."

"Thank you, Robert," Talia responded.

"Robert, you might be able to help us in a couple of ways," Jason said. "We have a few things to figure out, but we may need your services."

"You just name it," Robert said, pulling out his card with his number on it.

"Thank you," Jason said, giving his card to Robert. The girls had already gone in and were waiting for Jason.

After checking in, they headed to their rooms on the fourth floor. Chloe and Jana shared a room with a connecting door to Grandma Jean's room. Jason and Talia were across the hall. After taking their luggage to their room, everyone gathered in the girl's room.

"Since we didn't hear on the ride here about the pregnant woman," Grandma Jean said, "what happened?"

Jason looked at her and thought he best tell her and the girls what happened quickly. "Good thing you've had the midwife teaching you boys," Grandma Jean said. "Sounds about right."

"Chloe and Jana, we need to get the outfits unpacked and hanging up. According to the schedule, we need to be there to sign in by 5:00 p.m., and at 5:30 p.m., it's just us designers, and then we'll be given more instructions," Talia said, looking at her papers.

"Does it say anything about taking our garments over yet? When do we do that?" Jana asked.

"It says we'll be given a schedule regarding all of this," Talia said. "So, we'll all find out this evening. And we should all freshen up for the banquet. It starts at 6:00 p.m., and we can get acquainted with others."

"Jason, did Cole give you information about how we get to the convention center?" Talia asked. "The map shows it's about a half-mile. We could walk it, but then we don't know how late we'll be, and then afterward, the weather and it's dark outside…, and I don't know about Grandma Jean walking that far?"

"Let me get the envelope," Jason said, heading to their room.

"I can't believe we're here in Seattle," Chloe said. Jana nodded her head in agreement.

Jason came back with a paper in his hand. "We have a driver that will take us to and from the convention center when we're ready. I just have to call them."

"OK, so we have about two hours to rest. We should all be ready by about 4:30 p.m. Grandma Jean, is there anything you think you might need between now and the time we leave?" Talia asked.

"No. I'll hang up my clothes and take a little rest. Being on the plane, I didn't feel like I could close my eyes at all, even though I was tired."

"Well, we'll be able to get a good night's sleep after this evening's event," Talia said. "Tomorrow is a brand new day."

⁊   ℈

Arriving at the convention center a good twenty minutes early gave them all the chance to stand and look around. There were Valentine decorations everywhere, including hanging down from the ceiling. There were many bouquets of beautifully arranged flowers, and the smell was wonderful. They saw other people looking around, just as they were doing, and Talia wondered who and how many of these were designers.

She saw the huge marquee sign that said, 'Seattle's 10th Annual Valentine's Fashion Designer Show,' along with the date of February 14th at 1:00 p.m. Talia turned, grinning as she looked at Jason, who smiled back at her. He saw the joy that sparkled in her eyes.

Chloe, Jana, Grandma Jean, and Jason paused and moved to the side. It was Talia who would be signing in. As she was getting closer to the table, a young woman brushed past her with a few young girls pretty much on her tail. She didn't say 'excuse me' or 'pardon me.' Talia just looked at her with raised eyebrows, taking a slight step backward.

Two women were seated on the opposite side of the long table that was covered with a red tablecloth draped down to the floor. At each end was a small vase with red, white, and pink roses with greenery. As the young woman stepped right up to the table, with the young girls on either side, one of the women whose name badge said 'Elizabeth' spoke, saying, "Well, Sabrina Henington, it's been a few years since you were here as a contestant. Decided to try again?"

"Hello, Elizabeth, yes. And this year, I'm going to knock their socks off," Sabrina said in an uppity voice.

"Well, I'm sure you're going to try. You've had some time to improve, so we'll all be watching to see what you present," Elizabeth said, then almost in a whisper. "Just so you know, we won't have the same judges."

"It's alright. New judges don't scare me," Sabrina said. She signed her name and picked up her name badge along with her envelope, then once again, didn't bother to say, 'excuse me' or 'pardon me,' or 'coming through.'

With eyes wide, Talia just stood there and slowly turned her head to watch Sabrina march off down a long corridor. She turned back to the women at the table and took a step forward.

"Sorry about that. It's best to stay out of her way," Elizabeth said.

"No problem."

"OK, my dear, may I get your name, please?"

"I'm Talia Rose-Porter."

The other woman, whose name is Linda, spoke up, saying, "That's a pretty name."

"Thank you," Talia said.

After signing in, Elizabeth then handed Talia her name badge, saying, "This is your name badge, and you'll wear it around your neck like Linda and me. When you are here in the center, you'll wear it, including the banquet this evening. It sets you apart as a contestant. Inside the envelope will be name pins for everyone in your party. They'll also have to wear their pins here as well. There's information about Meydenbauer Center, along with a map showing some rooms you'll be in, including room number and time for your interview tomorrow."

"Is that when we also bring our garments in?" Talia asked.

"Yes. There's information about that in your envelope," Linda said. "You'll want to head up the escalator to the fourth floor and then go to your right, Room 403 will be on your left. Everyone in your party will go to the large waiting area behind us and past the stairs. There's plenty of seating."

"Thank you," Talia replied, then walked toward Jason. She put her name badge around her neck and then opened the envelope, taking out the name pins. Chloe, Jana, and Grandma Jean's first and last names were already on theirs since they were modeling. Two extra name pins were provided. Talia took a small marker out of her bag and wrote Jason's name on it.

Chloe looked at Talia. "How are you feeling?"

"Feeling a little overwhelmed at the moment." She looked at the girls. "OK, I'm scared." Jason put his arm around her and kissed the top of her head.

Looking at her, he said, "You'll do great. Take slow, deep breaths. See what's happening in this meeting, and then we'll get to enjoy a free meal, kind of like Villars." Talia smiled, remembering it was actually two free meals. She started to turn, when Jason pulled her back, gave her a big kiss, and then turned her toward the escalator. As Talia left, the four of them headed to the waiting area.

Room 403 wasn't exactly large. There were several short tables and chairs, enough for at least twenty people comfortably. Entering the room, Talia saw the young woman, Sabrina, sitting off by herself on the left side of the room, text messaging or something. She remembered what Elizabeth said, to 'stay out of her way,' but it wasn't Talia's nature to be rude. So, she sat down at the same table, but two seats away.

"Hello," Talia said, looking at Sabrina, waiting for a response. But there was none. *OK then, at least I tried,* Talia thought. She heard other voices and turned, seeing other designers coming in and sitting down. One was a young man, tall with glasses, wearing a bold pink shirt and black trousers with a black and pink polka-dotted tie. *That tie doesn't look that bad*, Talia thought. He came and sat down next to her. Smiling at him, Talia said, "Hello."

"Hi," he said.

"Is this your first time entering a contest like this?" Talia asked.

"Yes," he said, waiting a moment. "What about you?"

"I've never entered one of these before, either. I've gotten an invitation before but never entered until now. By the way, my name is Talia."

"My name is Rae, R-A-E." He saw Talia raise her eyebrows. "Ya, I know, my parents wanted to be different. Couldn't spell it the normal way."

"It's a nice name," Talia said.

The other women were pretty quiet, with only one or two talking.

೫

There were plenty of places for Jason, Grandma Jean, and the girls to sit while waiting for Talia and the other designers to return after their meeting. The round tables were big, and the chairs were comfy. Looking toward one of the inside walls was a huge water wall. It looked like one long planter at the base, and soft colors were changing behind the water. It barely made a sound but was quite mesmerizing.

The girls were on one side of the table, talking with Grandma Jean, and Jason on the other side, looking around, and noting where another hallway was and other doors leading to who knows where. He saw the red glass box for the fire hose reels and racks—

"Hello." It was a man's voice that interrupted Jason's thoughts.

Jason looked up and saw the man standing now, almost in front of him. "Hello," Jason said, sitting up straight.

"My name is John Marshall. I'm sorry, I saw your backpack with your insignia on it, and I saw you looking down the hallway checking to see where the fire hoses are, I presume?" John asked with a grin. "I'm a paramedic as well."

"Oh. My name is Jason Porter. Please, have a seat. It's a big table," he said, smiling. "Ya. Kind of a habit." Looking around, Jason then asked, "Do you need help?"

"Well, if something occurs while we're all here, I might. My wife is a fashion designer."

"Mine too. Where do you live?" Jason asked.

"We're from St. Cloud, Minnesota. Where do you call home?"

"The Midwest, such as yourself. We're from Des Moines, Iowa. So, are you a firefighter as well?"

"Right now, a paramedic. Going on five years, What about you?"

"I've been a paramedic going on sixteen years, and a firefighter for nine years, So you have family here with you then?"

"Yes, I have two sisters who are going to model, and then Gwen's best friend. And our daughter, Nikki, is with us. She's eight years old. Matter of fact, here she comes now." John smiled at her.

"Dad, you forgot your bag. You shouldn't walk off without it, you know," Nikki said, frowning at him in a scolding way.

"Yes, dear," John said, smiling at her. "Sweetie, I'd like you to meet Jason Porter. He's also a paramedic, and a firefighter."

"Hello, Nikki, it's nice to meet you," Jason said, smiling at her.

"If you do the job my dad does, do you see dead people?" Nikki asked.

"Nicole, that was inappropriate," John said to his daughter.

"It's alright," Jason said. "And the answer is yes. Like your dad, we do come across accidents where people died before we could get to them and help them."

"OK. In school, we were talking about what our parents do for jobs. I said my dad was a para-medic, and sometimes he sees dead people. My teacher and some kids thought that was awful, and some said, 'cool.' But I said it was sad because their families really miss them."

"Yes, they do," Jason said, looking at her with a solemn look on his face, then looked toward the floor. His thought turned to his sister, and his best friend, and then he thought when his own child would be going to school. Would they talk about what he did for a living…?

"Jason, I'm sorry. Kids are inquisitive, and things come out of their mouths sometimes before we can stop them."

"It's alright. I think it's OK that they question things. Hopefully, as adults, we can give them good answers."

"Well, we'll go back and sit down. We'll see you around." Jason nodded.

Chapter 15

The meeting room door closed, and everyone turned around to see a woman and a man walk toward the front of the room. Then the door opened again, and a woman walked in, heading to the front as well.

"Good evening. My name is Sara Walte. I am the Director of Sales & Events here at the Meydenbauer Center. And I wanted to take a moment and welcome you to Seattle if you've never been here before. Hopefully, you'll have some time while here to visit and see what we have to offer, and there is a lot.

"It's exciting for our center to hold this event once again, and many of us are looking forward to seeing the wonderful designs you've all created walking on the runway Friday afternoon. If you have any questions, I believe, in your envelopes, there is information about our center, and you can either call me or email me, and I'd be happy to answer your questions. So, with that, I'm going to leave and let your meeting begin."

"Hello everyone, my name is Arnold Schwartzenbaugh, not *Arnold Schwarzenegger*. I have never done any bodybuilding, nor do I think I need to, not at my age. And the fact that I couldn't spell my own last name until I got into junior high." Everyone laughed. "It was just too long. I simply signed anything as Arnold S." He waited a moment.

"The woman sitting beside me is my colleague, Mrs. Lorna Denton. Now, why I couldn't have had a nice short name, I have no idea." He smiled at everyone. "We were asked to participate in this year's fashion show contest due to our backgrounds in the fashion industry. Lorna and I have talked about how we got to where we are today, and it was because there were people who believed in us, saw what we had to offer, and gave us the opportunity to show our stuff."

Mrs. Denton then stood and spoke. "Arnold and I have been good friends for many, many years. As he said, when we were asked to participate in this contest, it was an easy decision." She paused a moment. "You've entered this contest hopefully because you believed in yourselves and what you can share with others. You are creative in the choices you've made with your designs that will no doubt appeal to people in their everyday lives.

"I've attended a lot of fashion shows, and I look at some of the clothing on the runway, and think, pardon my French, but 'what the hell is that.'" There was laughter. "We decided that, rather than stand here and 'preach' to you about fashion and style and what the difference is between the two, which you should know, we put together some information for you." Arnold walked around, passing out a small booklet to all the contestants.

"Now, we'd like to put a name to a face. So we'd like to have each of you stand and tell us your name, your company's name, and where you call home. Let's start with the last table to the far right and then the next person. We'll zig-zag up to the front."

The first woman stood up and said, "My name is Alice Monroe. My company is The Monroe Design Shop, and I come from Jackson, Tennessee."

"My name is Gwen Marshall. My business name is Marshall Designs, and I come from St. Cloud, Minnesota."

"My name is Jennifer Lily. My business name is Lily Designs, and I come from Pine Bluff, Arkansas."

"My name is Lindsay Peters. And my company name is Designs by Lindsay, and I come from Decatur, Illinois."

"My name is Mary Liktor. My business name is Fashions by Mary, and I come from Carson City, Nevada."

"My name is Nancy Becker. I come from Sydney, Nebraska, and my business name is Becker's Design and Fashion."

"My name is Robin Black. I come from Eugene, Oregon, and my business name is Black Creations."

"My name is Rae Arendt, that's R-A-E, by the way. As I was telling this woman, my parents just had to be different." There's laughter. "My business name is Designs by RAE, and I come from Wichita Falls, Texas."

"My name is Talia Rose-Porter. Yes, I hyphenated my married name. My business name is The T.E. Rose Shoppe. That's with two P's, and I come from Des Moines, Iowa."

It took the last person, Sabrina, a moment before she stood up, possibly thinking it was an inconvenience to her to have to do this. She didn't seem to care about the others, and it showed when she didn't bother to turn around and look at the other contestants. She stood, saying, "My name is Sabrina Henington. My business name is Creations by Henington, and I live in beautiful West Sacramento, California."

"Thank you, everyone, for introducing yourselves. Many of you have come from a great distance to be here, and we wish all of you the best of luck," Arnold said. "You have your envelope with various information in it, as well as the room number and time you'll have your interview tomorrow morning. That is a set time, and we ask that you please be on time, even a little early, just like you would for an interview.

"We'd like for everyone to please be in the central lobby by 8:15 a.m. Remember your name badges and pins for those coming with you. Bring your garments. We'll show you where they will be, in a protected room with a security guard. Yes, we take it seriously.

"Now, depending on when your interview is, you and your party will have some wait time. The center is setting up early tomorrow morning. Several tables will be filled with a variety of food, in the room where the banquet is this evening, so that everyone can help themselves. Once your interview is done, unless you need to do something with any of your garments, you are clear to leave and go explore until Friday morning."

Mrs. Denton then continued with, "As a heads up, even though I believe this is in your information packet, Friday morning, starting at 9:00 a.m., everyone needs to meet in the main lobby, where you'll be given further instructions. You'll then head to the large hall where your models will be practicing on the runway to get a feel for it and the music. We know it might be a little intimidating at first, but we want you to have fun with this.

"And you're all probably wondering who goes first, second, and so on. That will be provided to you Friday. Yes, we're going to keep you in suspense for a little while longer. But for now, we are done, unless anyone has questions." Everyone was looking around. "OK, we know we went over our time with you. Your people have been taken to the banquet room and are waiting for you there. So if you'll follow us, it's time to celebrate your being here."

The delicious aroma that drifted through the hallway as they were led toward the Center Hall room was heavenly, possibly because Talia was starving. The sandwich on the plane wasn't enough, and she wondered how the girls, Grandma Jean and Jason were faring.

All those in the banquet room were told the designers would be coming through the door momentarily, and everyone stood waiting for them. As soon as they walked through the big double doors, the applause started, with some whistling and flashes from photographers cameras. Once the designers found their groups of people, they headed toward their tables. Talia walked toward Jason giving him a big hug.

Valentine colors adorned the room. The round tables were covered in light beige table cloths, and each had a beautiful vase of flowers. The silverware was wrapped in red cloth napkins, and water glasses were filled. After several minutes of people talking, the room became quiet. There was the clinking of a glass to get everyone's attention. Once again, the designers saw Ms. Sara Walte.

"Good evening, ladies and gentlemen, and welcome to Seattle's 10th Annual Valentine's Fashion Designer Show." There was clapping. "We are pleased that so many could be a part of this event. My name is Sara Walte, and I am the Director of Sales and Events here at the Meydenbauer Convention Center. This year, we have ten contestants, one more than last year, so, maybe we're growing in popularity." Some laughter. "Our contestants come from all over the place, as close as Oregon to as far away as Tennessee, and everything in between. For me, I love seeing how creative designers can be, and hearing who and what inspires them.

"Now, the designers learned this at their meeting, but for the rest of you, tomorrow will be a day for interviews, which I believe starts at 9:00 a.m. and finishes around 4:00 p.m. When they are finished, unless they have something that needs to be done with an outfit, they are free to leave and enjoy the rest of their day and relax. Just so you know, I didn't pick the interview times. No way, not me." Laughter erupted. "Friday morning, the models will do walk-throughs on the runway to get a feel for the length of the runway and what happens with timing and music.

"This room will be set up for lunch for everyone starting shortly after 11:00 a.m., and I believe that by 12:30 p.m., the first ten models should be changed into their outfits and all that good stuff and get lined up. The show starts promptly at 1:00 p.m. Those who will wear more than one outfit, someone else will explain that Friday morning.

"But, right now, I'm sure your mouths have been drooling, just breathing in the smell of the food that has been prepared for you. We have some wonderful chefs here at Meydenbauer. This is buffet style, and we'll be starting with table number one, then two, and so on. You'll see the menu on the marquee near the start of the buffet line.

"So, without further ado, please enjoy the food, your evening, and the company that surrounds you. Who knows, maybe you'll make some new friends." More clapping as Sara went to sit at her table. Table one headed for the buffet. Soon it was Talia's table which was number four, so they headed for the buffet line, reading through the menu. Talia looked at Jason, Grandma Jean, and the girls with a big smile on her face. Everything looked scrumptious.

Designers' Valentine
Fashion Show Banquet
February 12th
6:00pm

MENU

Creamy Lemon Parmesan Chicken Piccata
Grilled salmon
Walnut Shrimp

Roasted Sweet Potatoes
Creamy Mashed Potatoes
Green Bean Almandine
Honey Garlic Butter Roasted Carrots

Garden Salad – assorted dressings
Artisan Bread w/Kerry Gold Butter
Black Bean Quinoa Salad

Fresh Strawberry Lemonade

Assortment of Desserts for your palate
Red Velvet Cake
Sugar Heart Cookies
Pink Vanilla Cupcakes
Caramel-Drizzled Brownie Hearts

As the evening wore on, a few people got up and left. Jason looked at Grandma Jean. It had been a long day for everyone, especially for her. He was ready to call it a night. "I'm going to call our driver and let him know we're ready to leave," Jason said.

"Sounds good to me," Chloe said. Jana agreed.

Jason made his call, and the five of them got up and headed toward the main door. While waiting for their driver, John approached. He was holding his daughter, who had fallen asleep. "Jason, it was nice to meet you. We'll see you in the morning."

"Nice to meet you as well. Tomorrow's a new day. You and your family sleep well."

 CB

Grandma Jean walked toward her room, and then turned around. "I'm usually up early. What time will we eat breakfast?" she asked.

"7:30-ish," Talia said.

"What time is your interview?" Grandma Jean asked.

"Mine is at 10:30 a.m." Talia then gave Grandma Jean a hug, wished her sweet dreams, and headed into her and Jason's room.

"When Talia gets done with her interview, we'll have lunch and relax. And then we can go see things. That gives us a half-day more than we thought, and we won't need to push on Saturday," Jason said. He hugged his grandmother telling her he was so glad she was with them, and then to sleep well and he'll see her in the morning. She opened her door and then turned to look at him. It was the look on her face, as she told him to enjoy his evening, then turned and went into her room. He looked at her door, wondering what that look was for.

Talia had already turned down the bed, and was sitting on her side facing the pillows. The only lamp on was on Jason's side of the bed as he came in and walked over to a chair laying his backpack down, then taking off his coat. Turning around to look at her, he saw what she wasn't wearing. She stood up and with a seductive look walked toward him. Looking her up and down, he gave her a deep, passionate kiss. It would indeed prove to be an enjoyable way to end the evening.

Chapter 16

Waking up with this new day of experiences in front of them, Jason held her warm body close to his and looked at her, saying, "If we didn't have to get up, get ready, eat breakfast, and out the door in the next full hour, I'd make love to you all over again." Talia gazed back at him, and then reached around his shoulder, tilting her head up so she could kiss him. Pulling her body closer, he grinned as her baby belly pressed against his stomach. He moved his arm down her back, and with his other hand gently rubbed her stomach.

"Surely this little one won't stop us from enjoying each other like we did last night," Jason said with a look of playfulness as he scooted down and caressed her belly, then kissed it and whispered to it. Talia giggled, as it tickled when he whispered to her stomach. Jason looked at her, moving back and wrapping his arms around her. Giving her teasing kisses, he moaned, knowing it was time to get moving. "We will continue this later," he said, giving her another kiss, then rolled onto his back and got up.

ςʑ

Talia buzzed Chloe's room and then Grandma Jean's to see if they were ready to go down and get some breakfast. It was about 7:20 a.m. They would need to leave by 8:00 a.m.

As they were eating, Talia said, "I was just thinking I should look at the garments one last time before heading over."

"Oh, you don't need to do that. Jana and I looked at them earlier, and they're fine. After hanging them up last night, they look great, and since we don't have to wear them until tomorrow, well, that gives them a little more time to… just hang there," Chloe said, with an odd smile on her face. "We even had Grandma Jean look at them quickly. We're all set. We have the small bag of notions, just in case, but they look fine. We're good to go."

It was the way Chloe spoke that sounded off. Talia looked at her, then Jana and Grandma Jean. They each had such an odd look on their face, and just smiled at her. "OK, what's going on?" Talia asked.

Chloe shrugged her shoulder and shook her head with a look of 'I don't know what you're talking about' on her face. Talia, again, just looked at the three of them with a raised eyebrow. "If something is wrong with one of them, I need to know now," Talia said with a voice of concern.

"There is nothing wrong with any of them, my dear," said Grandma Jean. "Don't you have any faith in your girls?"

"I've got enough on my mind without worrying if something is going on with one of my outfits," Talia said. Jason watched the four of them like a ping-pong game.

He looked at his watch, and then looked toward the door and saw that Robert was looking at them. He tapped his watch. He was going to take them to the convention center. "Ladies, it looks like Robert is waiting for us," Jason said, standing up.

Grandma Jean said she would wait in the lobby with Robert. Jason headed up with Talia, Jana, and Chloe to get all the garment bags, and soon they were heading to the convention center. Robert would be available to taxi them around during the day, as his wife was busy with friends. It gave him something to do as well, even though it was his day off, but he didn't mind.

 C&

After entering the convention center's main lobby, they noticed several other designers and their parties, all with their garment bags draped over their arms. It was Elizabeth and Linda who waited for them. When all the designers were checked in, except one, it was now 8:15 a.m. Elizabeth looked around and then asked if anyone remembered seeing Sabrina Henington. Everyone shook their head no. "Alright, we'll give her five more minutes, and then we'll head toward the dressing rooms."

It was 8:20 a.m., and no Sabrina. No phone call, nothing. Linda had everyone follow her. Elizabeth would stay behind and wait for Sabrina. Walking into the hall, everyone could see how large the room was. Linda told them this was where the fashion show would be as they continued walking. The large curtains were open, showing a full view of the stage. People were working on the long runway, putting down runners, etc. The group could see the three steps near the end of the runway, with a handrail. Other workers were lining up chairs on both sides.

Talia looked at Chloe and Jana with eyes wide, a big grin, and raised eyebrows. She could feel the excitement growing inside of her, still not believing they were here. They all continued through a pair of double doors, following Linda as she continued down a long corridor, and stopping where two security guards were standing. She moved half the group behind her so that everyone could hear as she introduced both guards, Charles Dawn and Pete Logan.

Charles explained that each designer and their models would come through the door to their assigned room. Once the garments were hung up, each bag would be checked, and any handbag they carried in. Linda called for Jennifer Lily to bring her garments and models, since her interview was first at 9:00 a.m. She took them in, showing them which dressing room they were assigned. Coming out of the room, Linda saw Elizabeth with Sabrina and her models behind her. Linda gave a quiet sigh.

Elizabeth moved toward the door where Linda stood, taking the colored clipboard from her, and told her to take Jennifer and her group so she wouldn't be late. "Linda is going to walk with each of you to your interview room, which is on the fourth floor. There are two separate rooms, and your interviews have been staggered by thirty minutes. You'll have a good hour with your interviewer. Make it count." Linda then left with Jennifer and her party.

"Next up is Nancy Becker if you and your models would come forward," Elizabeth said. She took them in, showing them their assigned room, and then waited for the security guard to check all their bags before heading back out into the hallway. "Nancy, if you and your models would head back down the hallway and wait by the door for Linda to return, she'll walk with you." Elizabeth waited a moment before calling on the next designer.

"Sabrina Henington, you and your party are next. If you would come forward, please," Elizabeth said. Sabrina was toward the back of the group. Her young models moved more quickly than Sabrina, who took her dear sweet time. It was clear to Talia that Elizabeth and Linda knew of Sabrina from the past, but she wondered what it was between them. It was like Sabrina had some point to prove to Elizabeth and possibly others.

It was quite annoying watching her. There was a snobbish air about her. Once she reached the door, Sabrina just looked at Elizabeth. Elizabeth smiled at her and then turned and walked into the room, doing the same thing she had done with Jennifer and Nancy. Minutes later, they came out of the room.

"Sabrina, if you and your models would head toward the door and wait for Linda, she'll be with you soon," Elizabeth said. Again, Sabrina walked past everyone with an air about her like people should know who she was. After Elizabeth's comment yesterday morning about Sabrina, Talia figured something must have happened that they are at odds.

"Next up, Talia Rose-Porter and models," Elizabeth said.

They were close to the door that would enter the dressing room area, and now they followed Elizabeth in. Elizabeth looked at the four of them, especially Grandma Jean, who looked back at her with a smile and said, "Yes, dear, I'm one of the models." Elizabeth nodded with a half-smile. She showed them the order on the wall in which the models would line up, and then she stood outside their room as she did with the others.

The room fit the four of them, including Charles, the security guard, comfortably. It had a small dressing table with several chairs to sit on. Hanging up their garment bags, they moved back. They saw Charles wearing latex gloves. Noting he was about to check the last bag, Jana, Chloe, and Grandma Jean started talking to Talia to draw her attention away from it and then hugged her as the guard closed that bag.

Talia took a step back with a slight grin, looking at the three of them with raised eyebrows. They then followed Charles out of the room. Jana and Grandma Jean gave each other a quick and quiet low-five, instead of a high-five. Walking back into the hallway, they heard

Elizabeth call for Gwen Marshall, who was next, working her way through with her models.

It was Pete, the second guard, seeing the insignia on Jason's backpack when he turned to walk away following the girls. Pete stopped Jason and said, "You're a paramedic/firefighter? I noticed you looking up and down the hallway. I can assure you, we're up to code. Everything is fine." It was Pete's tone, as Jason looked him in the eye and then down toward the gun on his hip, and back to his eyes. "I'm going to have to check your backpack." Others were looking on.

John was now standing there, watching.

"I'm sure you are up to code, and it's not a problem checking my bag. It's also a habit to observe everything, no matter where I am or we are, like you are with your job. I'm sure you want people to be safe and not be in harm's way," Jason said, looking at him. After Pete looked in his backpack, Jason then zipped it up.

"Would you like to check my backpack now?" John asked Pete, who turned to look at John, then back to Jason. John turned, so the insignia on his bag showed the paramedic symbol. John unzipped his bag for Pete to look in as Jason watched. When he finished, John zipped his bag closed.

"So, you guys all stick together?" Pete asked. That was odd coming from a security guard. Jason didn't know what it was as he looked at Pete, but something didn't feel right.

"I guess you might say we do. We're there for one another, no matter the station, or city, state, or country," Jason said as he looked at Pete, then John and nodded, then turned and followed Talia down the hallway.

Waiting by the door for Linda, they noticed that Sabrina and her models were nowhere in sight, unless Linda had already taken them.

While waiting for Linda, they peered around the door, looking at the vast amount of space and the work going on. Then they saw Linda walking toward them, so they started walking toward her. "You must have to move pretty quickly, getting people where they need to be," Talia said with a smile.

"Well, the first two, I did need to get them to their rooms quick, but everyone following will have a little more time," Linda said. "Now, you're Talia Rose-Porter." Talia nodded. "OK, we should have Sabrina and her models joining us."

"Sabrina saw her dressing room before us, and Elizabeth told her to wait here by the door," Talia said. "We thought you'd already come for her."

"No, I didn't," Linda said, looking around the room and then had them follow her. "She pulled this same thing a few years ago. I was surprised to see her yesterday. She comes from a very well-to-do family, and they feel they don't have to answer to anyone. You're expected to say, 'yes, ma'am' or 'no ma'am', and do as you're told. She's got quite the attitude. But I think it's more her parents, or her mother, that pushes on it. There are no manners, as you saw yesterday morning. She thinks she can come and go as she pleases, and doesn't want to follow instructions.

"We hoped she might have learned good manners from her grandmother on her dad's side. She passed a few years ago; she was ninety-two. I had the chance to meet her twice, and she was a wonderful woman. Smart, savvy, and had a sense of playfulness. She said she tried telling Sabrina that she was better than this. Better than what her mother was teaching her.

"Sabrina is just a very miserable person, and she's not doing herself any favors with her bad attitude. I wish things could be better for her. And honestly, I don't think this is what she ever wanted to do, but her mother has a tight rein on her and her brother. That's what's sad."

"That is most unfortunate," Grandma Jean said. Jason saw the look on her face.

Arriving on third floor, Linda said, "You have some time before your interview. You can relax a little. I'll come and get you fifteen minutes before it starts."

Walking into the room, they saw Jennifer and Nancy's people. They were sitting, talking, and eating. Also sitting at a table with her models was Sabrina. Linda was not sure how she didn't see Sabrina. She told Talia and her group to help themselves and also where the restrooms were. Linda walked over to Sabrina and was talking to her, but no one could hear what was being said. Then Linda left the room.

Seeing what there was for food, it all looked and smelled good. Even though they had a light breakfast, this made them even more hungry. Once the food was on their plates and a beverage chosen, they had their choice of tables.

Grandma Jean had her plate in hand, and she purposely walked by Sabrina's table and said, "You must know your way around the convention center to go off on your own, even though you were asked to wait." Sabrina barely looked up at Grandma Jean, giving her a snarly look. Then Grandma Jean went and sat down.

Chapter 17

"What, I'm hungry. I didn't eat much for breakfast because I was nervous," Talia said.

"I didn't say anything," Jason replied with a cheeky grin.

"No, you didn't. It was the way you looked at me," Talia said.

The time grew closer for Talia's interview. She got up and headed to the restroom. At 10:15 a.m., Linda came for her. The girls and Grandma Jean hugged her and wished her the best of luck. Jason gave her a big hug and a kiss, telling her she would do a great job and that he loved her so much. Talia started to leave, and then turned and handed her phone to Jason, saying she didn't want it accidentally making any noise, and then left with Linda.

Grandma Jean had a book, while Chloe and Jana had a different reading device. Jason sat quietly, looking at the three of them and then noted the exits around the room. After a few minutes, he stood up to stretch and walk around. His phone buzzed. It was a text message from Cole.

Cole: *Hope all is well. Received an email from the travel agent, Skye Chaundler, with an 'e,' that says, 'Found 3 or 4 other places you might like to visit if you have time today or tomorrow.' I'll get those to you soon.*

Jason texted back: *Skye with an 'e.' He must come from Montana, lol. Looking forward to the list.*

Cole: *Anything interesting happen on your way to Seattle? We've had a few accidents to contend with, but nothing major.*

Jason: *I had to help a woman who was almost 9 months pregnant on the plane. I'm glad we had that midwife come in and teach us a thing or 2.*

Cole: *She's to come next Monday for 2 hours. That will be interesting. I didn't know they still existed. But, what do I know.*

Jason: *Yes, they still exist, and a good thing, too. Talia is in her interview right now.*

Cole: *I hear she's a good designer.*

Jason: *She is. There's another designer here from St. Cloud, MN. Her husband is a paramedic. I met him, seems like a nice guy and a family man.*

Cole: *Hopefully, no one else will need your services while on vacation.*

Jason: *I agree, but I'm always prepared.*

Cole: *I'll get that list to you before noon, your time, today.*

Jason: *Thanks, Cole. Tell the guys there are a LOT of women here. There's even a man fashion designer in this competition.*

Cole: *Will do.*

03

As Talia entered the room, she saw a man and a woman. The man sat at a conference table, with the woman sitting at a different one. She had a notepad laid in front of her along with what looked like a small recording device. The man stood up, and came around the table, and introduced himself. "Good morning. My name is Norm

Shetler, and this is my assistant Juliet Adams." He reached for Talia's hand to shake it and then said, "You're Talia Rose-Porter?"

"Yes, that's correct," Talia responded. And then looked back at Juliet with a smile and said hello.

"Please have a seat. So is this your first fashion designer competition?" Norm asked.

"Yes, it is," Talia said.

"So, it's probably safe to say that you're excited to be here but also nervous about the whole process," Norm said. Talia nodded her head. "I was in your shoes a good many years ago, so I know those feelings well. I know it's also easy for me now to tell you to relax. I usually relaxed once I was done and out the door and could breathe normally," he said with a smile. Talia smiled back at him. So far, she liked him, but she still had this hour to go.

"You're from the Midwest. After going through many of the applications, there are a few of you from that region. I've had business between Des Moines and Chicago, a nice part of the country," Norm said. "Juliet is from Kansas. She's informed me of the many wonders of the Midwest, so I know to be careful what I say around her." Talia turned and smiled at Juliet. It was nice knowing there's another Midwesterner here.

"We think so as well," Talia said with a smile.

"So, were you born and raised in Iowa?" Norm asked.

"Yes, I was," Talia said.

"I'd like to find out a little more about you and your background," he said as he leaned back in his chair. She looked at him with a slight nod. He took a moment and then asked, "What made you want to become a fashion designer?"

Talia looked at him and took a slow, deep breath, getting her thoughts together. It was *déjà vu*; Jason had asked the same basic thing when they were on the train heading back to Basel. She smiled and then said. "I didn't know that I wanted to be a designer. I think my grandfather planted the seed to dream. He and I had many discussions when he'd see me daydreaming, and we'd talk about what people were wearing, things I'd see on TV and out in public. I told him I thought I could do a better job because some outfits looked terrible." For a second, her thoughts went back to her grandfather.

Norm looked at her and listened as she continued.

"Our conversations led me to telling him, then, that I felt like I wasn't good enough or deserving enough of anything I wanted, and that I doubted myself, and the voices of other people giving me their thoughts and opinions. I remember him looking at me, and he said, 'Don't allow other people's writing to be on your wall.' I wasn't sure what that meant. He could see it on my face, and he pointed to my head.

"In high school, I took a Family and Consumer class where we learned to sew, and I enjoyed it. In that class, I also found myself drawing designs, and I'd envision someone wearing it. I had a classmate that hated that class," Talia said, smiling. "She'd see me drawing, and it wasn't long before she asked if I'd come up with a design for her; a skirt and top. She liked my design, so we bought the material, and I sewed it for her.

"Little by little, classmates asked me to do the same. I even had a teacher have me design an outfit for her. As a senior in high school, the kids were telling me I should go to college and learn to be a 'fashion designer.'" Talia smiled, as did Norm. "So it started by taking that class and then turned into something I love doing, which is designing and sewing, and I'm grateful for that. I get to do what I love."

"I can hear it in your voice, that passion," Norm said, looking at her with a tilt of his head. "The next question will probably seem obvious to you, and I think it's obvious to me, but I'm going to ask. Who inspired you the most?"

Talia got a big smile on her face. "Definitely my grandfather." And then her smile started to fade. "His health was not good. I didn't know at the time that it would be the last time I'd see him. It was our last heart-to-heart talk. I can see him so clearly now, and hear his words.

"He told me, 'Whatever dream you have, design it. Be open to it.' He continued to look at me and then asked, 'What is the outcome you want for you and your life?' He passed a short time after that. Like I said, definitely my grandfather."

Norm just sat looking at her as if he was soaking in the words of her grandfather. "There are many designers who want to see their outfits on a particular gender or class of people. Who would wear your designs, and why?"

"Wow, that's a loaded question," Talia said, taking a moment. "Well, I'm not sure if the rich and famous are going to look at any of my designs and say, 'Oh wow, I gotta have that.'" Talia had a silly grin on her face. Norm looked at her with a smile. She was honest about it.

"I picture my outfits on a variety of people. Not everyone wants the same thing. I'd like to get to know the person, their background, and where they'd like to wear it. Is it for school, work, social gatherings, or something more important? I want to know how they want to feel when wearing one of my designs. I want them to describe that feeling they're looking to feel."

"Interesting that you talk about how you want people to feel when wearing something you'll design specifically for them," Norm said. "So, you'd be willing to design for different age ranges?"

"Yes, I would. Why not? Fashion and style are all over the place, and not just for a certain age. It's not just for those that can well afford hundreds of dollars for one design. I think there is something for everyone, whoever they are or their age. I know what it's like when money is tight," Talia said. "I may well be in that category of less than a handful of designers that wants to keep it in an affordable price range. Money is nice to have, and people need it, but people are important and how they feel about themselves."

Norm just looked at Talia, but she hoped she got her point across that for most people, 'money doesn't grow on trees,' and that everyone deserves to have something special in their wardrobe.

"I do have one last question for you before we go over the questions from the application," Norm said. Talia was quiet, as she had had this slight niggling that there would be more to these interviews. She wanted to be open and honest with all of her answers.

"My fun question for you is this. How did you come up with the name of your business?"

Talia smiled and sat up even more straight in her chair. "Oh, that was easy. When I last spoke to my grandfather, I told him that someday I would own my own shop. He looked at me and said, 'Sweetheart,' — that's what he called me— he said, 'Sweetheart, what is the name of your shop?' I smiled at him, and then hugged him and said, 'The T.E. Rose Shoppe.' I told him it had to have two P's in it because it looked cool." Norm laughed.

"My grandfather also laughed, but it was in his loving way. I told him I loved him, and that was the last time I saw him. I miss him. The T.E. stands for both of our initials, Theodore Earl and Talia Elizabeth."

CB

Jason sat back down. It was close to 10:50 a.m. Grandma Jean put her book back in her purse and stood up. She looked at Jason, and he looked up at her, smiling. "I'm heading to the restroom. I'll be back in a bit," she said, and started to walk toward the door. She turned and looked at Jason. "Be prepared." And she left.

Chloe heard her, and then looked at Jason as he watched his grandmother leave the room. She asked, "Be prepared for what? Does she think something's going to happen while we're sitting here?"

"She sometimes gets feelings about things before they happen," Jason said, then turned around to see where John was sitting. He saw John looking at him and nodded.

Chapter 18

Grandma Jean headed toward the restroom. She saw a few chairs along the hallway, as well as a small lounge area. There wasn't anyone around but empty chairs. After coming out of the restroom, she saw her sitting there, mumbling and crabbing to herself or someone. Grandma Jean stood there for a moment and then walked closer to her.

"Done so soon?" Grandma Jean asked.

"It's unbelievable that they would do that," Sabrina said disgustingly.

"Well, it can't be all that bad," Grandma Jean replied. "It is an interview where there are bound to be questions no one is expecting."

Sabrina stated in a bitter voice, "What would you know about it. You're old."

"Yes, I am. But I had to go on interviews when I was looking for work in my younger days." Grandma Jean walked to an armchair close to Sabrina and sat down. She was getting too old to have to stand and chat with someone who was acting so childish. "So what did they ask on the application?"

"They had specific questions on the original application, stating it was their way to get a sense of who we were before meeting us. I provided them basic answers. And then today, they asked a whole bunch of other questions."

"And you think it's unfair that they, what, changed their minds? How did you think the interview was going to go?"

"Short and sweet. No one will be prepared. They'll all muddle through and not tell the truth or make stuff up to sound good. But maybe that might be in my favor." Sabrina just stared straight ahead. "My family is very well-to-do. When I tell them about this interview, my mother, in particular, will not be happy. I'm expecting to do well here. I've had help from a top designer who's mentored me, groomed me."

Grandma Jean looked at her and then asked, "Why are you really here?"

Sabrina turned, looking at her with a peeved look. "I beg your pardon?"

"What I'm asking you is, why are you here at this competition? What's your goal?"

"I'm in it to win it, if you must know." She turned her head and looked straight forward, hoping this old lady would leave her alone and go away.

"Just to win?" Grandma Jean asked. "What's the prize if you win?"

Looking at Grandma Jean snidely, and in a quiet voice Sabrina said, "Each year, the amount of prize money goes up."

Grandma Jean nodded. "So you're here to win it for the money? That's it?"

Sabrina looked at Grandma Jean like she was deaf and said, "Yes. I just said that. And besides, my designs are going to shock the judges with how fashion is changing. It's all about the up-and-coming generation. My mother knows many of the design judges."

"So you're expecting to win because of your answers or because of your designs? Or because you're hoping your mother can persuade a judge's decision? Did you design any of your outfits?"

"I had help with them. Who doesn't? The judges can't NOT love what I'm going to be showing. And my models are young. That young woman you're with probably had lots of help. She doesn't look like she'd come up with much on her own. None of them do, except maybe that man designer, Rae."

"You must feel a sense of entitlement because your family is well-to-do. So many people don't have anywhere near what you have, yet they can make something of themselves and go on and succeed. Success is not always about how much money you're worth or a big house, or bullying your way through to get what you want," Grandma Jean said, looking at her, feeling a teensy bit sorry for her. "Let me ask you this, Sabrina. With all that you have, what are you grateful for?"

Sabrina did not have a nice look on her face. It was one of contempt as she crossed her arms in front of her and sat back in her chair, glaring at Grandma Jean.

"You can't come up with one thing?" Grandma Jean was waiting. "That's sad. I could probably give you a long list." Sabrina looked away from her, really wanting her to go away.

"How about, for starters, being grateful you are alive and breathing and walking on your own two feet. You can feed and bathe yourself. How about all the clothes you have? The roof over your head, did you pay for the house? You probably have a nice garage and a nice car to drive. You have heat in the winter and air conditioning in the summer when it's really hot. You have lights on in your house, are you grateful for those?

"How about you probably have someone cooking for you, and you haven't had to go hungry. Having a washing machine and dryer, so you have clean clothes to wear? Do you know how to do your laundry, or is it done for you? You probably received a good education. You know how to read and write. Have you ever had any pets that you appreciated having, who show you unconditional love? What about the vacations you've gone on, who paid for those? What about any bank accounts you have and how the money got in there?

"Everyone has something to be grateful for. All I asked you for was one thing, and you couldn't come up with one. You are so blessed compared to the millions who don't have anything or anywhere near what you have—the struggles they have, what they've lost. And just because you were given a certain name at birth, your name is not who you are.

"I had a friend once, a long time ago. Her name was Leota. She was much like you. Even in my youth, we had people of wealth, and some taught their children that it was OK to be selfish and rude and stuck-up. They lied, manipulated and bullied their way to get what they wanted. Many told their kids what they would do with their lives, not giving them a choice.

"Leota kind of got what she wanted, but lost friends along the way. She was miserable, rarely nice to anyone. She didn't seem to be grateful for what she had and what she could do to help someone else, human or animal."

Grandma Jean paused for a moment, and then said, "She grew old and sinister, and alone. After her parents died, she became angrier. Whatever it was, it had a grip on her. She couldn't seem to get past that her life was headed in a direction she never wanted, and the time she wasted. You need to figure out what you want and go for it, to follow your dreams." Grandma Jean got up and started to walk away, then looked back to comment and saw the tears in Sabrina's eyes.

"I'm aware of your grandmother's passing. I'm not your grandmother, but if I were, I would have kept after you to fulfill your dream, not your mother's. I know this is not what you are to do with your life. This is not the road you are intended to go down. I want you to know there is another door that will open for you. The timing is just about right." Grandma Jean turned and left.

₧ ₨

"I wondered when you'd get back. Did you get lost?" Jason asked with a smile. "I thought I was going to have to come find you or send one of the girls."

"No, just having a conversation with someone," Grandma Jean said.

"Well, Talia should be done in about ten minutes. It's getting closer to eleven-thirty," Jason looked at his watch. "Then we can fill up here. And Cole was going to get me a list of some other places to see. I should be hearing from him soon."

"I hope Talia's interview is going well," Chloe said. "I would be so nervous. I can't wait for her to get done and tell us about it." Jason smiled at her.

"I have to believe she's doing a great job up there," Jana said. "She's a good designer, and we all know that. All she has to do is be herself—" She barely finished her sentence.

Suddenly, **pop, pop**. Jason sat more upright in his chair and started looking around the room. He saw John do the same thing. The designers that were there earlier this morning were gone. The other designers wouldn't be back until after lunch for their interviews. So it was Sabrina and her party, Jason and the girls, and John and his people left in the room.

They both now stood up, with John walking over toward Jason with his bag. "I've heard that sound many times," John said. The others were also looking around, not sure what that noise was.

"Ya, me too. You don't have to be in law enforcement to know that was gunfire," Jason said. He picked up his bag and told everyone to stay in this room and don't go anywhere. He looked at Grandma Jean, and then he and John headed down the hallway and toward the escalators, not sure whether to go up or down. They started down and were stepping off, when a young man saw them. He asked if they knew where the paramedics were.

"We're paramedics," Jason said. "What the hell happened?"

"We don't know. It happened so fast," the young man said in a jittery voice as he turned, with Jason and John following him. They entered the large hall and headed toward the far end near an exit door. People were standing around. Jason and John saw a couple of men holding down another man on the floor. A second look and Jason saw it was Pete, the security guard, being held down and the gun laying on the floor.

"Charles," Jason said calmly.

As they approached Charles, he had his hands on the man's bloody abdomen, and half turned, looking at them. "How'd you get down here so fast? I just told someone to go up and get you."

"We've heard shots before. It echoes fairly loudly," John said as he and Jason knelt on either side of the wounded man and then took off their jackets.

"I assume you had someone call 911?" Jason asked without looking up. Both of their bags were open now, and they were putting on their gloves and getting out whatever supplies they needed.

"Charles, are you alright?" John asked, looking at him. Charles looked white as a ghost. More people were now gathering around, as well as a few staff from the convention center. There was a flash, and Jason looked up and saw someone with a camera.

"Would you all please just back up and give us space here. And stop with the camera," Jason said. "Someone go wait for the ambulance."

John put on the pulse oximetry, and then took the man's BP and checked respiration. Jason had Charles back away, which he gladly did. Jason said to John, "Let's see if we have an exit here." They worked together to roll the man gently so Jason could check, and there wasn't one. He shook his head no to John. The bullet was lodged inside, and this man would need surgery ASAP.

There was now a commotion as a couple of police officers were walking toward them. One went over to the two guys holding Pete down, and the other toward Jason and John. Someone had also placed several towels next to them. Jason pulled the bloody cloth that Charles used to pack the hole, and then replaced it with one of the towels as John kept up with the vitals.

They didn't have anything to start an IV with, since they aren't from the area. Thankfully, the man was still conscious, and they hoped he would stay conscious until other paramedics and ambulance arrived.

The officer bent over, asking where they came from, as he knew the guys from this area and knew John and Jason weren't. John briefly explained and then told him they would gladly show their ID after help arrived. The officer asked if he could do anything.

While holding his hand on the wound and bending closer to the man's ear, Jason said, "Sir, my name is Jason Porter, and my partner here is John Marshall. We're paramedics. Can you hear me OK?" The man slowly turned his half-opened eyes toward Jason and then nodded. "Can you tell me your name?" He started having a hard time breathing.

"John, grab the Ambu bag out of my backpack. Sir, my partner here is going to help you breathe with this mask on, alright? He's going to put it over your nose and mouth. It's going to help push air into your lungs." The man then looked at John. Jason took the stethoscope from around John's neck to get another BP and pulse reading and check respiration. They made notes to pass on to the paramedics that would arrive.

The officer heard over his mic that paramedics and ambulance had arrived and should be inside. He turned to see three paramedics and two EMTs coming through the double doors of the large hall heading toward them. As soon as they approached, Jason went over what they knew of the situation, what they were doing, and provided them with their notes. With the Seattle paramedics taking over, Jason and John could stop what they were doing.

Jason saw one familiar paramedic uniform, not American-made, and heard a voice he didn't think he'd hear for a while, a strong German accent. As the other paramedics took over, and the situation was under control, John and Jason gathered their bags and jackets. Standing up, Jason looked over and had to smile at the man smiling back at him.

In his strong German accent, he said, "Jason, first off, how the hell are you doing. And what are you doing in Seattle, Washington?" John looked at Jason and back to the German. Jason and the German gave a man-hug.

"Well, Jürgen Sussman, first off, I'm doing great. Remember, I was getting married? My wife Talia is a fashion designer in a competition here. What are you doing so far from home?" Jason asked.

"Oh, *Ja,* that beauty on your phone. I decided to do the work program for a week, like Adrian did with you before Christmas," Jürgen smiled. "My week is up tomorrow, and I go home."

The patient was now on the gurney and ready for transport by the EMTs, heading out. As the paramedics were cleaning up their stuff, Mark asked in a good-humored way, "So, Jürgen, you gonna stay and have a tea party with these two or what? And how do you know him?"

"Jason here worked with us for two weeks with this program in Germany. He and his two comrades did a damn good job. We run their, how do you say, their behinds off," Jürgen said, laughing.

"That they did. And one hell of an experience too," Jason said, smiling.

The paramedics were leaving now. Jürgen gave Jason another hug and a handshake. "It's really good to see you. I'll tell the others what famous person I saw today," he said, chuckling. As he was walking away, he said, "When are you coming back to Germany? We need you."

"Maybe in a couple of months. My lovely wife and I are planning our honeymoon, the one we never got to take. Jürgen, take care and have a safe flight going home."

"You too," Jürgen said. "*Auf Wiedersehen.*"

"*Auf Wiedersehen,*" Jason said, smiling.

The police officer stood there, still waiting to see their IDs. John pulled his out, and Jason pulled both of his out. John just looked at Jason and asked, "You got to do the work abroad program? In Germany?"

"That I did, and it was an amazing experience. One of the best parts was seeing the Porsche Museum. The other is, that's where I found and proposed to my wife, Talia. Well, actually in Switzerland," Jason said.

The officer just looked at the both of them, and then said, "You guys have all the fun."

Charles was on his feet and standing close to the three of them. The officer was going to take his statement. Charles looked at Jason and John and said, "Thank you for being here, and coming so quickly to the aid of that man. I've had nothing like that happen since I've been a security guard here. Ten years. And Pete, I don't even know what to say about him."

"Charles, we're also glad we were here to help," John said.

"We'll be seeing you tomorrow, I'm sure. It's the big day," Jason said.

After Charles shook hands with the both of them, John and Jason turned to head back up to the third floor. The people hanging around were mostly those that still had some work to do to get the runway and chairs set up and whatever else they needed to do, and now, clean blood up off the floor before tomorrow's show. Several feet inside the hall, Jason and John now saw Talia, Grandma Jean, and the girls, and one of John's sisters looking at them.

Chapter 19

Both men just stood there looking at the ladies. Talia was in front of the women looking at Jason with a blank look and arms crossed.

"How long have you been standing there?" Jason asked, looking at Talia, knowing she could get shaken by what she's seen. This one would be the worst, but he didn't know how much she saw. He had hoped that they would have just stayed upstairs.

"Long enough to see you roll him over. Just tell me that man won't die after getting shot in the stomach," Talia said as she looked to where he had been lying on the floor, with blood coming out. "And what about the security guard on the floor? We saw the gun laying there. Did he shoot that man?" She looked back at him. "Why did he shoot him?"

"First, I can't tell you about the shooting victim because I don't know why he got shot. But he has a good chance of making it, even though he lost blood and has internal bleeding. There was no exit wound," Jason said. "They'll have to get him into surgery as quickly as possible. The police will take care of the security guard. He won't be back here," he said, wanting to reassure her and the others.

Grandma Jean looked at Jason, and he looked back at her and asked quietly, "Did you know how bad this was going to be?" John looked at Jason, no doubt wondering why she would know what was going to happen. She was upstairs when shots were fired.

"No. I'm not privy to that type of information. You should know that by now." She turned and headed toward the escalator with Chloe and Jana following her. John watched Grandma Jean walk away, and then looked back at Jason. He wasn't going to say a word.

John looked at his sister Lori and asked, "Where's Nikki?" She pointed up and said, "She didn't see anything. She's with Vanna." He nodded.

Seeing her name badge, John said, "Talia, your husband has been doing this a long time, as you are well aware. He's damn good at his job, from what I can see just working with him now. I hope I can continue doing what I also love and care about, helping people when they need it most, wherever they are or wherever I am." He looked at Jason. "I'm glad we could work together on this. I'm going to go wash my hands." John headed out the door with Lori. Now it was just Jason and Talia.

She'd been holding in her tears, but now they flowed. Jason took that step and wrapped his arms around her. She put her arms around him, and they stood there. He looked at her, wiping away her tears, and kissed her. Jason's phone buzzed; it was a text from Cole.

Cole: *Here are 3 or 4 places that you might like to check out. I think they would be quite interesting. If you get a chance, maybe get some photos if you decide to see them?*

Jason: *Thanks, Cole. I would like to see these. Hopefully, they're not too far away. We need a good distraction right now. Just finished up helping a man who got shot here at the convention center.*

Cole: *OMG. No way! Hope he'll be alright, as well as the rest of you.*

Jason: *We are. I'll fill you in when we get back home. Tell Jim and Paul, I saw one of our German pm/ff's here. Right now, I have a wife to comfort.*

Cole: *OK. I'll tell them. Let me know how the sightseeing goes. Talk with you later. Be safe.*

"Why don't we go back upstairs, and I'll go wash my hands," Jason said to Talia. "Cole gave me a few places we can go see this afternoon. Two of them I'd really like to see for me, and one of them for Grandma Jean and the last one's for all of us." He put his arm around her as they headed toward the escalator. "Are you alright?"

"I'll be OK. I'll tell you about my interview later. I finished up sooner than I expected," Talia said. "When Chloe told me that they just heard some pop noises, and that you and John left in such a hurry, it scared me, and I wanted to come down. I know I shouldn't have, but I was worried for you."

"I'm alright as well," Jason said. "I would never intentionally get in the line of fire with anyone unless I'm protecting my family. I'll be the first on the scene of an accident if possible, and one of the first if a fire breaks out."

They entered the waiting/buffet room, saw Grandma Jean and the girls sitting at their table, and started walking toward them. They saw John and his group seated, having lunch. John nodded to Jason. Jason handed his backpack to Talia, telling her he would go wash up and be back in a few. Another man was getting a plate of food, turned, and saw Talia. He walked over to her. "We just heard about the commotion down in the large hall," the man said.

"Mr. Shetler, this is my husband, Jason Porter. He's a paramedic/firefighter. He and Mr. Marshall, also a paramedic, are the ones that helped the man downstairs," Talia said. He looked at Jason and was about to shake his hand, when Jason held up his hands, showing some blood on them.

"I'll be back in a bit," Jason said, giving Talia a quick kiss. "And then we'll talk about this afternoon."

"Mr. Porter, thank you for your service. It is greatly appreciated," Norm Shetler said.

"Thank you," Jason said, and then he turned and left.

"Well, Talia, I'm going to go eat my lunch. Have a good rest of your afternoon. Seattle has a lot to see," Norm said.

"Thank you. We look forward to doing some sightseeing. I'm excited about it. Maybe I'll get inspired. And thank you for such a wonderful interview," then she walked to the buffet table to get some lunch and headed to her table.

⋔ ⋕

Walking back into the room, Jason saw the cooks putting out fresh food. It smelled good, and made him hungry. He filled his plate and walked over to their table.

"I thought you fell in, and I was going to either come in and rescue you or have John go in after you," Talia said, grinning. The girls giggled, and Grandma Jean smiled at the two of them. They continued to eat.

"Ha, ha," Jason said with a silly grin. He wasn't going to tell her he needed to text Cole about a surprise he wanted to do for her, hopefully before they had to return home next Tuesday. With his head tilted down, and his alluring smile, he looked at Talia and said, just loud enough so that even the two girls heard, "Now, had there been a shower in there, I would have texted you to join me." Jason took hold of Talia's hand, kissed it, then leaned toward her and kissed her lips.

The girls looked at Jason and then Grandma Jean with eyes wide, not sure where to look. She gave them a sideways glance and said, "It's OK, I have selective hearing and sight when I want to."

"So, when we're done here, we can head out and go see a few things this afternoon, and then we'll see what the evening brings," Jason said, looking at all of them. Chloe was the one to ask where they were going.

"As my mother used to tell me when we went somewhere and I asked where, she'd say either 'down the road a piece' or 'you'll see when we get there,'" Jason said. "After a while, I stopped asking, but these will be interesting for all of us." When they were finished, Jason said, "If you ladies care to make a restroom break, do that. I'll do the same, then I'll call Robert and let him know we're ready."

They headed down to the main lobby to wait for Robert. It was cloudy and cool outside, but at least warmer than Iowa in the middle of February. Getting into Robert's vehicle, they headed south on Interstate 405. Their destination would take about thirty minutes if traffic was flowing nicely.

"So, Robert, do you know where we're going?" Grandma Jean asked. She wasn't able to sense anything from him as to where they were heading.

"I do indeed. My wife and I have been to these very places several times. I think you'll all appreciate them." Robert talked about and pointed out various sites along the way. Soon they were crossing Lake Washington on the E Channel Bridge onto Mercer Island. He told them a little about Mercer Island, and that it was named after Judge Thomas Mercer back in 1860. Soon they crossed Lake Washington again, this time on the Homer M. Hadley Memorial Bridge. Robert could see in his rear-view mirror how big the girls' eyes were, looking at the length of the bridge and all that water.

He continued telling them briefly about the bridge's history, which was named after the man who was the pioneering engineer from Seattle, Homer M. Hadley. Robert told them it was a floating bridge, and the world's first that connects Seattle to Mercer Island. It's also commonly called the I-90 floating bridge. He could see that both Chloe and Jana preferred their eyes looking straight ahead, rather than looking around.

"So Robert, when was this bridge built, and how long is it?" Jason asked, looking out his window, enjoying the view.

"It was built in 1989. It's the fifth-longest bridge of its kind, and is around 5,800 feet. That's well over a mile long," Robert said.

They were coming to the end of the bridge, when Jana asked if they would be crossing back over that bridge, and Robert said, "No, not that one," and left it at that. They arrived at their first destination and parked. Everyone got out of the vehicle and followed Robert across the street. He looked at them and said, "This area, including where we parked, is called Occidental Square. There's this small park, and all these nice shops, places for people to sit and relax and ponder about whatever is on their mind. But this will have meaning for you, Jason."

He stood there for a moment and then told them about it. "This entire sculpture was inspired because of the deaths of four Seattle firefighters back in early 1995 that battled a warehouse fire, and it's called the Fallen Firefighters Memorial." Jason walked up to each statue, looking at it and walked around each. Soon, Talia, Grandma Jean and the girls were also walking toward them along with Robert.

"They're made of bronze, aren't they?" Jason asked, and Robert said yes. The girls, including Talia, were taking several photos. There weren't many people around, which, he was glad.

"I know it isn't a very big memorial, kind of small, but I'm glad that you got to see this," Robert said as he walked closer to the figures and Jason. "There are a lot of memorials for fallen firefighters across the country."

"It didn't have to be big. Thank you, Robert," Jason said. "Robert, would you mind taking a couple photos of us here?"

"Not at all," Robert said. He took Jason's phone and took a picture of all of them with each statue. When it was done, he asked if they'd like to at least walk down the one side and back up the other, and then they'd head to the next place. Grandma Jean did well in walking. When they finished, they headed for Robert's vehicle. It's so nice having someone else do the driving who knew where they were going.

Robert found parking at the next place, and they followed him down the sidewalk until they came to it. He explained that it's called the Garden of Remembrance. It's a memorial in honor of the over 8,000 Washington state residents who've died since World War II. Robert Murase designed the entire memorial.

Robert said his dad's name was on that wall. He fought over in Korea. Jason and Grandma Jean both looked at him.

"My husband, William, fought in Korea," Grandma Jean said as her eyes misted over. Jason put his arm around her. Robert nodded his head. They continued walking along the wall, stopping and reading the inscribed messages and looking at the names. When they were finished, Robert wanted to show them one last passage on the wall from a poem.

FOR THE FALLEN

They Shall Not Grow Old

As We Who Are Left Grow Old.

Age Shall Not Weary Them

Nor The Years Condemn.

At The Going Down Of The Sun

And In The Morning,

We Will Remember Them.

—Laurence Binyon

Chapter 20

Before getting in Robert's vehicle, Jason told Robert he was going to text his two partners, Jim and Cole, about this first excursion. He attached a couple of photos for them to share with the guys, as well as photos from the Garden of Remembrance.

Jason then texted: *We're heading to the Museum of History & Industry, and then the chocolate place after that. Looking forward to it. Maybe I'll send a photo.*

Arriving at the museum, Jason looked at Grandma Jean as they were getting out of the vehicle and saw the smile on her face. The building itself was impressive, and even before they started walking toward it, Robert stopped them and said, "My wife and I have had a membership to the museum for a long time. We used to go more often with the kids when they were growing up, but they've grown and moved away. We try to go at least twice a year. After you told me about wanting to come here, I made a phone call, and with my membership and the OK from my wife, you can all get in free."

"Robert, are you sure about this?" Jason asked.

"Yes. I am happy to share this with you. You've all been wonderful, and I've been enjoying your company when not with my wife," Robert said, smiling. Jason reached out and shook his hand. Talia walked up to him and hugged him, and the girls and Grandma Jean told him thank you.

After following Robert inside, he spoke with someone at the main desk, and then they set out, walking and looking. There was a lot to see. They listened to the short artifact audios while looking at the exhibits behind glass. Some displays were about Salish Baskets and the Petticoat Flag, the Arctic Club Stained Glass Panels, and the "Iron Chink" Salmon Butchering Machine, and Starbucks. In 1971, three friends started it. They came up with the name from the book *Moby Dick* by Herman Melville. It was the first mate's name, 'Starbuck.' The Navy Periscope was quite interesting. They each took a turn looking through it, giving them a 360-degree view of Seattle. This was a fun one, to have a picture taken while looking through a periscope.

The most interesting for Jason, as a firefighter, was that he couldn't imagine so many buildings that were wood, but then it was back in 1889. He could see how easy it would be for them to go up in flames, and fast. They all sat in a room watching the short, seven-minute video about the Great Seattle Fire of 1889. It was a hot June, and there was very little rain. They learned how the fire started in a woodworking shop. A glue pot had boiled over and ignited wood chips and turpentine, and soon spread to a liquor store, which exploded. And then a domino effect, setting entire blocks on fire.

All those buildings were built of wood. The city's water supply was low, so there wasn't enough water pressure, and many of the water pipes were made of hollowed-out logs and burned. A lot of the hydrants were made of wood, so naturally, they burned too. The fire destroyed twenty-five blocks of downtown Seattle in less than a twenty-four-hour period. People were very grateful that day that no one died. The next day, the government and business leaders got together and made plans for a better, safer, and more prosperous future.

They stopped at the MOHAI Mercantile and browsed, finding a few goodies there. Talia found some wonderful teas, picking one out. Jason agreed with her choice. It was called Lavender Orange Grey. Then a chocolate threesome, and a book titled *Do One Thing Every Day Together – A Journal for Two*. Jason leaned down, kissing his wife.

When they finished on the inside, they headed outdoors. Robert wanted to show them the large clock on the north corner. As they walked to it, he told them that the clock is fifteen feet tall and was built in 1913, getting moved to this location now, its new home, at Lake Union Park. It's called the Carroll's Jewelers Street Clock.

Talia had to smile, and walked around it, seeing the name Carroll's on each face of the clock. Jason watched, smiling at her. Without the S, she thought of Carroll, where her Aunt Joan and Uncle Dave live in Iowa. They've lived there their entire lives. Talia and her brother, Kurt, lived there for a short time before moving to Des Moines with their parents. After that, they spent a lot of time with their relatives and played with many neighborhood kids making friends. Talia had Robert take a few photos of them all standing in front of the clock.

It was time to head for the last treat of the day until Saturday. This one, Jason kept under wraps, not telling any of the girls. He was excited about seeing their faces when learning they'd all get to go on this tour. He had no idea exactly what a chocolate tour was. Robert pulled up close to a door, then turned and looked at Jason with a smile. He said he was dropping them off here and would return well before closing time at 6:00 p.m. He'd pick them up near the front entrance. Stepping out onto the sidewalk and looking up at the building with the company name, they turned back to Jason, smiling and eyes wide.

They were right on time for their tour. The girls stood looking at Jason, and then looked at the sign: Theo Chocolate Factory.

"How did you learn about this place?" Talia asked, smiling and hugging her husband. He gave her a quick kiss.

"Cole sent me a few other places that he learned about from the travel agent here, and I wanted to surprise all of you," Jason said. "I told Robert that I wanted all of us to experience this. So, ladies, if you're ready, why don't we go in and see what this is all about." He walked to the door, opening it, and the smell of chocolate was quite aromatic. Everyone was required to wear a hairnet. They were given a brief history of the building, dating back to 1905. It was originally a trolley barn, and then after 1941, it served as offices, storage, a repair garage, and a warehouse. It was also Redhook Brewer for twelve years. Jason saw the look Talia gave him, knowing he probably wouldn't have minded having a beer, but that would have to wait.

Their guide continued telling them that since 2006, Theo Chocolate Factory is most proud to be the first organic, fair trade, bean-to-bar chocolate maker in North America using only the highest quality chocolate, which comes from the world's best cocoa beans in the Democratic Republic of Congo. Relating to cocoa and cocoa farms, they touched on the social and government issues, also stating this company believes that to help make our planet a better place, they would be the ones to do things differently. Before continuing, the guide asked if there were any questions, to which Grandma Jean raised her hand.

"Where does the name Theo come from?" Grandma Jean asked.

The guide answered, "A good question. It comes from the Theobroma cacao tree, which is a fruit tree, and its name means 'food for the gods.'" The guide went through the fifteen-step process, explaining each while everyone watched that machine do its job.

When the tour finished, it was time to go and see what was inside the retail store, known as the "Flagship Store." As they walked in and looked around, it was like chocolate heaven. Chloe and Jana walked in one direction, while Grandma Jean saw a couple of sofas. She was going to sit down for a bit. She liked chocolate, but just wanted to watch everyone. Talia wandered, and Jason sat with Grandma Jean for a few moments next to a beautiful fireplace.

"Why don't you go find your wife and see what goodies she's found," Grandma Jean said. Jason got up and headed toward Talia. She had several chocolate bars in her hand.

"So, what flavors did you find?" Jason asked. Talia showed him, and he smiled. "I think I'll like the Gingerbread Spice and the Peppermint Crunch. I'm not sure about the Turmeric Spice, in chocolate?" looking at her. "Any others you want to try?"

"No," Talia said. They saw Chloe and Jana, each with several chocolate bars in their hands. The girls headed to the counter to pay, as did Jason and Talia, and then walked over to Grandma Jean and asked if she wanted anything. She said no, but she was glad they found some wonderful treats to remember this place by. It was about 5:45 p.m., and they headed toward the front door going out. It was dark out, and they saw Robert standing by his vehicle waiting for them. He asked how it went, and they all started talking at once. He just smiled at them, and then they all headed for the hotel.

೮೦ ೮ಠ

Arriving at the hotel, and getting out of Robert's vehicle, Talia turned to Robert and said, "I want to invite you and your wife to the show tomorrow. That is, if you don't have anything else planned. You have been so kind in driving us back and forth and taxiing us around. You feel like family."

"Talia, thank you. My wife and I would very much like that. We've never been to a fashion show. But don't outsiders need a ticket to get in?" Robert asked.

"I spoke to someone earlier today, and your names are on the guest list," Talia said, smiling.

"Thank you so much. My wife will be excited to hear this. It starts at 1:00 p.m., correct?" Robert asked.

"Yes, but you'll want to come early and find a good seat," Talia said. Robert nodded, and she shut the door, heading inside.

Rather than go out and try to find something to eat, they all agreed to order something from a restaurant that would deliver. They gathered in Chloe and Jana's room and enjoyed soup and sandwiches, and talked about this afternoon and what they'll be doing tomorrow. It's the big day.

"I can't believe tomorrow is Valentine's Day, and we get to be part of the fashion show," Jana said, with a big grin on her face.

"It does seem dreamlike," Talia said, looking at them. "Had I done this the last year or two, I'd know what was going to happen. I know I didn't thank you, Chloe and Jana, for telling Jason about the envelope and getting him involved. I was scared, because I honestly didn't think I was good enough to go up against anyone else. I was afraid to show my talent. I love designing for people and have them tell me it makes them feel wonderful and special to wear something they just thought about and not find it anywhere. I enjoy sewing, but of course, the two of you have me beat."

"Talia, ever since I've known you, I was, well, kind of jealous of you because you could design," Jana said. "My creativity in coming up with something, like you do, just wasn't there. I'm much happier taking your designs, making a pattern, and then sewing the outfits.

That's what I enjoy doing. And I don't mind being 'behind the scene,' so to speak." She looked at Talia with sincerity.

"I'm glad we're here, because I've never seen a fashion show. And now, I get to be in one, and with a design I came up with, with some help," Grandma Jean said. "And with that, I'm going back to my room to watch a little Seattle news, and then to bed. It's been a wonderful but long day for me." She stood up, and then Jason and Talia hugged her. Chloe and Jana did the same.

"I think I'm going to go back to our room and relax, and maybe watch a little news myself," Jason said.

"I'll be there in a moment. It has been a long day, but a good one," Talia said. She asked Chloe and Jana if there was anything they needed to do or talk about before morning. They looked at each other and then back to Talia.

"I really can't think of anything," Chloe said. "I think getting a good night's sleep, having a good breakfast in the morning, and then let's go and enjoy our fifteen minutes of fame after lunch." She smiled, as did Jana nodding her head.

"Alright then, we'll have breakfast before eight. I'll see you in the morning," Talia said. Both girls smiled and bid her good night with her handsome husband.

ॐ

There was enough light this morning from the security lights outside. Talia lay in Jason's arms, his body warm against hers and her baby bump. Under the blanket, her arm lay across his chest, feeling the rise and fall of his breathing and his steady heartbeat. She could feel her heartbeat match his. Looking toward the window, she remembered the first time she lay beside him in this same position, only facing an open fireplace with the flames dancing, and she smiled a big smile.

She felt him move, and looked at his face to see him looking back at her in such a loving way. Talia propped herself up and leaned over his chest, kissing it, and then up to his lips. He wrapped his arms around her, and then one hand caressed down her back. He kissed her passionately, making love to her again. Her heart was so full of love for him, and his for her. He taught her that, when they made love in the cabin for the very first time in the mountains of Switzerland.

Jason whispered in her ear, "I love you so much!"

"I love you. Happy Valentine's Day, my love," *she* said softly.

"It's like Christmas morning all over again. I'm so grateful for you being in my life," he said, still with his arm around her, holding her and gently rubbing her stomach. Jason saw the clock on the nightstand, showing it was 7:00 a.m.

Talia also looked over at the clock and then back to him. "And I'm grateful to have you in my life, but we're going to have to get up now." Giving him a quick kiss, she scrunched up her nose. "I'm just so happy being here with you, the girls, and Grandma Jean. I hope she's enjoying all of this, because I know I am, especially this part." He leaned down, kissed her once more, and then got out of bed. He walked around to her side, and the two of them headed for the shower.

Chapter 21

After breakfast, Robert was waiting to take them to the convention center. He told Talia that he had told his wife about going to the show that afternoon, and that she was so thrilled, and was going to tell her friends a fashion designer had invited them. Talia smiled. When they arrived at the center, they saw the other designers and their people. Sabrina was even there with her girls. Soon, Elizabeth and Linda walked toward them and said, "Good morning, everyone, and Happy Valentine's Day to all of you." Everyone reciprocated the same and clapped.

"We're going to check you all in, and then we're going to head to the large hall so we can get this morning under way," Elizabeth said.

As they walked into the room, it was completely decked out for a special Valentine's show, and the atmosphere felt joyful. The chairs on either side of the runway made it feel real. There were still people working on finishing touches. The judges' long table sat on a riser several feet from the end of the runway, and there were other tables and chairs scattered around the room. The group walked toward the runway, and saw a woman walk down the three steps toward Linda.

"I'd like to introduce all of you to your choreographer, Jackie Glen." She turned back to Jackie. "You've been a choreographer for the last twelve or thirteen years?"

"Actually, today, February 14th is the start of my fourteenth year," Jackie said with a big smile.

"So, are you ready to get started with your new models?" Linda asked.

"Yes, I am," looking at the large group. "OK, who are all my models here? If you would first line up in front of the steps for me, we'll get started in just a few moments." The models lined up, waiting for instructions from Jackie.

Linda turned to her now smaller group of ten designers and the few other people who accompanied them. "While Jackie is working with the models," Linda said, "the rest of us are going to sit back and watch and learn." They headed over to some tables and sat down.

Jackie explained the process, and with the help of her assistants, everyone watched them as they walked down the runway, stood for a moment, completed a 360-degree turn, and then walked back toward the stage. Now it was the models' turn. Jackie had them follow one another about five feet apart toward the end of the runway on one side, and then walk back on the other side toward the stage. They would each get to do the turn later when they practiced individually.

Jackie's models were usually under forty years of age. When it came to Grandma Jean, who Jackie had been watching, she walked over to her. Both Chloe and Jana watched, as did Talia and Jason, not sure what was about to happen, and the others watched as well.

"Good morning. May I ask your name?" Jackie asked with a slight tilt of her head.

"My name is Jean Porter," Grandma Jean said, looking at her with confidence.

"It's nice to meet you, Jean. You might be one of the oldest models I've had the opportunity to work with. Would you be willing to tell me what your age is?"

"Not at all. I'm eighty-eight."

"Well, I have to say that you don't look like you're eighty-eight. And honestly, if I can look this good when I'm your age, I'll be tickled pink," Jackie said with a smile, and then turned toward the rest of the group.

"OK then. We're going to practice walking with the music first, as a group in line, and then we're going to practice one at a time. This will allow each of you to walk down, stand for a moment, turn completely around and then head back toward the stage. I want you to pretend you hear the announcer read your name and company name, and go through the description of your outfit. Do not hurry this process. I want you to enjoy it. After all, you are the models, and the clothing you wear are the stars of this show, so showcase them." She looked back at Grandma Jean with a smile.

It was time to add the music. Again, everyone watched Jackie's assistants to get the feel of the music. They were also told there would be no high-stepping like they see professional models do. She didn't want anyone looking that silly or uncomfortable. Jackie told them to stand up straight, no slouching, breathe from the stomach, and smile.

After rehearsing for about two hours, it was after 11:20 a.m. Jackie felt good about how everyone did, and told them so, specifically looking at Grandma Jean. She said lunch was being served on the third floor where the banquet was held. All models would need to be back down in their dressing room, getting ready, and the first set of ten would get in line, ready to go, by 12:45 p.m. The schedule for line-up was on each dressing room wall. The show starts at 1:00 p.m., Jackie and her assistants would be around to help anyone who needed it.

Also, if anyone had questions, they could come and see her near the judges' table. They were dismissed. Everyone was milling around talking, and the excitement grew. Little by little everyone headed upstairs to have lunch.

☙

While eating, Talia looked at Chloe, Jana, and Grandma Jean and asked, "How are you feeling about this now? We're just under an hour away from this thing starting."

"I'm a little nervous, but excited," Jana replied.

"Me too. Knowing that the three of us are up there doing this makes it easier. I think it's going to be fun," Chloe said as she looked at Jana and Grandma Jean, taking hold of her hand.

Jason had to ask, "Grandma, what are you thinking?"

She looked at her grandson with the biggest smile he'd seen in a long time, not counting the look on her face at the museum. "First, I'm having a hard time believing that I'm even here with all of you. Second, I get to wear something I designed. And third, I love it." They all laughed. "Just make sure you get plenty of pictures so I can show off to my friends." Lots of photos had already been taken since first boarding the plane in Iowa.

Two of Jackie's assistants came into the room and told the models it was time to go and start getting dressed. Everyone stood up, giving hugs, and you could hear all the "good luck" wishes going around. The excitement was really building for everyone now. The designers were asked to stay in the room, someone would come and get them.

John, Gwen, and their daughter Nikki came over to Jason and Talia's table and sat down, as did Sabrina, which kind of surprised them. There was small talk. Talia excused herself as she headed to the restroom, not knowing if there might be an intermission somewhere.

When she returned, she sat down, taking hold of Jason's hand. It was about five minutes later when Linda came for the designer' family and friends taking them down, leaving the designers to stay put and wait for Elizabeth. At least five to eight minutes passed and Elizabeth walked into the room and asked them to follow her.

෨　ෆ

The designers walked with Elizabeth toward the large hall. When they moved through the large double doors into the room, it grew quiet, and then there were flashes from cameras and clapping. Jackie's assistants guided each designer to their spot to sit with their family members and watch. There would be five designers on either side of the runway. People settled down as they saw Norm Shetler come from behind the stage curtain, dressed very nicely, and was handed a microphone. He walked a little way down the runway, looking around at the audience, and everyone became silent.

He smiled and then started by saying, "Good afternoon and Happy Valentine's Day to all of you." The clapping started, and he continued. "We especially want to thank our ten fashion designers who entered this year's contest and have this opportunity to showcase their talents and creativeness." Norm paused.

"How many of you have ever wondered what or where Valentine's Day comes from?" He looked around the room with a smile. "It has a rather dark history to it, from a very long time ago, possibly dating back to the third century. There are some tales, as history goes, that it's named after St. Valentine, a Roman Catholic martyr. It's said that he was put in jail for marrying people secretly even after he was forbidden from doing so. And while he was imprisoned, folklore has it, that St. Valentine fell in love with his jailer's daughter." There was some laughter. "Before his life was ended, he let her know by writing a note and signing it, 'From your Valentine.'

"So, Valentine's Day has existed since the Middle Ages and has become very popular worldwide. It celebrates romantic love by giving gifts, usually sweets, cards, beautiful flowers, and couples spending time together, and even marriage proposals. Today, we celebrate Seattle's 10th Annual Valentine's Fashion Designer Show." Norm continued speaking while two men walked down the steps on either side of the stage with roses, walking to each designer and handing each a rose. There was clapping.

"So, a few things before we get started. First, this contest is being recorded live. So any designer's, who would like a copy, please let Sara Walte know. Next, I'd like to introduce to you our judges." He walked a little further down, looking at the judges, and everyone looked toward the long table with the man and woman behind it. "They have at least twenty-seven years of judging between them. One is from New York, and the other is from Georgia. Please give a warm welcome to Arnold Schwartzenbaugh and Lorna Denton." They both stood up, and there was clapping. The designers looked at one another with eyes wide and mouths open.

He continued by saying, "I had been asked before this show got started to introduce each of the designers to you." He looked on both sides and then said, "So, after I announce your name, would each designer please stand for a moment and be recognized." With his large index card in his hand that he pulled out from his inner coat pocket, he started with Mary Liktor and her company name. Once each designer was introduced, and the clapping subsided, he then walked down the steps, turning toward the stage announcing, "We ask that you please hold your applause throughout the first half of the show. We'll let you know when intermission is before continuing with the second half.

"Ladies and gentlemen, we present to you this year's designers and their collection of wears."

As the music began, the curtains opened up to reveal beautiful decorations setting the stage. Out walked the first model to the center of the stage, and with Jackie's cue, started down the runway with ease. The announcer was Sara Walte.

One by one, as the first ten models began to stroll down the runway, it was fun to see where each designer may have been heading with their creation. The model before Chloe was to walk, may have had a little stage fright. It was different when there wasn't a whole room full of people watching you. Jackie stood down on the floor off to one side of the steps and spoke softly to her. She told her to imagine that morning in practice, take her time, and enjoy it.

It was one of Jennifer's models, and in moments, she walked toward the end of the runway, forgetting to complete her 360-turn before heading back to the stage. Chloe was next, waiting for the cue from Jackie, and then she started down the runway. She had a smile on her face, and was enjoying the experience. Sara told the audience Chloe's name and company name, and then proceeded with the description of what she was wearing. She read that it was a long, flowy, two-layered skirt made from natural linen fibers in two different colors, complementing the simplicity and style. The top skirt was draped open in the front with two hidden pockets on both sides, and the soft floral linen top could be tucked in or left out for comfort.

The outfit resembled a piece of clothing from the Victorian era. Chloe was so enjoying herself as she did her 360-turn, slow and easy, then turning and gliding back to the stage. Talia had a closed grin on her face, feeling proud of this design, she knew she had no control now over what Chloe, Jana, and Grandma Jean would do. After taking a couple photos with his phone, Jason took hold of Talia's hand, kissing the back of it.

The last one in the first set of ten was one of Sabrina's younger models. She did a nice job of modeling, although the piece she wore didn't quite seem age-appropriate. After the first ten models were done, there was a pause preparing for the next ten. Once they were lined up, each waited for their cue from Jackie. There were so many wonderful pieces of clothing, styles, and colors presented. Many fabrics used were natural fibers, and others were synthetics. Each model walked down, posed, making their full turn before heading back. Rae's male model looked like a natural, and was attractive and tall.

Jana was second to last in this set, and now had taken her place, waiting for Jackie to cue her. Once she started down the runway, she glanced toward Talia, giving her a slight smile and seeing Jason with his phone camera. Sara read Jana's name and company name, and read the description of her outfit. Jana heard some of the description of her outfit, that the slacks or trousers were made of tweed, black with threads of forest green and indigo, and pockets. Her button-down V-neck blouse, tucked in at the waist, was made of a Georgette fabric with full-length sleeves rolled about three-quarters of the way up over the sleeves of her Merino wool jacket in an elegant dark green, with the lining in a lighter floral green silk fabric.

The last model was one of Sabrina's. Unlike Sabrina's first model, this one tried doing some kind of squirrely walk, getting to the end of the runway a little too soon, turning around, and then walked back with an abnormal gait toward the stage. Talia and a couple of other designers glanced toward Sabrina, who had her head in one of her hands, slowly shaking it back and forth. Talia almost felt sorry for her. Almost.

It was a few moments, and Norm walked up onto the runway with his microphone and announced that there would be an intermission of fifteen minutes, and then the second half of the show would begin. People stood up to stretch and most likely use the restrooms, which Talia needed, and Jason followed.

Chapter 22

The sound of a gong signaled the intermission was over. Norm Shetler walked out on the runway again, with his microphone in hand. He looked around, seeing that everyone was taking their seat, and then announced, "Welcome back. I believe we'll get started with the second half of this incredible show." He smiled and reminded everyone if they could hold their applause until the end, that would be great. Norm then walked to the end of the runway and down the steps, heading toward the judges' table.

The music began, and the stage curtain opened again. The first model waited for her cue from Jackie, and soon took her walk down the runway. Talia paid close attention to the fabrics and how each would feel, even as Sara announced what the models were wearing. At the end of the runway, the model did her turn, paused a moment, and then walked back toward the stage. The next model was in place, ready for her walk, as did the others waiting their turn.

Soon it was Chloe's turn. She was the last in this third set. She would be modeling something very dear to Talia's heart. Talia sat up a little straighter in her chair, glancing at Jason, then back to the stage, watching intently. Even after choosing which outfits she wanted to show, Talia knew Chloe would look amazing in it because the style of her maid-of-honor dress was just like this one, except Chloe's dress was navy blue and a different fabric. Chloe looked good in anything she wore, even in her jeans and whatever top she would wear.

Chloe had checked in with Jackie earlier that morning to ask a question, not knowing if it would even be allowed, but to her surprise and Jackie's delight, she thought it was a wonderful idea and would talk to the announcer, Sara Walte, and the DJ. Talia would have no inkling of what would occur, just thinking Chloe would walk down the runway, do her turn, and head back. No one else would know either.

The music started softly with the hint of the song, and then the lights in the large hall dimmed slightly except for the lights over the runway. Chloe then walked to center stage and stood, waiting for her cue from Jackie. Sara was given her signal from Jackie and announced, "Our next model is Chloe Chang from The T.E. Rose Shoppe." Chloe walked the few steps forward and then stopped near Sara. Talia looked at her, wondering what was going on and why she stopped. Did she now have stage fright? Talia then heard the "ooh"s, "ah"s, and whispers. She held onto Jason's hand, and he put his arm around her and kissed her cheek. None of the other designers yet had presented a wedding gown.

Sara continued, "Chloe's A-line shape gown is cut close at the waist, gently widening down to the floor with a full chapel-length train all made from wild tapestry silver brocade, as is her strapless corset with white satin cross ties. Her bolero cover is iridescent organza, with three-quarter-length sleeves dusted with tiny crystal sequins."

Chloe received her cue from Jackie, and then started to walk the runway as the music crescendoed. She carried the same bouquet Talia had on her wedding day, red and white roses with long satin ribbons. It was the voice of a wonderful and talented, Black woman, singing this beautiful song. Chloe walked slowly with the music.

Jason closed his eyes as he listened to the words. He remembered the first time he saw Talia's face, and then opened his eyes as he looked at her now, and she looked back at him, with those same captivating eyes. It was magical. Chloe reached the spot where Talia and Jason were sitting, and then paused momentarily.

It was behind Devils Tower when he gave her that first gentle kiss, his own heart fluttering like the wings of a butterfly. It took his breath away, wanting her in his life. Chloe did a full turn, flaring the skirt and train, while someone who had been waiting their cue presented Talia with a small bouquet of miniature red roses. Chloe looked at both Jason and Talia, giving a slight nod and seeing Talia's tears. Jason took her hand, kissed it, and then kissed her lips in front of everyone.

Chloe continued toward the end of the runway, with the song continuing. Jason remembered when she came to him at the cabin, and he lay with her that first time. The pure love he felt filled his world. He knew he would love her forever. With a second complete turn, Chloe walked back toward the stage, standing as the song ended.

Many people in the audience, including Robert and his wife, looked toward Talia and Jason and couldn't seem to help themselves and clapped. Talia buried her head in Jason's shoulder, and he hugged her, smiling.

Talia looked at him, wondering if he had something to do with this, and asked in a quiet voice what she had just been thinking. He shook his head no and said, "I wish I would have thought of this myself. I didn't know anything about this, but I loved it, and I love you."

The music continued with a little more upbeat feel as the last ten models, one by one, took their turn down the runway, wearing some very creative designs. Talia liked them all, except one. She didn't know who would wear it, but learned there is something out there for everyone, no matter how strange-looking.

Grandma Jean's turn was coming up, and Talia was getting a little nervous, hoping she would do well walking, even though it wasn't exactly her kind of music. She was proud of her, that she designed an outfit for women in her age range, and that anyone wearing it would feel beautiful. Still holding Jason's hand, she looked at him, taking a slow, deep breath. Jason raised her hand again to his lips and kissed it. Little did Talia know, Grandma Jean had her own agenda for the runway.

₧   ₨

Grandma Jean was the second to last model, with one of Sabrina's girls, Leslie, last. No one knew what the lineup was, except for Jackie, the models and the designers. A quick decision was made to switch Grandma Jean and Leslie, since Leslie wasn't feeling well and had to use the restroom. Jackie texted Sara the last-minute change.

Leslie wore a more age-appropriate outfit, looked very cute, and did a nice job on the runway with a full turn, a very quick pause, and then hastened her walk back toward the stage. Talia wondered why the switch, and hoped that Grandma Jean wasn't feeling ill or got scared.

Jackie also spoke with the DJ letting him know of the change, and that the last model was probably his grandmother's age, so the style of music needed to change. Grandma Jean walked toward center stage, looking wonderful, and waited for her cue. She glanced to her right, as if looking at someone off stage, giving a nod, and a slight smile on her face. Talia noticed this, and presumed she was looking at Chloe and Jana.

Sara was given her cue to announce the last model, as was Grandma Jean, given her signal to walk. "Our last model this afternoon is Jean Porter. She is the grandmother of fashion designer Talia Rose-Porter of The T.E. Rose Shoppe. Jean Porter designed her outfit with some guidance from her granddaughter. Her slacks are made from 100% European stonewashed linen in milk-white, with side pockets and elastic waist. Her no-collar, black V-neck button-down blouse is made from Chambray, a lightweight, plain-weave cotton with tulip sleeves. And the waist-lined jacket is made from soft moleskin peachskin dress making fabric. The jacket's color is burgundy red with a floral 100% silk lining."

Talia smiled as she watched Grandma Jean nearing the end of the runway, getting ready to turn completely around and then pause. Talia hoped she wouldn't get dizzy and fall, but she did well with her turn, then opened one side of her jacket, placing her hand on her waist so the lining showed.

She turned and headed back toward the stage, then stopped halfway as two young men walked toward her. Turning back toward the judges, she stood still. Talia sat with her mouth open and glanced at Jason, who was smiling and just kept watching his grandmother with a little shake of his head. He heard Talia mumble, "What is she doing?" as her hand moved up to cover her mouth. She looked back at Grandma Jean. There wasn't anything Talia could do but sit in her chair and be silent.

Talia looked across the runway at Rae, and he seemed just as surprised with eyes wide and nothing he could do. The two young men were Rae's models. One of them had a beautiful long coat hanging over his arm, while the other carried a long-stemmed yellow rose. They helped Grandma Jean take her current jacket off and slip the coat on. One of them turned to head back toward the stage, while the other gave Grandma Jean the yellow rose and held out his arm for her to take as he walked with her to the end of the runway.

Sara continued, saying, "Jean's knee-length tunic is a beige linen with a gold loop linen blend with a camel-colored silk lining, an ensemble any woman would enjoy and be proud to wear for any special occasion." Jean did a complete turn, and then she and her escort walked back toward the stage where her escort left her to stand by herself facing the audience. Everyone stood and applauded. She stood for a moment, and then headed off stage.

Norm walked toward the bottom of the steps and announced, "Ladies and Gentlemen, we are going to have all the models walk one last time." He looked at Jackie, giving her the signal for the models to walk. "And here you may continue your applause." As the models followed one another down, they lined up on both sides of the runway facing the audience, and then crisscrossed facing the audience again before both sides together walked back to the stage, lining up in two rows. The clapping continued, with flashes from cameras, and then the models were led off the stage.

Norm walked up onto the runway, and everyone became silent. "Since this is a competition and the number of garments rose this year, I was informed the judges would need a little time deciding on who our winners will be. I'm certainly glad I don't have to make any of those choices as I've done in the past." He looked at the designers and smiled. "Yes, I've been a judge." The designers looked surprised. "Our judges have left the room to consult with each other, so this shouldn't take too long. This will give everyone a short break. Designers, we ask that you do not go back to your models' rooms. We wouldn't want any 'what were you thinking' talks," Norm said, and everyone laughed.

Talia got up, saying she had to use the restroom. Jason thought that was a good idea. When they came back to the hall, Robert and his wife came up to them, and he introduced his wife, Lynne. She was thrilled being in the presence of fashion designers, and feeling giddy about it. She'd taken a few photos with her phone, eager to show her friends. Talia asked her if she had some favorites this afternoon.

"Oh, heavens, yes. At least a good handful. There was a lot I wouldn't wear, and some I'm sure I wouldn't be able to afford. But I loved the outfit your grandmother wore, and that beautiful tunic looked wonderful on her. It must have been so fun helping her with those." Talia looked at her and smiled, then looked at Jason.

"Yes, Jean knows what she likes. She has quite a mind of her own," Talia said.

"May I ask, dear, could we get a picture with you and your husband? I understand you're a paramedic and a firefighter?" Lynne asked, looking at Jason.

"Yes. I am," Jason responded, smiling.

Rae came back into the large hall, and Talia stopped him, introducing him to Robert and Lynne. Rae took a photo of the four of them, and then Lynne wanted a picture with Rae, who was tickled to have his photo taken with a guest. He looked at Talia, knowing she was just as surprised about his models and her grandmother. Walking back toward the runway, Talia and Jason chatted with a few other people. Then John and Gwen walked toward them with their daughter. John and Jason shook hands.

Gwen asked, "So, Talia, how far along are you?"

"I'm almost five months. Baby is due in June," Talia said.

"Do you know if it's a boy or a girl?" Gwen asked.

Looking at Jason and smiling, Talia said, "We aren't sure if we want to know the sex. In a way, we want to be surprised."

"Oh, I hear you. John and I were the same way. Although he kind of wanted to know, but I didn't," Gwen said. "But no matter which it is, you'll love that child with all your heart. You're their parent, their teacher, their coach, and confidant and protector. But I think right now, we should go back to our seats. It's been almost twenty minutes. I wonder how much more time they need. I'm nervous and excited about the outcome."

"Well, good luck to both of us. There were a lot of wonderful designs, and I think we can all be proud of what we accomplished," Talia said. John and Gwen turned, heading toward their seats. Jason stood for a moment, watching them, and then looked at Talia with a solemn look as he also looked at her stomach. She knew what he was remembering. Talia looked into his eyes and reached up for a kiss. He took her hand, and they headed back to their seats. Norm stood on the runway, getting ready to announce that the judges had made their selections.

Chapter 23

Norm walked to center stage, and everyone grew quiet. "We are moments away from announcing our four prize winners in this year's Valentine contest. We thought it was appropriate that all the models have the opportunity to watch." The curtain opened, and the models were sitting on risers. "Each year, we have been entertained with the designs created and presented. This year..." He paused for effect. "...we have been captivated, in more ways than one, by ten talented designers. Would all of our designers please stand." The clapping began, and then he motioned everyone to hold their applause. "It was a game-changer after last year's contest, and the decision was made to add a little twist, stir things up, something the contestants hopefully wouldn't see coming this year.

"The designers were all asked the same questions on their application, so the judges could at least get a sense of the designer. Those were real questions, but during their interviews, each were asked new questions," he said as he looked at the designers and then the rest of the audience. Talia kind of figured that might happen, and possibly the other designers thought this as well.

Norm continued, "The judges wanted to get a feel for them on a different level, one that showed honesty, attitude, integrity, emotion, and passion. We've had eyes and ears all around the last couple of days. We learned that sometimes we hear things we don't want to hear, the profound impact it can make on us, and what we are meant to do. We would be better off following our own path in life, instead of what someone else chooses for us. It's difficult 'going against the grain,' as the saying goes, finding your joy in what makes you feel alive and grateful.

"We would like to ask our designers to please come up on stage and line up behind me." The designers headed toward the steps by the stage. Jason took hold of Talia's hand, kissing the back of it as he looked at her with loving eyes and a smile. Once they were all lined up, Norm stood off to the side near the edge of the stage. He continued. "This was not an easy decision for our judges, as you could tell by how long it took them." He smiled. Jackie and her three assistants stood at the far side of the stage, holding flowers. Looking at the cards and envelopes he held, Norm then looked at the designers and then back to the audience.

"Designers, ladies and gentlemen, it is time to announce this year's four Valentine fashion designer winners. Best of luck to all of you! We'll start with our fourth runner-up. This prize is worth $2,000.00, along with a gift card of $300.00, and it goes to..." There was a slight pause. "...Alice Monroe of The Monroe Design Shop, Jackson, Tennessee." The applause started as she was asked to step forward. He handed her a pink envelope and hugged her. An assistant brought her a small bouquet. Norm then had her step back to his right side.

"Our third runner-up, receiving a prize worth $4,000.00 and a gift card of $500.00, goes to..." Another pause. "...Gwen Marshall of Marshall Designs, St. Cloud, Minnesota." Again, everyone applauded as she stepped toward Norm, receiving her pink envelope and an assistant bringing her a small bouquet. She then stepped back by

Alice. With eight contestants remaining, they moved closer together. Norm smiled at them, looking at their faces in anticipation of the name being called next. Some had their eyes closed or heads tilted down. Talia looked at Jason, knowing how much he loved her, and knew she did her very best.

"Our second runner-up, receiving a prize worth $10,000.00 and a gift card of $500.00, goes to…" an even longer pause, "Rae Arendt of Designs by RAE, from Wichita Falls, Texas." Rae's eyes got big, and the look on his face was one of shock as he walked toward Norm, who handed him the remaining pink envelope as he shook his hand, and an assistant bringing him the last small bouquet. He raised his bouquet in the air with a huge smile on his face. The clapping continued, and Rae joined Alice and Gwen. One remaining winner left. The group moved a step closer to each other. Now seven designers left.

Norm looked at the designers and then toward the audience. "The judges and I have been friends for a long time. We've seen fashion come and go, and sometimes we've tried to understand what some designers were thinking with their outfits. And, honestly, they really could have used some help." There was laughter from the audience as Norm himself chuckled. "It takes someone to think about the needs of others, and not themselves and what they have to gain. One designer stood out and made me think back to why I became a designer in the first place, and the joy I could bring to others, and the smile on that client's face at what I designed for them. People of all ages are important, from the very young to our elderly. And when we can make them feel special, that they matter, that is huge in my book." He paused as he looked at the remaining designer's.

"Ladies and gentlemen, this year's top winner and first prize recipient of $35,000.00 and an interview with *Rising Fashion Magazine* showcasing her designs is…" the longest pause ever, "Talia

Rose-Porter of The T.E. Rose Shoppe, Des Moines, Iowa." There was the thunder of people clapping. Talia just stood, unsure she heard her name right, and then looked at Jason, who stood up clapping and whistling. Mary and Robin were on either side of Talia. They turned toward her, each placing a palm on her shoulder. She brought both hands up, covering her mouth and nose, with eyes wide and tears forming. She turned to see Chloe, Jana, and Grandma Jean with huge smiles, clapping and cheering.

Talia started shaking, and then saw Norm holding his hand out to her to step forward. He handed her the red envelope, giving her a big hug. And then Jackie brought a larger bouquet to her, hugging her. Talia just stood there, and then looked down toward Jason. He had his phone out, taking some pictures. Other flashes were going off. The models all stood, and the designers then gathered around her. It took several minutes before the audience quieted down.

Norm asked the winners if they would please take a walk on the runway. Talia was first, with Rae following, then Gwen and Alice. More clapping as the four of them stood on the runway, and then they turned and walked back toward the stage, lining up. Norm announced that this was the show's conclusion, and they looked forward to next year's contest and for everyone to enjoy Valentine's Day. He asked the four winners to please wait a moment.

Judges Arnold Schwartzenbaugh and Lorna Denton walked over to the steps leading up to the stage, walking up them. They congratulated all four winners. It was overwhelming for these four designers to have this much attention. People in the audience were standing around, waiting and watching. A couple of photographers from local newspapers approached the winners, Norm, and the judges, wanting to get pictures. Then the reporter from *Rising Fashion Magazine* came. She'd seen the show from start to finish, now asking

Talia if she would be available in about thirty minutes to meet by the judges' table for her interview. Talia said yes, and the reporter left. Most models had gone back to the dressing rooms to change, and some designers went with them. Arnold, Lorna, and Norm said they would also meet back in thirty minutes and then left.

Chloe, Jana, and Grandma Jean walked over to Talia, giving her hugs and telling her congratulations and how proud they were to be part of it all. They were going to change, but Talia told them not to. The photographer would probably take some pictures of the outfits they wore. It wouldn't hurt to leave them on for a while longer. Talia looked toward Jason, and headed down the steps as he walked toward her. The tears came as he hugged and then kissed her.

"You won, my love," Jason said, smiling and hugging her, and feeling very proud of his wife. He wiped her tears.

"I'm stunned. I can hardly believe it, and now a reporter from a fashion magazine will interview me. My heart is beating so fast, and I feel like I can't breathe," Talia said, shaking.

"Take some slow, deep breaths. The hard part is done. We'll have to get a video of this show to share with family and friends. They may not believe us otherwise," Jason said. He felt a tap on his shoulder, and turned around, seeing Robert and Lynne. They congratulated Talia, with Lynne hugging her. It was so exciting to see this firsthand. Lynne wanted one more photo, if she could, with just her and Talia. Robert then let the two of them know he would be available to get them back to the hotel when they were ready; call him. He and Jason shook hands, and Robert hugged Talia. And then they left.

John and Gwen, and Rae, all came over chatting for a few moments. Gwen and Rae both couldn't believe they won as well, even though it wasn't first place. But it was the experience of being here, and sharing their designs and talents that meant the most, and making new friends. Rae said they were flying out tomorrow; they had to get home. He gave both Gwen and Talia a hug, and then he left.

John and Gwen would stay until Sunday and then fly home. They thought maybe they could all meet for breakfast. They had a little sightseeing of their own to do on Saturday. And come to find out, they were also staying at the same hotel as the Porter group, but hadn't crossed paths. They headed back toward the dressing rooms. Chloe, Jana, and Grandma Jean were sitting down, waiting for the next thing before changing. Talia said she had to use the restroom before talking with the magazine reporter. The girls were fine and would stay put.

ဆ   ☙

Returning to the large hall and walking toward a table, Talia saw the magazine reporter approaching with her photographer. Norm, Arnold, and Lorna were at the judges' table, standing and talking. The reporter asked the three of them to join Talia and Jason. After they sat down, she introduced herself as Lola Fenmore, and her photographer's name was Marc Seaborne.

Lola asked Talia if Marc could get some pictures of her models. Talia said yes, as long as they were alright with it. Marc provided a waiver for each to sign, permitting their photograph to be taken. He took them up on stage. After taking several pictures, the girls and Grandma Jean went to change. Lola started her interview with Norm, and then drew in Arnold and Lorna since they were the judges. *They seem so natural at this,* Talia thought as she watched and listened.

Lola asked how they chose the four winning designers. She wasn't writing a lot, but Talia saw the small recorder, no doubt wanting to get all the information correct.

Arnold and Lorna explained what they were looking for, saying there were a few designers they were impressed with, and one in particular whom Norm interviewed. Norm said, "The reason we all got into design was what Talia talked about in her interview with me. It reminded me why I became a designer in the first place. It was how I wanted people to see themselves and feel when wearing one of my one-of-a-kind designs. I never intended to make multiples of the same thing, much like what Talia described to me." Jason took hold of Talia's hand, watching her, hearing what they were saying about her. Her eyes were glazing over, and he kissed the back of her hand, not afraid to show how much he loved her. Talia looked at him with a smile.

Norm continued, "When I said that sometimes we hear things we don't want to hear and the impact it can make on us, that was a light-bulb moment for me, at least," he said as he looked at Arnold and Lorna. They nodded their heads in agreement. Norm turned slightly and looked at Talia as he talked. "And when I spoke of learning to follow our own path instead of what someone else tells us we should do; we find our joy and what truly makes us happy, and we're better people for it, just as your grandfather told you."

He then looked at Lola. "I said we had eyes and ears around yesterday. A conversation was overheard between two individuals. One spoke of this very thing, choosing our own path, not the one chosen for us. And then there was a simple question: 'What are you grateful for?'" Lola just looked at Norm as he continued. "After all the interviews and the three of us discussed all the contestants, well..." He smiled, and turned to Arnold.

Arnold picked up where Norm left off, saying, "We had a good idea who our winners would be. But of course, we needed to wait until all the models walked the runway. We had to see the designs and feel what the designers were feeling." He turned to Talia. "And I absolutely loved that your grandmother had the wardrobe change on the runway. It was a bold move, and I was impressed with her. She reminded me of my Nana, who passed a few years ago. She would have loved wearing a tunic like that one. And it looked to me that you and Rae had no idea she was going to do that, or that his two models were in cahoots with her? I loved it, and I loved what she designed, and that she took you by surprise."

"Oh, you have no idea," Talia said, smiling and looking at Jason.

Lorna spoke up. "The one that clinched it for me," she said as she looked at Lola and then Talia, "It was your wedding gown design, the style and fabric, and of course, the song that played. I loved it."

"That was my wedding gown," Talia said.

Lorna turned toward Jason. "Mr. Porter, I watched you watch your wife. It seems two little birds shared a heartfelt story about you two." Lorna looked back at Lola. "I believe we chose well."

"So, Talia, your models; two are friends?" Lola asked.

"Yes, good friends, and both are my employees," Talia said.

The interview went on for another twenty minutes regarding Talia's upbringing, what made her decide to be a fashion designer, and then how she and Jason met. They gave the short version. Norm commented that Jason and another of the designers' spouses, both paramedics, helped save a man's life yesterday morning.

The interview soon ended. Lola asked Talia about taking her picture, including her husband, if it was alright. Marc took them up on stage. When finished, they headed back to their table. Lola told them she would get the interview written up soon, include the photos and send her a proof copy by email. If there were any changes, they could let her know before it went to print. She planned on getting it in the next issue, which was April. She congratulated Talia again and told her she'd be in touch, and left. Norm, Lorna, and Arnold congratulated Talia again, and also left. The girls and Grandma Jean came out carrying their garment bags, and sat down at the table.

"Talia, are you alright?" Chloe asked, reaching over to the small bowl that had the Hershey Kisses in Valentine colors. She unwrapped one popping it into her mouth.

She looked at Chloe, not saying a word at first. "I'm still trying to take it in. My mind is kind of numb from this afternoon, and that I won," she said with a half-smile.

Scooting his chair closer to Talia and putting his arm around her, Jason said, "It's been a long day and an amazing afternoon. I've never seen anything like it. And you three models did a great job. I loved watching you, and you looked wonderful."

"So, Chloe, I'm wondering what possessed them to play that song?" Talia asked, with raised eyebrows.

"I heard it over a week ago, and then it kept popping up in my head. I told Jana about it, and well, we thought it would be amazing. It was like it was meant to happen. We talked with Jackie, giving her a quick background on the two of you. We didn't know if we could even have it played. It was a long shot, but she loved it." She waited for Talia to say something.

Looking at Talia, Jason spoke up, "I loved it. It was beautiful, and it almost brought me to tears. And you heard what Mrs. Denton said." Talia nodded her head, lowering her eyes.

"I know, and it was beautiful. But I just wish you would have said something to me," Talia said, quietly.

"That would have taken all the surprise and fun out of it. It was meant for the two of you. But, if there were others in the room, and it touched their hearts as much as it touched yours, and to have Jason look at you that way, then it was worth not telling you ahead of time."

"And the small bouquet of roses was my idea," Jana said.

"Then I should say thank you to you both. It was very unexpected and sweet," Talia said with a half-grin. She then looked at Grandma Jean, wanting to say something about her little surprise with a quick wardrobe change on the runway. Just when she was about to say something, Grandma Jean spoke.

"I know what you're going to ask. You're wondering when and where we had time to design and sew a tunic? And why weren't you told?" Grandma Jean looked at her with her knowing look. Talia looked at Chloe and Jana, and they averted their eyes.

"I found my fabric several years ago and envisioned it being that tunic, but neither my machine nor fingers were working the way they used to. I asked them to help me." She looked at the girls, then back to Talia. "The timing for this was right. I thought about telling you, but this wasn't for you. You'll see in due time." Talia just looked at her, wanting to ask who it was for.

Jason said, "I think right now, we should do something about food and celebrate." Jason's phone rang, and he saw it was Robert.

"Hello, Robert."

"Hello, Jason. Lynne and I were talking. If you guys have something planned for this evening, it's alright, but we'd like to invite you to our home for dinner. We have a couple of friends that are joining us. Is this something that might work out for all of you?"

"Well, hold on, everyone is here." He told them what Robert just asked.

"Robert, we would all like that very much, but you said you lived in Seattle. Isn't that a little far for you to come?"

"We moved to Medina over two years ago. We aren't that far from your hotel. I can pick you up at the center in a bit and bring you here, and then I'll take you back to the hotel afterward. We would love to have you join us."

"OK, then. You have five guests coming for dinner," Jason said, smiling.

"Wonderful. I'll be on my way then."

Chapter 24

The evening with Robert and Lynne was nice and relaxing, with good food. Two other couples joined in, and were delighted to meet a fashion designer and her family. As the evening ended, Robert took them back to their hotel. He asked what things they planned on seeing tomorrow, being Saturday, so he would know which route to take, and told them he would pick them up in the morning when they were ready to leave.

It was getting late as they briefly gathered in Chloe and Jana's room. Grandma Jean opened her connecting door, and Talia retrieved the digital picture frame so they could upload their photos.

"So what is our game plan for tomorrow?" Jana asked.

"On our schedule is going to be The Space Needle. You can't come to Seattle without seeing it and going to the top, I hear," Jason said. "Then we decided on Chihuly Garden and Glass. Cole got a good package deal for us with Anisha's help. And then we'll get some other recommendations while you three are still here, before leaving on Sunday. But why don't we all turn in and get a good night's sleep. We'll get the rest figured out in the morning."

From their room, Jason called John to see if they were still up for having breakfast together, or had other plans. John said they would meet downstairs around 8:00 a.m.

Talia sat at the small table, looking at the first-place red envelope. Her bouquets of red roses lay on the table making the room smell wonderful, and with that pop of color. Jason had changed into his light sweats and of course no shirt. He walked up behind her, kissing her on top of her head before sitting down in the other chair.

"You're quiet," he said looking at her. "Are you going to open it?"

"I'm nervous. I've never won anything before." Talia continued to stare at the envelope. "When Norm said how much the first prize was, along with the magazine interview, and then had that suspenseful long pause, and we're all holding our breath, all I could think of was food. I was getting hungry." She now looked at Jason.

He chuckled, as he didn't think that was what she was going to say. He leaned over and kissed her and then asked, "Do you want me to open it?"

She looked at him and then slid the envelope toward him. He turned it over, gently opening the flap, and pulled out two pieces of paper. One was the check for $35,000.00 paid to the order of Talia Rose-Porter, and showing First Prize Winner in the memo line. He slid it toward her. There were also two tickets for a Seattle Harbor Cruise. Jason smiled, not saying anything, but turned them around so she could see what they were. He held onto the other piece of paper for a moment. She looked at the check and the tickets with eyes wide, like it was Christmas again, and then there was a huge smile on her face.

"I know we're in Seattle. That's real. But the show this afternoon felt like a pipe dream. I'd come and show my designs with the others, and then we'd have a few days and head home. I never dreamed I'd be the one winning first prize. I see this check with my name on it, and I'm…" Talia looked at her check.

"Yup. I can see you're in shock," he said with an amused look. "This paper says that funds can be directly deposited. And to please call or email Sara Walte for further information and instructions."

"I think that's a good idea. And I want to get a picture of the five of us tomorrow with me holding my check. When will I ever get to hold ‚a check that large again," Talia stated with a silly grin.

CS

Talia came out of the bathroom and saw Jason sitting up in bed with his stethoscope draped down his bare chest. She smiled at him, and he asked, "Do you want to see if we can hear the baby's heartbeat?"

"Yes, Doctor Porter," she said with a large grin and eyes wide.

"Why don't you lie down, and let's take a listen." Talia lifted her top over her small plump belly. Putting the eartips in his ears, Jason took hold of the chest piece, placing the bell on her stomach and slowly moved it around. Talia watched his face for a sign that he heard something. His eyes closed as if concentrating, and then he stopped. A slow smile showed Talia that Jason heard it. Keeping his hand steady on that spot, he gave the eartips to Talia. It was such a wonderful, steady sound, the baby's heartbeat. This turned out to be the best Valentine's Day gift anyone could have had.

ᘒ   CS

Jason watched her sleep while still holding her in his arms. The soft light peeked through their hotel window. Her breathing was steady with the rise and fall of her stomach. He remembered when she was in the hospital, and how grateful he felt when she breathed on her own after the ET tube came out. That fear of losing her was almost too much for him, as well as his child she was carrying. With that incident behind them, they now looked forward to being parents. He's amazed, watching her body change before his eyes. Her belly looked like a small soft, light pink pillow, and he smiled, knowing he was going to get to watch more changes unfold and be there for the birth. He's wanted to be a dad for a long time. He drifted back to sleep, holding the love of his life.

⚃

Jason's phone buzzed. It was Jim, his partner, texting: *Morning. I know it's early. Nadine and I were wondering how it went yesterday with the fashion show. We'll be gone for most of today with the kids. Have a good one.*

It was 8:30 a.m. Iowa time, 6:30 a.m. Washington time, when Jason looked at his phone. They would have to get up, even though he would just as soon stay in bed with his beautiful pregnant wife. However, he was looking forward to some sights they'd get to see today, especially with Grandma Jean. Spending time with her is a treasure, and soon she'd have a great-grandchild. Jason hoped she would be around for many years to come. He also thought about his grandfather, and the time lost due to his work schedule and filling in when one of the guys was gone or sick since he didn't have a wife and kids. It was 7:10 a.m., and time to get moving. He turned his head to see Talia looking at him.

"Where were you just now?" she asked.

"I was thinking about my grandfather, wishing I'd spent more time with him." He looked at her.

"I thought I heard your phone buzz earlier," Talia said.

"Ya, it was Jim. He and Nadine were wondering how the fashion show went yesterday. They have a family day planned today as well. But I wonder if it will be as much fun as what we're going to do and see," smiling back at her, giving her more kisses as he gently caressed her warm stomach.

"I was just thinking, we'll have to get some photos of me as this belly of mine expands," grinning at him and rubbing his strong arm.

"Well, why don't we go shower and get dressed, and then I'll take a few photos of that beautiful bare belly of yours. I like the idea of seeing photos of this pregnancy progressing. Then one day, we'll show our son or daughter where they got to spend the first nine months of their life, inside of you, and we'll put stories with them. We can add those to our photo albums as well."

"I love you," Talia said, kissing Jason, and then started moving to get out of bed until Jason pulled her back and gave her a big hug and a kiss.

"I love you more," he said, smiling at her, and then released her. She sat on the edge of the bed and then turned back to Jason, looking at him with eyes wide. And then she looked down.

"What?" he asked, sitting up straighter and reaching his hand out to her.

"I think I felt a flutter." She waited a moment to see if she could feel it again. Smiling at him, she said. "Jason, I think I felt the baby move."

Jason scooted closer to her, putting his hand on her stomach where she indicated, wondering if he might feel it as well. They were both silent and still. At the moment, Talia wasn't feeling anything. She looked at Jason's face as he looked up at her with a slight shake of his head. "I'm a little jealous that you could feel the baby move," he said with a mopey look on his face.

"I'm sorry. I hadn't noticed this feeling until just a moment ago. I was worrying so much about preparing for the fashion show, and then the last several days. And then, I kind of forgot that I'm pregnant. Geez, did that sound weird or what," Talia stated, as she stood up looking at him.

"You look absolutely beautiful to me," he said with a smile. "I guess I'll feel our baby move soon enough. But, right now, we need to get moving if we're going to join the others for breakfast."

⅚⎈⎈⎈⎈

Before heading downstairs, Talia asked Jason not to say anything about the baby moving. He agreed, but said, "You remember my grandmother seems to know things."

"I know. Sometimes it's just weird." Scrunching her nose.

"Ya. It's her little secret, how she knows. So, we ready to head down?"

Two big tables were pulled together with Chloe, Jana, and Grandma Jean, who were already eating, along with John and his family, just sitting down with their breakfast. Talia and Jason got their food and sat down.

"It's good that the two of you could join us," Grandma Jean said, looking at them with a slight grin.

"Well, we slept in a bit," Jason said as he noticed her looking at Talia. "Morning, everyone. John, Gwen, good morning. Nikki, how are you this morning?"

"I'm good. I thought my parents would never get out of bed. I was really getting hungry, and they stayed in bed hugging and kissing one another," Nikki said matter-of-factly with a crinkle of her nose as she ate her eggs and toast. Everyone chuckled.

"Nicole Danielle Marshall," Gwen said, with eyes wide and looking embarrassed. John grinned, knowing anything could come out of his eight-year-old daughter's mouth.

"Well, Nikki, sometimes that's what moms and dads do. That's because they love one another so much," Jason said as he glanced at Talia.

"I'll be glad to go home tomorrow. I miss my friends. We have show-and-tell sometimes, so I want to tell my teacher and friends about Mom getting a prize for her clothes, and some of the fun stuff we did here," Nikki said.

"So, Jason, what all do you have planned today?" John asked, and the two talked about their plans. It was a nice breakfast, visiting with the Marshall family. John's sisters, Vanna and Lori, and Gwen's best friend, Josie, talked about how they've supported Gwen when others snubbed their noses at her. But maybe now their opinion will change.

"Talia, your designs were amazing. I loved the outfits, especially your wedding gown design," Gwen said as she took a sip of her coffee.

"Thank you. Your pieces were also beautiful. And that was my wedding gown," Talia said. "I was inspired by things I saw in Switzerland. Chloe and Jana did most, if not all, of the sewing. I wasn't sure I wanted to share it, but then I thought if there were a bride-to-be who couldn't find what they were looking for and this sparked joy in them, then I would work with them and come up with a one-of-a-kind affordable gown." The ladies all continued talking.

John enjoyed talking with Jason about the work abroad program. Jason told him what he and his comrades did while in Germany, also telling John as the others listened that he and Talia hope to go back soon before the baby is born.

"You went across that ocean?" Nikki asked with eyes wide.

"Yes," Jason said, smiling at Nikki. "Would you like to travel someday across the ocean?"

"I don't know. We got to see a really big map of the whole world. And then our teacher had a globe so we could all look and watch it go around in circles. Do you know how much water there is?" Nikki asked Jason, looking at him.

"I do know. There is a lot of water on our planet. Did your teacher ask you if there was someplace you'd like to visit that's not here in America?" Jason asked. Everyone was quiet, and watched his interaction with Nikki.

"She did. I had a classmate tell her he wanted to go to the country of Hawaii. I gave him a stupid look. I told him my mom and dad went there on a trip without me." She looked at her parents like, 'how dare you go without me.' She looked back at Jason. "I told Curt that Hawaii was a state and part of America." She continued talking. "Then, my friend Maggie said she wanted to go where the polar bears were. But I forgot where they live."

"Do you know where the Arctic is?" Jason asked, looking at her. She looked at him and shook her head no. "You know how the earth is round?" Nikki nodded intently, listening to Jason. "If you were to look at your globe, you go to the top of it, and you'll see that the Arctic is way up there, and it is really big. It covers a lot of miles. And that's where the polar bears are. Did you know that's also where the North Pole is? Where Santa Claus lives?" he asked, smiling at her.

"I knew he was from the North Pole, silly," Nikki said, grinning at Jason.

"So could you imagine if Santa Claus had a bunch of polar bears pulling his sleigh instead of reindeer?" Jason asked. Her eyes got big, and she turned toward her dad.

"Wouldn't that look funny to see eight polar bears pulling Santa's sleigh?" John asked his daughter.

"So, Nikki, if you could travel anywhere you wanted to, where would it be?" Jason asked.

"My teacher asked me that too. I like animals. Maybe, Af-ri-ca? That's a big place. So, it has lots of animals, right?" Nikki asked Jason.

"Yes, it is a very big country with lots of animals," Jason responded, smiling.

"Well, something we plan to do today is to go visit the Seattle Aquarium so she can see the ocean animals," John said. Nikki smiled at her dad. "And, if we don't get moving, it'll be lunchtime."

John and his family stood up, as did Jason. The two of them exchanged ID cards and shook hands. Then Jason asked Nikki if he could shake her hand. She smiled, shaking his hand, and then they left.

Talia called Sara about making the direct deposit.

"I'm going to call Robert in a few minutes so he can pick us up," Jason said, then looked at Talia. "Do you want to get to Sara's office and get that taken care of?"

"Yes, I do. No sense in having such a large check on me or my bag. Oh, I want all of us to have a picture showing this check. I'm going to ask that employee if they could help, and then I'll head to Sara's office." With the five of them gathered together, and Talia holding her large check, the employee took a picture of them.

Chapter 25

After leaving Sara's office, Talia headed for the front lobby where Jason and the girls were waiting for her. With today's adventure, everything would be within easy walking distance, even for Grandma Jean.

When Jason spoke with Robert, he told him about the first place he wanted to go, telling Robert it was also a surprise for his grandmother. As they started crossing the Evergreen Point Floating Bridge, Robert saw the nervous looks on Chloe and Jana's faces in his review mirror. He remembered from a couple days ago that they were not keen on crossing the large body of water on the Hadley floating bridge.

"So, Robert, how long is this bridge?" Grandma Jean asked looking out her window.

"This bridge is just a little over 7,700 feet long. According to our Washington State Department of Transportation, it made it to the Guinness World Record with the title of being the longest floating bridge anywhere. We're quite proud of our floating bridges."

"So, I don't understand," Talia said. "You call them floating bridges, but what are they floating on? I mean, we're driving on cement. There must be hundreds of cars and trucks that travel on these bridges all day, every day. That's a lot of weight. Why not one of those big suspension bridges?"

"Ah, like maybe the Golden Gate Bridge," Robert smiled at Talia in his mirror. They were nearing the end of the bridge on the Seattle side as Robert continued to tell them why it was better to build a floating bridge, rather than the traditional fixed bridge or a suspension bridge. As Robert drove, everyone looked out their window. Soon he pulled into a parking lot that was across the street from The Space Needle. Once they got out, they saw the monstrously tall structure as it reached for the sky.

"Robert, do you know how tall it is?" Jana asked, looking up at The Space Needle.

"Oh, let's see, I think it's around 605 feet. It's built to endure strong winds up to around 200 mph. And as long as we don't have earthquakes over a magnitude of about 9.0 on the Richter scale, it should stay standing for a very long time. It's made of steel, so pretty strong, sturdy stuff."

Chloe looked at Talia and Jason, and asked if they were going to the top, unsure if that was something she wanted to do, seeing the elevators on the outside. Yet, she sat by the window on the airplane, looking out. Even Jana had a look of uncertainty.

"Lynne and I have been up to the top many times. It's a smooth ride, not as fast as you think. And there is an elevator operator who talks to you while going up," Robert said, looking at Chloe. "I promise you, this is something that will be a real treat for you. It's beautiful looking out, and a memory that you'll have for a long time."

Talia and Jana were taking photos, along with some pictures of the looks on Chloe and Grandma Jean's faces. Jason had a big smile. Talia asked Robert if he could get the five of them with The Space Needle behind, if he could fit it in. After taking some steps back, making sure they all fit, he took a few pictures. Everyone looked at them quickly and liked what they saw. Robert had them follow him across the street, heading to the Pacific Science Center. Once inside, Robert pointed toward the exhibit Jason told him about for Grandma Jean. Robert said he would pick them up later today when they were ready, and he left.

"Grandma Jean, we do have a few other things we'll go do, but when we saw the information about this exhibit, we wanted you to see this," Jason said.

"And I wanted to see them," Talia said, smiling at her.

Grandma Jean stood there looking at both of them, then toward the door into the Tropical Butterfly House. She was surprised. Turning around, she had a big smile on her face and hugged her grandson. "Thank you so much."

"You're welcome," smiling back at her. "But, just so you know, before we go in, it was Talia that wanted you to see this." Grandma Jean turned to Talia and hugged her, telling her thank you.

Once inside, it was amazing to see these little creatures flying around. Some were in the trees, some sitting on rocks, with a few sipping nectar from a small container with water and fruit. They took their time looking at it all, being careful where they stepped as well.

Their photos captured these little ones, some finding their way onto Chloe and Grandma Jean's arms. One landed on Jana's shoulder, and she slowly turned her head to look at it while Talia took a picture. The girls giggled when they saw two butterflies land on top of Jason's head, and he stood there quietly, then turned to look at the girls as they took a photo of Jason's little adornments.

One beautiful orange butterfly settled on Talia's stomach, fanning its wings. The staff that was inside told her it was called a Cruiser.

Jason took a photo of both beauties, the Cruiser and his wife, as she looked down at it.

"Anytime we can admire what Mother Nature has given us, I think it's important to seize the moment," Grandma Jean said to Talia and Jason. "This was so special, and a surprise to me, since I am usually aware of things and events. But I had no sense of this one."

Talia wished she knew how Grandma Jean knew things, and just at that moment, it was like Grandma Jean read her thoughts by the way she looked into Talia's eyes. It gave her goosebumps. Jason asked his grandmother if she wanted to stay a bit longer or move on to the next thing. She was ready for the next thing, and said it would be a fun show and they could sit.

Jason told the girls to be careful not to take any hitchhikers out the door with them as they checked each other along with the butterfly staff. Next, they headed for the planetarium. After that wonderful show, they were all getting hungry. "Robert told me that the closest eating place is called Collections Café. It's just on the north end of the Chihuly building, so a block away. We can eat there," Jason said.

"When was he going to be back?" Chloe asked.

"He said he has an appointment somewhere in the vicinity later this afternoon, and when we're ready to leave, I'll call him. He figured it might be an early evening for us," Jason said. "We'll have to play it by ear."

"Well, I'm getting hungry. Let's go see what this Collection Café has to eat," Talia said.

⁖ ⁗

It was a nice lunch, and to be able to rest a bit. The group was ready for the next leg of their sightseeing journey. They headed for The Space Needle. Heading inside, they found the podium to show they had tickets. It was time to get into the elevator, along with about fifteen other people, including the elevator operator that would take them to the all-glass observation deck at the top, 520 feet in the air. The maximum capacity for an elevator is twenty-five people. Jason kept an eye on the girls to ensure they were alright riding to the top, even though the elevator ride was about a 42-second ride. The view going up was pretty awesome. Of course, the best was yet to come.

Once everyone got off the elevator, they could walk all around and take their time. There were floor-to-ceiling glass walls, which allowed for a full scenic view with nothing blocking it. The entire glass floor revolved, which was weird, allowing visitors the opportunity to see the elevators coming up and going down.

More photo opportunities looking out those windows, and of each other standing on the see-through floors. Even Grandma Jean was enjoying this and smiling. There was a lovely staircase leading down to the 500-foot level where more glass walls, and another revolving floor, were. They were all willing to walk down slowly to that level, making sure Grandma Jean made it down as well. She wanted to do this. The girls took pictures of her walking down the steps so she could show her friends. They'd spent a good hour at the top, enjoying it all. It truly was an experience, and made for more wonderful memories with photos to share.

"So, Jana, are you glad you came up with us?" Jason asked.

"I have to admit, yes, I am glad. I was uneasy about the ride up, but it wasn't as bad as I thought it might be. I did close my eyes once or twice. My stomach got in knots standing on the glass floors looking straight down, and I had to grab onto Chloe's arm." Jana said, looking over at Chloe.

"Well, I'm ready to head down. I saw the gift shop," Talia said, smiling.

"Me too," Chloe said and then asked, "Grandma Jean, how about you?"

"I am. This has been truly wonderful, and I can't wait to tell my friends that I got to go to the top of The Space Needle. You'll have to share your photos with me, as they may not believe what I've seen or that I was in the fashion show. When I told them, several of them had smug looks on their faces, not believing me," Grandma Jean said, looking at Talia.

"Sara said she'll let everyone know when the video is available. I'll let you know, and then we could have an evening with you and your friends, and they can see it. But, I think I'm ready to go back down." Talia said, looking at Jason.

"Ladies, why don't we head for the elevator," Jason said with his hand pointing toward it. While waiting, there was a commotion behind them. Jason turned around to see someone falling to the floor. He went over to see what he could do to help, telling them he was a paramedic. A family member told him that their sister had hypoglycemia. He knew there was a medical person on each floor, just in case, but someone else needed their help on the other side.

Jason opened his bag, taking out his BP cuff and stethoscope, and asked if they had eaten anything today. They said it had been quite a while since they last ate. They weren't from this area. Jason said he wasn't either. They looked at him, so he quickly pulled out one of his ID cards and gave it to them.

He knew if they waited for medical aid, the woman's blood pressure could drop further and she would be in more trouble. He pulled from a deep pocket inside his medic bag, a small bottle of Dex4 tablets, which was glucose, telling them what they were. These were large orange-flavored tablets that dissolve when sucked on, which help raise low blood sugar. After a few minutes of sucking on several of those, Jason asked how she felt; she still felt a little shaky and her vision was a bit off.

He asked if any of them had something she could eat until they got down to the ground. They didn't, and neither did Jason's people. Usually, she knew when it was about to hit her, because her vision would change seeing an aura of color, and get the shakes. It didn't happen often, but when it did, she had to eat, like now. Jason gave her another glucose tablet to suck on.

Giving her a few more moments, he took her BP again. It had come up a little, but she was going to have to get food in. He told them he would ride down with them, for which they were grateful. Helping her stand up slowly, one of her siblings took hold of her arm, staying close to her. The medical aid still hadn't come, but others would let them know what had happened and that there was a paramedic that had helped.

Getting on the elevator and heading down, Jason kept a watch on her, talking with her. They were on the ground floor in less than a minute. They thanked Jason for being there and helping, and then took her to get food. After they left, Talia gave Jason a hug and a kiss. Chloe and Jana just looked at him.

"What?" Jason asked.

"Talia mentioned that there were times when someone needed help now, and you stepped up lickety-split. Just like on the plane, and then the convention center," Cloe said.

"That's what I'm trained to do. I can't second-guess, waiting to see if someone else or other medical help will arrive in time. If I'm first on a scene, I do what I can for them. Their life may be hanging in the balance," Jason said, sounding a little miffed. "I'm sure you would be grateful that I came to your aid if you needed help now, when no one else was around, right?"

"Oh, gosh, ya. It's just seeing you take action. I didn't mean anything by it, Jason," Chloe said. "I'm sorry."

"I know you didn't. Why don't we head over to the gift shop, and then we'll head for Chihuly Garden." Talia took Jason's hand as they headed for the gift shop.

Chapter 26

Leaving The Space Needle gift shop with a few souvenirs in hand, they walked toward the outdoor garden of Chihuly. Admiring it, they considered which to see first: the garden, the glasshouse, or the gallery.

Jason's phone rang. It was Robert, and Jason put him on speaker. He was checking in to see how things were going. Jason told him they just got to Chihuly's, trying to figure out which to do first. Robert suggested they circle by walking through the garden first, seeing everything during daylight, and then heading into the glasshouse. Then they would enjoy the displays and listening to the audio in the gallery, which would give them background about Chihuly Garden and Glass. It's something that he and Lynne have done. And then they can all head back out to the garden when it was dusk and see everything lit up. It would be spectacular, colors they might not even imagine, and could be inspirational to someone.

Robert asked if they had plans for dinner that evening. If not, he and Lynne would very much like to have them back, and then he could take them back to their hotel. It took little to convince the five that they liked that idea a lot, so it was agreed. Robert said it might take them at least a good two hours with Chihuly. When they were ready to leave, Jason could call, and they would meet at The Space

Needle valet parking. Again, everyone agreed and thanked Robert for also inviting them back for dinner.

"OK, you heard the man," Jason said, smiling. Once they entered, they could now wander, look, admire, and take photos. With every turn of their heads, there was an incredible display of color, no matter how small or large. There were also beautiful plants, ferns, perennials and vines, along with so many wonderful glass creations displayed among all the vegetation. It was truly incredible to see this in person. They worked their way through the Glasshouse, seeing more blown glass in vibrant colors and shapes. Chihuly Garden and Glass, gallery and landscaping, have 45,000 square feet combined. The Glasshouse itself is 4,500 square feet and a good forty feet tall.

You could hear all five of them periodically saying, "Wow. Look at this. Come over here. You gotta see this one." Inside the gallery, there were many rooms: Glass Forest, Northwest Room, Sealife Room, Persian Ceiling, Chandelier, Millie Fiori, and several others. They each had a favorite room. Grandma Jean had to sit down twice. The others decided to join her and rest a moment before going to the next thing.

They were in awe of how each piece was meticulously glass-blown, and each unique in design and color. It was simply beyond anything they'd ever seen. It was getting dark outside, and they wanted to head back to the Glass House and Garden like Robert said. But first, they stopped at the gift shop and found a few other little gems.

Heading out and walking back to the Glass House and Garden, they continued to be captivated by what they saw with everything lit up. It was incredible, and so worth seeing. This was also a treasure, and their smiles showed it. Jason called Robert to let him know they were ready to go, and they headed over to The Space Needle parking.

☙

The meal that Lynne and Robert served was as wonderful as the night before, along with some yummy desserts. They invited a few other friends who were kind and funny and enjoyed meeting a real-life fashion designer and a paramedic/firefighter. Lynne told their friends about the fashion show and how fun it was to see it all in person, never having seen such a thing before. She especially enjoyed seeing Jean on the runway and the two young, good-looking males that escorted her.

Since Robert first picked the group up from the airport, he wondered how Talia and Jason met and about her shop. After being enlightened about their growing up and then Europe, it made Lynne want to travel a bit more, even if it was to see their kids who all lived out of state. The farthest Robert and Lynne had been was to South Padre Island, Texas.

Grandma Jean told them how Jason helped the pregnant woman on the plane, with Jason briefly explaining. Of course, everyone then looked at Talia, seeing she was expecting, and hopefully a planned trip back to Europe. They asked how far along was she, and if it was really safe for pregnant women to fly. They were just glad that Talia's husband was a paramedic. Jason told them about Jéan-Paul, a doctor in Europe, a good friend and mentor he's worked with many times in the States, and abroad.

Not having asked the night before, Talia asked Lynne about her work. She said she was a helper at a school for disabled children, and worked part-time in a bakery. She loved baking, as everyone could tell by the desserts served, and how colorful and delicious they were. In Medina, they found a Farmers Market where Lynne enjoyed taking and selling her desserts and baked goods. Friends were always available to help set up tables. They enjoyed interacting with people who walked around, finding various goodies to buy.

And Robert had been an over-the-road truck driver for a long time. He had regular routes he drove, but also enjoyed when it took him outside of Seattle. Sometimes, it took him at least 300 miles away. After retiring a few years ago, Robert still wanted to drive, and found the perfect part-time job where he could drive people around and talk with them. And he was so glad that on the day Talia, Jason, the girls, and Grandma Jean needed someone to pick them up from the airport, he was the one.

It was another fun and wonderful evening with new friends, but it was getting late. Robert asked what time the girls and Grandma Jean had to be at the airport. They said their flight was to leave at 10:55 a.m., so they had to be at the airport well over an hour before. Robert said he would pick them up at about 9:00 a.m., giving him plenty of time to drive to the airport.

⁎   ⁏

After getting back to the hotel, Talia checked with the girls and Grandma Jean to see if they needed help with the garment bags; they said no. They were ready to fly home tomorrow, even though they would have loved to stay longer. Chloe and Jana wanted to upload their photos to the digital frame, so Talia brought it to the girls' room, and then told them breakfast would be shortly after 8:00 a.m., and with that, she went to her and Jason's room.

Jason was lying in bed when Talia came in. Her light was off, but he left on his light. He watched her change, and then she headed to the bathroom. After coming out, she stood looking at him while he looked back at her. He moved the covers and she got into bed, cuddling up next to him, laying her arm across his chest and twirling some of his chest hairs with her fingers. With his arm around her, he kissed the top of her head and then looked at her again.

"What?" Talia asked, looking back at him.

"Nothing. I love looking at you, a lot. I'm just feeling content with you in my arms. Have I told you lately how much I love you," he stated. She looked at him with a big smile, reaching for a kiss.

"*Ti amo anch'io, più di quanto saprai mai ever,*" Talia said.

"OK, so I know what *Ti amo* means, but what else did you say?" Jason asked with a quirky grin and raised eyebrows.

Looking into his eyes, she said, "I love you too, more than you will ever know." With a big grin on his face, he gave her another kiss and hugged her.

"I need to learn Italian," he said, smiling at her.

"We'll have to work on those. But if you hear something often enough, and then know what it means—" Before she could finish, he kissed her some more and then nuzzled her neck. She giggled. Jason put his hand gently on her stomach. With both feeling total contentment, they closed their eyes. It had been a long and awesome day.

Barely asleep, suddenly, Jason's eyes opened wide, turning his head toward Talia.

"Did you feel that?" he asked in a loud whisper.

Not yet asleep, she turned her head toward him with a smile. "I did," looking back at him. She placed her hand on top of his.

"Oh, my god. That's incredible. I just felt the baby move under my palm." Talia moved the blanket away from her stomach and watched Jason. His face showed sheer joy now that he actually got to feel the baby move. He looked at her stomach, as if he would see a foot or something, and then felt another slight movement. He leaned down to talk to her stomach in a normal but quiet voice.

"Hello in there. I'm your dad. I'm here with your mommy, and I love you so much," as he felt another slight movement. He looked at Talia, and she could barely see the tears in his eyes from the lamp's soft light, which he now shut off. He laid back down, drawing her closer to him. She heard him say, 'wow' a few times. Smiling at that, she fell asleep as he did.

ଓଃ

"It's funny what things occur just when you're about to fall sound asleep," Grandma Jean said at breakfast, not looking at either Jason or Talia.

"Didn't you sleep well, Grandma Jean?" Chloe asked, looking at her and then Jason and Talia, wondering why she said that.

"Oh, I slept just fine. Quite peaceful, in fact," Grandma Jean replied with a slight smile.

Jason just looked at her. He knew she knew the baby had moved. He looked at Talia and mouthed the words, "Should we tell her she's right?"

Talia grinned with a slight nod.

"Since you already seem to know, yes, something did occur before we fell asleep," Jason said. Jana and Chloe looked at Jason, then Talia, and then Grandma Jean with eyes wide.

"What did she already know? She didn't say what she knew. And if it's intimate, we don't need to know," Jana said, knowing she was blushing.

"My grandmother sometimes senses things," he said, looking at Jana, and then back to his grandmother. "Talia felt it yesterday morning, but I felt it last night," he said in a sensual, teasing voice, looking at Chloe and Jana, letting them wonder for a second if it was something intimate, which it was. Then he said with a smile, "I felt the baby move."

A squeal came out of Jana and Chloe's mouths, and then they covered their mouths. Their eyes were now wide with excitement. Several other guests looked over at the noise before turning back to their breakfast. Looking at Talia, both girls grinned from ear to ear.

"What did it feel like? Was there a lot of movement or a little? Did your stomach move?" The questions came as they looked at Talia. Chloe reached over to squeeze her hand. They were like sisters, all three of them, Jason noticed. They had become part of his family as well, even though they worked for Talia.

"Jason, what did you do?" Chloe asked, and then realized that might have been intrusive.

"I had my hand on her stomach, and then soon I felt this flutter or slight brush movement under the palm of my hand." He took Chloe's hand and showed her the very light sensation he felt, on her palm, giving her goosebumps. Her eyes got big. "It was pretty amazing," he said, smiling. It was funny, because Jana put her hand out, and Jason did the same for her and grinned. Grandma Jean watched. She knew that feeling very well, as did William when he first felt their baby move, that being Jason's dad, Jeff. They didn't have any other children. Jeff was an only child.

"Do you know the sex of the baby?" Chloe asked, not helping herself and smiling.

"No, we don't know. We want to be surprised," Talia said, looking at Jason. She then looked at Grandma Jean, wondering if she knew the sex. Grandma Jean looked back at Talia, but Talia had no idea whether or not she knew, and felt she wouldn't say if she did know. It would be Grandma Jean's secret.

Chapter 27

Robert picked them up at 9:00 a.m. and headed for the airport. There was chit-chat about what they got to see and do, and spending two lovely evenings with Robert and Lynne. They looked forward to Talia and Jason coming home so they could all get together and share their photos with family and friends. They especially were looking forward to the contest video and could hardly wait for that.

Arriving at the airport, Robert pulled up to the United Airlines drop-off. Robert and Jason unloaded their luggage, and the girls thanked Robert again for driving them around and the two wonderful evenings. It was fun spending time with them and their friends. Chloe and Jana each hugged Robert, and he smiled.

"Do you want us to go in with you and help get your luggage checked in?" Talia asked, looking at the girls and Grandma Jean.

"I think we'll be alright," Grandma Jean said, smiling. "I have the girls to help me. We'll be together, and it won't be long, and we'll be home. Jeff will be there to pick me up." Looking at Jason and he nodded.

Chloe hugged Talia. "Talia, this has been an incredible trip, sharing all of this with you and being in the fashion show, wearing two of your awesome designs. I love what I do, working with you and Jana.

Thank you. We'll see you at home in the next few days." She also gave Jason a hug.

"And I love what I do. Thank you for this trip and this experience. I've had a blast," Jana said. She also hugged Talia, and Jason, and turned to take her luggage. They waited for Grandma Jean, who turned and looked at her grandson and granddaughter-in-law.

"This has been the best trip I've had in, like, forever. You've made me feel so alive, and feel like I can still do anything at my age," she said with a heartfelt smile.

"Grandma, I love you more than anything," Jason said. "I would do anything for you, and I'm so glad that I, we, got to share this with you. You mean the world to me." He hugged and kissed her cheek. Talia walked up to her, also giving a hug and peck on the cheek.

"We'll have that party soon, and share all our wonderful photos and experiences. I'm so glad you were part of this. Something I would have loved to share with my dad and grandfather if they were here, to see what I've accomplished," Talia said, with eyes misting over.

"Then I'll say it for all three of us, even though the other two aren't here any longer. As your elders and your family, we are very proud of you and love you. Good things will come your way. You'll see," Grandma Jean said, then, taking hold of her luggage handle, she turned to follow Chloe and Jana inside. She stopped briefly as the sliding doors stayed opened for her, partially turning around, looking Talia square in the eye, and then she said, "Help is on the way."

"Grandma Jean, what does that…" Talia was asking as Grandma Jean turned and walked through the doors. Jason heard it, and Talia turned toward him with her mouth open, and then said. "What did she mean by that? Help is on the way. Do I need help? Does someone else need help? Are you going to need help? Jason that makes me nervous."

"I'm not sure," he said, taking her by the shoulders. "She wouldn't have left it at that if we were in harm's way." They turned and got back into Robert's SUV, sitting in the seats they had been riding in.

☙

Robert could now speak openly after leaving the airport to head for the Seattle Harbor for Talia and Jason's cruise. "I didn't want to say anything in front of Jean, Chloe, and Jana, but Lynne and I have to leave and go out of town until late Monday evening. A very good friend of ours has been put in the hospital, and her husband is beside himself, not knowing what to do. They've hardly spent any time apart in the last fifty years. We know he's scared. He called us early this morning to see if we could come."

"Robert, of course, go. You should have told us earlier. We would have gotten the girls and Grandma Jean to the airport," Talia said, now with a look of concern.

"I know. Lynne told Tom we'd be there later this afternoon. It's about a two-hour drive from home. We'll be leaving before noon. She had a few things to do this morning," Robert said, glancing back at them in the rear-view mirror. "I also wanted to tell you I have someone who is willing to take you where you want to go. I've had the flexibility to take you places, unlike the other part-time driver. This person works in Madison Valley. I told her you were taking a harbor cruise, that she could meet you at Acres of Clams when it got back to port. There's seating near the back and patio side. You can decide if that's where you'd like to have lunch. I hope you don't mind, but I'd like to send her your photo, so she'll be able to recognize you."

"Do you remember her name?" Jason asked.

"Oh, dear, let me think here," Robert said.

"Robert, it's OK. You focus on driving," Talia said with a smile. "I'm sure if she has our photo, she'll find us. Who else looks like my handsome hubby?" She giggled as Jason reached over and took her hand, grinning and shaking his head.

✣ ✤

Robert stopped just past Pier 55. "You two have a wonderful harbor cruise. I know you'll enjoy it. Lynne and I have been on some of these over the years, and we never tire of being on the water. There won't be that many people on board with it being February."

"Robert, thank you for driving all of us around the last several days. We are grateful for the time we've spent with you and Lynne, and what we've gotten to see," Jason said. "Let us know if Tuesday works to take us to the airport."

"I'll let you know for sure. Right now, it's hard to say with Tom's wife in the hospital," Robert said.

"Could you text us and let us know how she's doing?" Talia asked.

"I can do that," Robert said, smiling back at Talia. Through the open passenger front window, Jason shook hands with Robert, and then Talia and Jason headed hand-in-hand for the departure dock.

Only a dozen other people were waiting. They still had a little time before boarding. They wandered toward the backside of Pier 54, seeing steel gray benches looking out over the bay. Seagulls were hovering above the water before landing to float on it. Talia stood at the fence that kept people from falling in and then turned up her nose at the strong fishy smell. Jason walked over toward the end of the fence and looked around the corner to see what was there. A large patio with various tables and chairs was set up for anyone's outdoor dining experience, with a view of the fireboats, larger ferries, and cruise ships.

"When we get back, I think we can sit on the patio side so that woman can find us easily," Jason said, walking back to Talia. "The sunshine feels good, providing it stays shining." Putting his arms around Talia, he kissed her. He looked at his watch, and then they headed for the departure line.

❧

The cruise would start at 10:30 a.m. Once on board, Jason and Talia walked to the front of the ferry to sit like they had when they took their Rhine River cruise, but then decided to walk toward the back. As the ferry left the dock, there was live narration spoken by Jonathan, one of the tour guides, about what they were seeing. He had quite the sense of humor, telling stories and facts. He talked about the skyline of the Emerald City, the historic neighborhoods, the shipyards and terminals, and the Washington State ferry fleet. People asked a lot of questions, and he answered them all.

It was fun to see a few of the cruise ships up-close, and they were HUGE, according to Talia, who looked at Jason with a smile. Their ferry went through Elliott Bay and Seattle Harbor.

Seeing Seattle from this point of view was an enjoyable experience. And seeing Puget Sound and then the Cascade and Olympic mountain ranges was also amazing. The waves were a little bouncier than they experienced on the Rhine River, which meandered from Germany down through Switzerland. Talia looked at Jason, and he knew what she was thinking. He wrapped his arms around her, and then, all too soon, they were headed back to the harbor.

Following the other passengers off the ferry, they walked around the back side of Pier 54 to the Acres of Clams patio. It was close to noon. Talia was getting hungry, and her stomach was making noises.

"Sorry, I should have eaten more at breakfast. But I was thinking about the girls and Grandma Jean getting through all the airport stuff," she said.

"I probably should have eaten more as well," Jason said.

Just after boarding the ferry, and before leaving the dock, Talia hadn't felt her phone buzz, but then felt it again and she showed Jason the text from Chloe. They got their luggage checked and got through security fairly easily, until Grandma Jean got annoyed about taking off her shoes and coat again, placing them along with her handbag in the bin to go through the x-ray machine. But seeing that her stuff did come through the other side, she was OK. They were just waiting to board their plane. Talia texted Chloe back, wishing them a good flight home, and to let her know when they landed, and that Jason's dad should be there to pick up Grandma Jean. Chloe responded with a big thumbs-up and then said they were now boarding. She would text when they landed.

☙

They saw a round table that was sitting partly in the sun. Talia sat facing the bay, and Jason faced the dock, seeing the fireboats. There were less than a handful of people sitting at a larger table, and after a few moments, they got up and left. Talia and Jason chatted about the tour and what they might see or do the rest of today and tomorrow. They were both watching for the woman that Robert said would find them.

Then, a woman came around the corner and stopped a moment, looking at Talia with a smile on her face. She walked over to them and said, "I was on the tour boat and saw you, and I remembered you were one of the designers from the fashion show this past Friday. There were so many wonderful outfits." She paused. "I'm sorry, where are my manners. My name is Janet Barnes." She reached out to shake Talia's hand.

"Nice to meet you, Janet," Talia said, and before getting another word out, Janet spoke again.

"It was so much fun, watching the whole show. I had a friend invite me who works at the convention center. I'll tell you..." she was looking around, "I was secretly hoping you would be the one to win, and you did," Janet said with a big smile on her face.

"Yes, I did. It was a surprise to me," Talia said, looking back at her and then Jason.

"I took some photos with my cell phone, especially with your grandmother wearing that gorgeous outfit, and then she changed into that longer jacket with the help of those two young men. Oh, I could have eaten them both up."

"Yes, they were helpful," Talia said, smiling.

"I was wondering, would you be a dear and sign my program?" Janet asked, looking at Talia with a look of 'pretty please.'

"Sure, I'd be happy to," Talia said, smiling back at her.

Janet whipped out the program from her bag and laid it on the table with a blue pen for Talia to use. Signing her name on the front, Talia then gave the program and pen back to Janet.

"Thank you so much. I can't wait to show my sister. Well, I best leave you two alone." With that, Janet turned and headed back the way she came.

"You're welcome," Talia said loudly, then looked at Jason, who was grinning at her with big eyes.

"What?" Talia asked.

"I thought she was going to be the woman who was going to take us where we wanted to go. I was holding my breath, hoping she wasn't the one," Jason said with raised eyebrows and a goofy look on his face.

"Ya, I was thinking the same thing," Talia said. He took hold of her right hand and kissed the back of it.

Within minutes, Jason noticed a movement out of the corner of his eye and slowly turned his head to the left. A woman was standing several feet away, looking at them. He quickly noted her height, a good inch or so taller than Talia, medium build, kind of short medium-blonde hair, and about Talia's age. She wore jeans with white sneakers, a dark green raincoat with a hood, and a large black handbag over her shoulder. A cell phone was in her hand, and Jason wondered if this was the person Robert spoke of.

Talia was looking off in the distance at a large cruise ship, not seeing that Jason was looking at something or someone behind her. The woman had an uneasy look on her face, looking at them and then back at her cell phone. Jason saw her looking at the back of Talia's head, but before he could say anything, she spoke.

"Qu'est-ce que je vois, assis à côté de moi? Mais deux petits amis, heureux comme on peut l'être." She spoke softly in almost a rhyme.

Chapter 28

Jason sat up a little straighter, looking directly at the woman with a guarded look, ready to protect his wife. The woman was silent, still looking patiently at the back of Talia. He saw Talia lower her head and close her eyes. Within a moment, she took a slow, deep breath and had a comforting look on her face as she replied, *"L'un est Talia, l'autre Skye. Deux petits amis, heureux comme on peut l'être."*

Jason's eyes got big looking at Talia, and then saw the woman's eyes glisten as she stood there waiting. Talia turned toward Jason, and he saw the tears in his wife's eyes. There was recognition from both women. Turning around in her chair, looking at the woman, Talia stood up. They walked to each other, giving a big hug with more tears.

Standing up, Jason looked at the two of them, not knowing what was happening. Wiping her own tears, Talia took a step back. She looked at the woman for a moment, slightly shook her head, and held the woman's one hand.

"How did you know it was me?" Talia asked the woman quietly, looking at her.

"I wasn't for sure. Your photo was provided to me by a client, and your name," she said.

"You haven't changed a bit," Talia said.

"You either. You're just as pretty as ever," the woman said, now with a smile.

"Talia," Jason said as he took a step toward his wife. "Who is this?"

Looking at the woman, Talia said, "She is a childhood friend who had to move away, and I missed her." She turned to Jason and said, "This is Skye Chaundler." Looking back at Skye, Talia said, "This is my husband, Jason Porter." Skye reached out her hand to shake his. He was feeling a little more than confused, and now by her name.

Skye looked at Talia with a tilt of her head, and a slight grin, trying to recall from memory, and in a quiet voice asked. "So, is this the same Jason Porter you talked about way-back-when?" Jason looked at his wife now with a sly grin. "You had a huge crush on him. I remember, any time your parents talked about going on vacation," Skye got this look on her face with a bigger grin, "your eyes would get big like saucers, and then you'd get all tongue-tied. You always said you were just looking forward to vacation and the fun places you'd get to visit."

Jason continued looking at Talia, now with his arms crossed against his chest. He hadn't known this before from any conversations he had had with Kurt. And, apparently, Talia didn't tell Kurt either.

"Oh, I don't know if I got tongue-tied," Talia said, with eyes wide and now blushing as she looked at Jason. "Oh, it's getting a little warm out here." He gave her a sensuous smile, thinking it was cute that she was blushing. He never really knew for sure if she liked him in their younger years, but when they were older and on vacation, Kurt would nod to Jason in a fashion that said Talia was looking at him and must have liked him.

It was then that Jason looked back at Skye, still a little confused, and asked, "So, you're Skye? What's your last name again?"

"It's Skye, with an e, Sierra Chaundler with a 'u' after the 'a.'"

"Were you born in Montana or lived there?" he asked, looking at her with a puzzled look.

Talia looked at Jason with a questionable look, and then looked at Skye and back to Jason and asked, "How do you know Skye? And she's not from Montana."

Jason looked at Skye, "I don't know her." Then he looked at Talia. "Cole said he's spoken with Anisha Moten from some travel agency here, and she said she was working with someone named Sky. Cole sent me some information and said he got an email from Skye, and it ended in 'e.' I joked, asking if he was from Montana, hence the big 'sky' country." Jason looked back to Skye.

"Well, I wish I would have known about that email," Talia said, feeling a little confused herself.

"Mr. Porter, I think Talia and I can clear up a few things and get caught up." She looked at Talia. "But why don't we go inside and get something to eat, and we can talk. I'm sure you're hungry, and so am I," Skye said.

"Call me Jason, please," as he picked up his backpack. He saw Skye looking at Talia's stomach and then turned to walk back the way she came, with the two of them following. Once inside Acres of Clams, Jason saw all the gorgeous wood on the ceiling, the walls, and the huge scalloped-designed bar. It was beautiful. The three sat down at a big table by one of the large windows looking out over the bay. Talia sat by the window with Skye across from her, and, of course, Jason seated next to Talia.

The server brought water and menus for them. As the girls were looking it over, Jason saw the server's name was James Todd and decided to ask him a question.

"So, James," Jason said as he looked at him, "As we walked in, I saw the beautiful wood bar. Is that mahogany?"

"You are correct. All the wood in the bar is mahogany. We reclaimed it when we renovated Acres of Clams between 2014 and 2015. And we saved the wood from the old restaurant and used it on the faces of the fireplaces. There are two, and each is visible from all sides."

"Have you been here a long time?"

"Yes. I've worked for Ivar's for over fifteen years and love it. I'm a single guy, born and raised, here in Seattle." He asked if they needed a few more minutes to decide.

Everything on the menu looked great, and finally, James could place their order. Jason also ordered a beer, and Talia looked at him with a grin and then looked at his chest. He smiled back at her, giving her a wink, which Skye saw and thought, *There is going to be a lot of catching up to do.*

"Before the two of you reminisce," Jason said, as he looked at Skye and then Talia, with his arm on the back of her chair, "You want to tell me what you said to one another outside? It almost sounded like a rhyme." Lowering his head, he looked at Talia. "Your mother speaks French, and that's what the two of you were speaking, am I not correct?"

"Yes," Talia said, and then looked at Skye, who gestured that the story should come from her. Looking back at Jason, Talia said, "When I was little, this was before our families ever met in Basel, Mom, Dad, Kurt, and I used to live in Carroll until I was about eight years old. Mom would often speak French to Kurt and me, having us reply in French back to her. She wanted us to learn another language.

"Skye and her family lived just a couple of blocks from us. There was a big park where all of us neighborhood kids would play. Skye and I developed a friendship that continued even after we moved, and then before they had to move, and that was…" Talia looked at Skye to help her remember. James returned with Jason's beer.

"I was going to be in the ninth grade when we had to move. You were going into eighth grade," Skye said, and then she looked at Jason.

Talia continued. "We came up to Carroll a lot and stayed with my Aunt Joan and Uncle Dave Rose. You met them at the wedding. Skye and I continued to hang out together. We were five months apart. I missed the deadline for starting school because of where my birthday fell, and I had to wait until the following year.

"Anyway, we'd go to the park and sit on a picnic table on either side of my mom, and she would smile and say this rhyme looking at us. *'Qu'est-ce que je vois, assis à côté de moi? Mais deux petits amis, heureux comme on peut l'être,'* which means, 'What do I see, sitting beside me? But two little friends, happy as can be.' The second part…" Talia looked at Skye to say the whole thing. "'*L'un est Talia, l'autre Skye. Deux petits amis, heureux comme on peut l'être.'* And it means, 'One is Talia, the other Skye. Two little friends, happy as can be.'"

"Mom made up this rhyme, and every time we were at the park, she would say those words and then help us say it. That went on for several years until they moved," Talia said. "And it stuck."

"I loved listening to her speak French," Skye said, smiling. "I just thought it was the coolest thing."

"Wow." Jason didn't know what to say at first. "And you both remembered that after all these years of not seeing one another?" James brought their food. They each got something different. It looked amazing and smelled so good, and now their taste buds could celebrate. "OK, we eat, and you continue to talk. I want to hear the rest of the story," Jason said.

Qu'est-ce que je vois, assis à côté de moi?
Mais deux petits amis, heureux comme on peut l'être.

L'un est Talia, l'autre Skye.
Deux petits amis, heureux comme on peut l'être.

What do I see, sitting beside me?
But two little friends, happy as can be.

One is Talia, the other Skye.
Two little friends, happy as can be.

ꟸ ꟹ

"So, Skye, why did your family have to move?" Jason asked.

"My dad was a contractor building bridges. Several years before, he had a good friend who moved out to Astoria, Oregon, and was doing well. He finally talked my dad into uprooting us and moving. Although it wasn't the whole family."

"How many in your family?" Jason asked.

"My parents, of course, six kids, plus a dog. I was the youngest. There are thirteen years between us. They thought they were done at five, and then I came along." She saw Talia and Jason both grin. "My two older brothers were already married before we moved, one to Minnesota and the other one to Kansas. They've hardly kept in touch."

"Was that Martin and Bo?" Talia asked, looking at Skye. She nodded.

"Kate, my older sister, got married after attending community college. That was just before we moved, and they didn't stick around, they moved to Idaho. Matt is single and still works in the Astoria area."

"What about Jules and your parents? How are they doing?" Talia asked, then seeing a sad look on Skye's face.

Skye got real quiet, lowering her head, and her eyes misted over. "Jules died several years ago. It was hard on all of us, but Dad took it the hardest. They didn't want to stay in Astoria anymore, even though Matt still lives there. Too many sad memories, and then Dad had been having health issues, and the doctors said he needed a dryer climate, so they moved to Santa Fe, New Mexico," Skye said, looking out the window, obviously missing her family.

"Oh my god, Skye, I'm so sorry about Jules." Talia reached over and took Skye's hand. "What happened with her?"

"I don't want to talk about it right now," Skye said, and then tried eating another bite. Talia glanced at Jason and then back to Skye. They knew all too well about losing people they loved.

"So, when was the last time you two kept in contact?" Jason asked, looking at Talia and then Skye as they continued eating.

"It's been a long time," Talia said, "I wish now I would have done a better job keeping in contact with you. You were one of my best friends."

"I'm just as guilty, Talia. I could have done the same. I started a letter to you, then family stuff came up, school, and then work, and time just got away from me. And here we are, how many years later? But, I never forgot about you."

"Me neither. But, what are you doing here in Seattle?" Talia asked.

"Well, after I went to community college and received my AAS degree, I worked as a secretary for a long time. I got tired of it. I knew there had to be something better for me. I've always wanted to travel, so I decided to attend travel agent school at night. After completing it, I had a friend who lived here in Seattle, and she told me to get my butt up here," Skye smiled. "I found a job with an agency in Madison Valley, and that's where I met and work with Anisha Moten," she said, looking at Jason. "I live in the next suburb called Madrona, so I live fairly close to work and not too far from Lake Washington."

"So the person who gave you our name and photo, was that Robert Anders?" Talia asked as she was finishing up her salmon and chips, and drank her water.

"It was," Skye said. "He mentioned he has been a driver the last several days for some nice people. He didn't tell me the names."

"How do you know Robert?" Jason asked.

"Robert and Lynne, his wife, have come into the agency, and I've helped them with a couple of trips. They're very nice people, easy to talk with, and interesting. Robert said that he and Lynne were invited to a fashion show last Friday afternoon by one of the designers, and that Lynne was so excited. And then they invited these people to their home, twice, for dinner. At first, I thought that wasn't such a smart thing to do.

"It wasn't until this morning that he called me explaining the whole thing, and that he and Lynne had to be gone for a short while. He was so sincere in asking for help with this nice couple, taking them to see a few more things before they had to fly out Tuesday." She looked at them both.

"When did you learn it was me?" Talia asked.

"Robert sent your name and photo to me about forty-five minutes before you were to dock, not much time. I just kept looking at your photo, and then thought, 'help is on the way.' And then realized I had to get a move on and drive down here." Talia and Jason looked at one another. That's the exact phrase Grandma Jean said to Talia. "Anyway, it didn't seem real until I spoke the rhyme and waited for you to reply," looking at Talia. "I thought your husband was about to—"

"You did have me a little concerned," Jason said, looking at Skye. "You kept staring at the back of Talia, and I was going to protect my wife. And it surprised me when Talia responded to you in French." Skye nodded.

"I'm sorry," Skye said. "But, I had to make sure. No one else would know that rhyme." Her voice sounded a little off.

"Skye, it's OK. I'm so glad you were the one Robert asked, mostly because I didn't know you lived here," Talia said. James returned to pick up their plates, and asked if everything was alright. Then he asked if they had room for dessert.

"I saw something that looked like a strawberry shortbread. I think that would hit the spot. You want to split it with me?" Talia asked Jason.

"I can do that," he replied. Skye decided on a small dish of vanilla ice cream.

Skye looked at Talia's stomach and asked, "Are you, by chance, pregnant?"

With a big smile, Talia said, "Yes. I'm almost five months along."

"Congratulations to you both," Skye said, smiling at Talia and then Jason. "So, when will this arrival happen?"

"In June," Talia said. Jason took her hand and kissed the back of it, looking at her. It was obvious how much they loved each other. Skye longed for the same thing, wondering if it would ever happen for her.

They'd been enjoying their desserts and finishing up with them, when James brought a drink to Skye. Looking at the glass, Skye said, "I'm sorry, but I didn't order a drink." Looking up at him, the smile on Skye's face went away, and she started looking around the room. Jason saw this and sensed something wasn't right as he also looked around, but for whom?

"No, miss, I know you didn't," James said. "There was a nice gentleman that came in about twenty minutes ago. He sat at the far end looking at you, and then ordered this for you just before he left about two minutes ago, saying you like slow-gin-fizz? He didn't want to bother you with your clients, but said he would catch up with you later." And then James left.

"Skye, what is it?" Talia asked, now concerned for her best friend.

Chapter 29

"I tell you what, I think we could head out and go to one of my favorite places first, and then figure out where else you'd like to go. But I'll need to use the restroom," Skye said as she got to her feet and looked around again. It was nearing two o'clock.

"I'll come with you. I seem to frequent the ladies' room a little more often now," Talia said, smiling at Skye. Jason stood up to let Talia go by. James brought the check, and Jason took care of it. When the girls came back, he went to use the restroom.

Skye headed out the front door as they walked toward Pier 55. Even now, Skye was looking around, and Talia and Jason just looked at one another. They followed Skye across the crosswalk as she made her way to a large parking lot and then came to her car. It was an older Jeep Cherokee, like Jason's. As they stood outside of her jeep, waiting for her to unlock the doors, Jason had a smile on his face, looking at Talia as he opened the front door for her.

"How do you guys feel about maps?" Skye asked, looking at Talia and then Jason in her rearview mirror.

"Well, they're fun to look at when finding someplace you want to go," Talia said. Skye smiled and then headed out of the parking lot. As they drove through the streets, it was nice to look out the window, not worrying about where you were going in an unfamiliar city and how you would get there. Like Robert, having Skye do the driving, knowing where she was going, was perfect.

"And how do you feel about walking?" Skye asked the two of them.

"We've done our share of walking," Talia said, and then, smiling, said, "And hiking."

"So, Jason, your backpack has the insignia of paramedic and firefighter on it. How long have you been one, and do you carry that with you a lot?" Skye asked.

"Yes, I do. It comes in handy when needed. I've been a paramedic for about sixteen years, and a firefighter for nine."

"Twice, since we've been here, someone needed his help before other paramedics could help," Talia said.

"Really. Can you do that?" looking at Jason in her mirror as she was turning down a street.

"Yes. But as soon as paramedics arrive, we give what information we gathered, and they take over, and we back off unless our help is needed," Jason said.

"Actually, it's been three times," Talia said, looking out her window. Skye looked at her and then at Jason in the rearview mirror.

Skye found a parking place and then shut off the engine, turning in her seat. "Who did you have to help?" she asked out of curiosity.

"The first one was on the plane coming here after leaving Denver," Talia said. Skye's eyes got big. Jason then filled her in on that situation.

"So what were the second and third ones?" Skye asked, wanting to know. Jason told her about the man who was shot at the convention center and that he had help from another paramedic, whose wife was also a fashion designer, until the Bellevue paramedics arrived. And then he told her he also saw one of his German comrades who was doing his week abroad in Seattle, but headed home to Germany this past Friday morning. This piqued Skye's interest. Then Talia started to tell her about The Space Needle incident, and Jason finished that story.

"So your job never sleeps," Skye said with a grin, and then she turned to open her door.

"No, it does not," Jason said.

Coming around to the front of her car, she explained they were in the Pike Place Market area. They crossed the street, following Skye as she told them about the many businesses, naming a few of her favorites. She stopped in front of her most favorite shop, Metsker Maps. Talia and Jason just looked at Skye, and then looked in the window. It didn't look like much from the outside, but they would soon find out differently. Skye asked Talia for her phone and took a picture of the two of them under the business sign.

"Ready to see where your next big adventure might take you?" Skye asked, smiling at them. They walked inside, and Skye watched their faces, grinning at them. "What do you think?"

Eyes wide, Talia said, "This is great. I love this. How did you find this place?" She looked around.

"Well, working for a travel agency helps. When a client comes in telling me where they'd like to go, I check our racks first. They usually like actual maps and books. If we don't have them, even though I can find it on the internet, I tell them I'll get what they need to finish planning their trip. The internet is nice, but I come here and find that treasure for them. It's nice to have a hold-in-your-hand item," Skye said, looking around. "There's a lot here, and I enjoy looking through all of this."

"Skye, how are you?" one of the clerks asked. Skye turned around to see her favorite clerk.

"Molly, it's nice to see you. It's been weeks," Skye said. "I'd like to introduce to you one of my dearest, childhood best friends. This is Talia Porter and her husband, Jason Porter."

"Actually, it's Rose-Porter," Talia said, smiling.

Molly gave Talia a curious look, and then one of recognition. "You were that fashion designer from the Valentine show last Friday. I was there. It was so wonderful. I loved it." She turned to Skye. "Oh Skye, you should have been there. It was so much fun." She turned to Talia, and then Skye looked at Talia.

"Thank you," Talia said. "I didn't know Skye lived here."

"Um, could I get a picture with you? I have some friends that rarely believe much of what I tell them. I didn't get hardly any photos at the show," Molly said, smiling. "Oh, could we also get your handsome husband in a second photo?"

"I think we can handle that," Talia said, looking at Jason with a smile and winked at him. Skye took a couple of photos with Molly's phone.

"Well, I'll let you all browse. And if there is anything I can help you with, please, just ask," and then she walked away to help another customer.

"Alright, so I do have a few things I need to find for some clients. You two look around to your heart's content," Skye said.

Talia and Jason just stood there, looking around, not sure where to start. But the smiles on their faces said this was a good place to imagine the possibilities. All kinds of maps and globes in different sizes and books galore and other treasures, oh my.

Something Jason thought about after talking with John's daughter, Nikki, and where she might like to go, was that he wanted to give her a globe of her very own and let her dream. After looking at so many, Jason decided on one. He showed it to Talia and told her what he was thinking. She loved the idea. He would have it shipped to Nikki in care of her dad in St. Cloud, Minnesota.

Skye was close by as she watched them, and took two photos without their knowledge. As they continued looking, they saw and asked Skye if she'd take a few different pictures of them among the maps, globes, and everything else, including the globe he was going to send to Nikki. Jason texted John to get their address, and to let him know to expect a box for Nikki.

Then there were a few other photos, with Skye included with the help of her friend Molly. They thought it was funny that you could have fun in a large map store. It was great. They found a few treasures for Europe and the US. They couldn't believe the time they spent in this store, but it was well worth it.

With items ready to be checked out, Jason said, grinning, "Some serious money can be spent in here." Talia agreed, giving Jason a hug and a kiss.

"OK, you two. You sure do a lot of kissing from what I'm seeing," Skye said, feeling a little envious.

"Can you blame me? You wait, Skye, there's someone special for you to call your own." Talia took hold of Skye's hand to reassure her. "It will happen when you least expect it."

❧ ❧

Leaving Metsker Maps, they stood under the canopy, and Skye asked, "What would you still like to do today?"

"We've seen some pretty amazing things here," Jason said, looking at Talia as he put his arm around her. "For me, being here in Seattle with my beautiful wife. The whole experience of the fashion show, and spending time with Chloe and Jana, who feel like family, and my grandmother." He looked at Skye. "Seeing the joy on her face when she walked down the runway wearing her own design, priceless." Looking at Talia, he had a sigh of contentment and asked what else she wanted to see.

"I thought about the big Ferris wheel or maybe the aquarium," she looked at Skye, "but I'd like to just spend time with you before we have to leave on Tuesday."

Skye smiled and said, "Well, since one of my other favorite shops is closed today, we'll have to bypass that one. But the other is also so delicious and unique. What I'd like to do is take you up to Piroshky Piroshky. It's not too far away, and we can walk."

"What's a Piroshky?" Talia asked.

"Well, you'll have to wait until we get there," Skye said, motioning for them to follow her. "I think you'll both like this place. We can pick up food and then head to my apartment? I can take you back to your hotel later, and pick you up tomorrow and do whatever you'd like."

"I'd love that," Talia said, giving Skye a big smile. Jason could see how much she missed her best friend.

Approaching Piroshky Piroshky, and before walking in, Skye took their photo under the business sign for another fun memory. Then Jason did the same with the girls. Following Skye in, there was a line of people ahead of them. Jason was right behind Talia. She turned partly around to look at Jason with big eyes and a goofy grin, and then nudged him to see the long line behind them. The place was small. It almost seemed cramped for the number of people lined up to place an order. There was a pandemonium of sounds coming from the roar of heavy fans, and you could see and hear the bakers call out with orders being placed fairly quickly. It was like a well-oiled piece of machinery with every part working in harmony.

They took steps closer to the ordering line. The bakery shelves were full of all kinds of baked goods, from sweet to savory. The aroma was incredible. You would have to make your selection pretty quickly, no standing around thinking about it. How would they ever decide what to choose? Checking out each row of goodies, Skye made a few suggestions. When it came to their turn, Skye ordered a couple of the hand-held pies. The Chicken Curry and Rice and the Beef and Onion, and then she wanted to try the Moscow Roll and the Fresh Rhubarb Piroshky. Now it was Talia's turn, and oh dear, this was no easy task.

"Everything looks and smells so good," Talia said to Jason. "How am I supposed to choose?"

"I tell you what, you pick out whatever items you want, and I'll get a couple different things, and then we'll share at Skye's place," Jason said. Talia nodded. Between the two of them, they chose a Ham, Cheese & Spinach, the Bacon, Hash Brown, Egg and Cheese, Beef and Potato, and the Smoked Salmon Paté because it was shaped like a Salmon. And then they picked a couple of sweets, the Marzipan Roll and Cinnamon Cardamom Braid, along with an Apple Cinnamon Roll and a Moscow Roll. They couldn't resist. If there were anything left after dinner, they'd share them for breakfast.

After leaving Piroshky Piroshky and walking back to Skye's jeep, she unlocked the doors and they got inside. Putting her key in the ignition, she saw the single black flower under the windshield wiper on her side. Staring at it, she looked around, and then she got out and threw it to the ground.

"Skye, what was that?" Talia asked, and then looked back at Jason. He saw it too.

"It was just a black flower. Someone probably put it there as a joke," she said, not smiling. Then she put her head down for a moment and took a breath.

She told Jason there was an insulated bag behind his seat, if he could grab it and put their food in it to keep them warm. Backing out, Skye told them it would take about thirty minutes to get to her apartment.

Skye talked about Piroshky Piroshky from what she knew. She told Talia she should go online and check them out. There was a short interesting story. This gave Jason a little time to look back through the photos on his phone. Cole had texted him about the email from Skye with an "e" and places to see. When Jason texted him back, he said it sounded like Skye was from Montana. Now he could text Cole that he knew where Skye was really from and send a photo or two.

Chapter 30

Jason texted Cole: *How's it going? You and Jim doing OK? Just thought I'd tell you we had another interesting day.* He didn't expect Cole to get back to him right away. He was probably busy. Jason was looking out the window when his phone buzzed.

Cole: *All is well here, except for the cold and snow.*

Jason: *It rains off and on here. Most everyone who lives here wears a heavy raincoat with a hood.*

Cole: *So did Jean and the girls get onto their plane alright?*

Jason: *They did. However, my g'ma had a little issue taking off her coat and shoes again to get through security. It shouldn't be long before we hear they made it home safely.* There was a pause.

Cole: *I checked their flight and weather. Looks like they should land in the next fifteen minutes if they're on schedule.*

Jason: *Good. I kind of lost track of time.* Jason sent two photos to Cole, but didn't say anything about who was in the photo.

Cole: *Wow. She is pretty. Who is she?*

Jason: *She is very pretty. And you're not going to believe me, but this is Skye Chaundler.*

Cole: *What?*

Jason: *Ya. This is Skye with an "e." Remember I joked about Skye and Montana? Well, Skye is from Talia's hometown. They were best friends. Skye's family had to move to Oregon when she was in the 9th grade. They lost touch after that.*

Cole: *Jason, I'd like to hear more about her, but I have to leave right now. I have late dinner plans.*

Jason: *Hope she's pretty.*

Cole: *Ya, well, she is, and her husband is tall. Lol. It's Jim and Nadine. They invited me over for a late dinner.*

Jason: *Tell them hi from Talia and me. Enjoy your evening.*

Cole: *You also.*

⚃

Skye headed down a tree-lined street, and then pulled into an alleyway and then a small parking lot. She parked her jeep, shutting off the engine. Just then, Talia's phone buzzed. It was Chloe, and they had just landed. She was not looking forward to getting off the plane and then heading outside, where it was cold and snow was still on the ground, even to get into her dad's car quickly. They wanted to make sure that Grandma Jean's son was there to pick her up before they left. She'd let them know, but have to find their luggage first.

Getting out of the jeep, Jason looked around at a few other vehicles and then the back of the building. It looked like a very large house, maybe a mansion, that was three stories, and the second and third floors had balconies. A door on the first floor faced the parking lot, but Skye walked around to the side of the building where there was a large outside light on. She then opened a large door, with a ceiling light hanging down, and walked through with Talia and Jason following.

"This is where I live," Skye said. "I'm up on the second floor." They walked to the top of the stairs, where there was a nice landing and entryway. Jason figured it was a good four feet by six feet, and noticed another set of stairs leading up to the third floor. Skye unlocked the door, pushed it open, turning on a hall light, then a kitchen light walking into the kitchen. Talia and Jason followed and could see into the dining room.

Skye had Jason put the food bag on the counter and then asked if he would please lock the door. After locking the door, and turning back toward the kitchen, he saw the long carpeted hallway which blocked the sight of the dining room.

Looking around, and letting her eyes adjust to the dim light coming from a window into the dining room, Talia said, "Skye, this looks nice."

"Well, it's been home. I have a roommate, but she'll be moving in about a month, and right now, she's gone home to her parents for the week," as she took their coats and hung them up along with hers in the hall closet. Skye then grabbed a couple of plates and glasses, out of the cupboard, and silverware and napkins. She took the food out of the bag, still feeling the warmth. The kitchen into the dining room was open with the exception of the counter between the two. Skye walked over and flipped the light on over the dining room table.

"We can probably heat your food in the microwave if you'd like. And I don't have a lot to drink, mostly water, some milk, and coffee," Skye said.

The wood dining room table was a nice size, so there was plenty of room for sitting and elbow room, unlike Talia's little kitchen table she had in her apartment before she and Jason got married. Their parents bought them a bigger table with chairs as a wedding gift. Sitting down to eat, it was Jason that asked the question.

"So Skye, when we were at Acres of Clams, and our server brought that drink to you, your happy face went away pretty abruptly," Jason said. "Is everything alright?"

She looked at Jason, then Talia, and back to Jason. "It's nothing. I'm fine." She continued eating, then not looking at either of them. Talia looked at Jason with a sad look.

"I've learned to trust my instincts and what I see. I'm pretty observant, being a paramedic. Your pupils changed, along with your carotid pulse, your heart rate, and your breathing, all showing me signs everything wasn't fine." Talia watched Skye's reaction to what Jason had said. She knew her husband pretty well, and knew he was concerned about her best friend.

Softly, Talia said, "Skye, it wasn't hard to see that it upset you. You seemed... on guard, looking around. And when we headed outside, you looked around some more like you were anticipating a confrontation."

"You can't help. So let it go," Skye said, sounding somewhat defensive.

"I can't do that. We can't do that. This makes me nervous for you, and now it scares me. I don't want anything to happen to you. Who is this person?" Talia asked, pleading.

Skye looked at Talia and shook her head. She was going to keep it to herself, but Jason knew Talia wasn't going to let it go. After the assault on her and the intervention from Nadine, he knew Talia wanted to get to the bottom of this now, especially since they would be heading home soon and Skye would be left to her own defenses. They were all but done eating. Several minutes passed, Talia looked at Jason. He nodded to her.

"Skye," Talia said, "I want to tell you something that happened to me."

Jason's phone rang, and he saw that it was his dad. He excused himself from the table. Walking toward the living room and talking to his dad, he saw the balcony door, and opened it up and walked out, then closing the door. The air was cool and damp. Then his grandmother wanted to tell him they had landed safely, and it was a good flight with no mishaps, but it was sure cold outside. Jason smiled at the short conversation with her, and before she said goodbye, she said, "Jason, keep watch," and then hung up. What was he supposed to watch for?

He turned to look back through the living room window, watching Talia, and then turned to look down at the parked cars. The sun would be setting soon, and he now saw someone crouch down on the back side of Skye's jeep. He wondered what they were doing, so he took his phone out and started recording. This person moved from the back of the jeep to the right rear and then near the right front, and then stood up, heading toward the side of the building. Jason headed back inside.

He saw the girls wipe their tears as he went to sit back down, now not sure how to tell Skye what he saw. But at least he had a short video he could show her to see if she knew who it was. It concerned him enough that he was thinking he needed to call the police. And then the thought ran through his head as to why Skye might have some fear. Jason was getting ready to say something when there was a heavy knock on the door. Skye jumped. Then another knock on her door.

"C'mon, Skye, I know you're in there. I saw your car outside," the man said.

ಶಿ   ಲ

"Skye, do you want me to answer the door?" Jason asked as he now stood up. He motioned for Talia to stay sitting, as he could see she was scared, with eyes wide.

"No," she answered back, and then walked to the door with more pounding on it. She barely got it unlocked when the door handle turned, and the door opened, almost hitting her. She started to back up as he followed her, and then she stopped. He was so close to her face.

"What do you want, Devon?" Skye asked in a shaky voice, still facing him. "I've told you repeatedly to stop coming here and to stop following me. I'm not your girlfriend. I never was."

"Awe, that's what you say, but I know that's not what you really think. C'mon, we had plenty of good times. We hung out together. Too bad your friends couldn't see what a good guy I was," Devon said.

"We went out a handful of times, but I was never your girlfriend. I don't want to be your girlfriend. I didn't appreciate how you treated my friends or me, and I lost them because of you. They won't talk to me. You need to leave me alone," Skye said, getting more upset. "And stop putting things under my windshield wipers."

Devon didn't see Jason or Talia because his view was blocked by the long hallway. Talia now put a hand over her mouth.

"You like those flowers. And you're blaming me because your friends don't want to talk to you? Too bad," Devon said sarcastically. "So who were those people you were having lunch with at Acres today?" Devon asked in a demanding voice. She looked at him with disgust.

"It's none of your business! And how do you know I was at Acres of Clams?" Skye asked as she took a step back staring at him.

"I have my ways, and I'm going to make it my business," Devon said in a stronger voice. Jason had heard enough. He held up his phone with the camera aimed toward the two of them, and then walked around the corner and clicked two photos. It took Devon by surprise, and he got furious. Putting his phone in his back pocket, Jason took a couple of steps toward Devon now, getting between him and Skye, and motioned her to get behind him.

"Who the hell are you?" Devon asked angrily, trying to stand taller than he was and walk toward Skye. Jason had a good four inches on him with a stronger build, blocking his way. This little man was not going to get away with threatening anyone.

Getting into Devon's face, and in a low voice, Jason said, "Let's just say I'm going to be your worst nightmare. You don't listen very well when someone sends you the message that they want you to leave them alone, to stop harassing them and following them and whatever else you're doing, illegally." He glared at Devon.

"I don't know what the Sam hell you're talking about," Devon said. It made Jason think of Tim, the pizza guy. And there are many stupid, arrogant men out there.

"Really, well, maybe we can rectify this situation real quick here," Jason said, his patience with this guy ending. Not wanting to say Talia's name, he said, "Honey, take Skye into her room and call the police, now." Talia got up and moved toward Skye.

"What, why?" Skye asked, knowing there would be repercussions for her from Devon after they leave. She'd be alone, and that scared her.

"I think you'll find out when they get here," Jason said. "Please do as I ask." His tone changed, which Talia had never heard before.

Devon tried moving to the front door to leave, and Jason grabbed him as he started struggling to get away. The girls headed toward

Skye's room quickly, while Jason took a strong hold of Devon's shirt, forcing him into the dining room to sit on a chair.

"You're not going anywhere. And you have some explaining to do when the police get here," Jason said. Devon tried again to move and get out of the chair, but it proved pointless with Jason. Devon was a punk and a bully.

"I don't know who you think you are keeping me here. I can leave if I want to," Devon said, trying to get up, again. But Jason wasn't going to let that happen.

"Why, so that when we're gone, you can come back later and harass Skye even more or try to harm her because she doesn't want anything to do with you? That don't fly with me, and you can damn well bet it won't fly with the police," Jason said.

It was about ten minutes when there was a knock on the door. Jason called for Skye to answer it. She looked out the peephole and saw two police officers standing there. She opened the door, backing up.

"Are you Miss Skye Chaundler, the one who called for help?" one officer asked.

"Yes, I am," Skye responded, motioning for them to come in. Talia was standing near the wall by Skye's bedroom, trying to stay out of view. They waited until Skye closed the door and then followed her around the corner.

"So, what seems to be the issue here?" the other officer asked, looking at Skye. "You said a possible domestic situation?"

"I did," she responded, now looking at Jason.

Jason pulled out his phone and said, "Officers, I have something I think you need to see, and you tell me if this isn't illegal." Devon tried getting up, and one officer put his hand on Devon's shoulder, holding him down. The officers watched the video and then looked at one another.

"Sir, can I ask your name, please?" the officer asked, taking out a notepad.

"Yes, I'm Jason Porter."

"I'm Officer Troy Bennett, and this is my partner, Officer Cal Lockner."

"Cal, why don't you go down with Mr. Porter and check this out. I'll stay here and keep an eye on good old Devon Potts," Officer Bennett said, looking at his suspect. "So Devon, it's been a good long while."

"You ain't got nothin' on me, so you might as well let me go," Devon said, then looked at Skye with a sneer. After hearing what Devon's last name was, that made Skye angrier. She looked at him with disgust, taking a step closer.

"Potts. Your last name is Potts? On top of everything else you've done to me, you're a lying, conniving asshole. Your life must really suck!" Skye said and then looked at the officers. "He told me his last name was Sanders."

"Devon has a rather shady and long, nasty past," Officer Bennett said, looking at her.

Jason headed down with Officer Lockner. He saw two patrol cars, and then Officer Lockner headed to his car, getting out some equipment. Jason stood and watched.

"What made you decide to record Mr. Potts?" Officer Lockner asked as he was preparing his detector and mirror and then put latex gloves on.

"I was actually out on the balcony speaking with my grandmother while my wife and Skye were talking. After getting off the phone with her, I stood there enjoying the air and looked down, watching some people head down the alley. Then I looked at the cars and saw someone at the back of Skye's jeep. I wondered what they could be doing. It could be nothing, or it could be something. So I thought I best record it.

"We spent the day with Skye. She and my wife were best friends when they were young, from back home," Jason said. "They hadn't seen each other for a long time."

"Where do you call home?" Officer Lockner asked as they walked toward Skye's jeep.

"Iowa. We were here for a fashion show over at the Meydenbauer Convention Center. My wife is a fashion designer," Jason said. He watched the officer with the detector and heard a little click. With the lighted mirror, the officer showed Jason the small tracking device. Reaching under the bumper, he removed the small oblong device, placing it into an evidence bag, shaking his head.

Then he moved toward the rear right wheel, doing the same. There was no click, but saw where a device had been stuck to the wheel well above the tire. Next, they moved to the right front wheel. There was a click. Another tracking device was found and removed. The officer placed it in a second evidence bag. He did the same thing on the left side, but didn't find any other devices. He then continued with his long detector pole under the jeep, but found nothing else.

"OK, except for these two tracking devices, the car is clean," Officer Lockner said, taking off his gloves. He wrote in his notepad. "So Mr. Porter, what do you do back in Iowa?"

"I'm a paramedic/firefighter," Jason said. The officer nodded, looking at Jason, and then smiled.

"We've got some buddies across the pond over at the police station and the fire station in Bellevue. You wouldn't know anything about a gunshot at the convention center this past week, would you?" Officer Lockner asked, smiling.

Jason grinned and then nodded, saying yes. "And you call that a pond? Pretty big pond, if you ask me. Iowa is a landlocked state. We have some ponds, but not as large as Lake Washington."

Officer Lockner said, "There were two of you working on a downed man. We heard from Mark, one of the paramedics who arrived to take over. He said they had some German paramedic who was working with them, and that the German and one of the unknown paramedics who helped knew one another."

"That would have been Jürgen Sussman," Jason said, smiling.

"And then one of the officers, Chris, waited for ID badges and heard the conversation about working abroad. He actually got jealous and wouldn't shut up about it." Officer Lockner chuckled and then reached out his hand to shake Jason's hand.

They walked toward the side of the building to head upstairs. Once inside, Jason walked over to Talia with his back to the others, putting his arm around her, and kissed her. Officer Lockner showed Officer Bennett the evidence bags, and then he walked over to Skye showing her the tracking devices, telling her where they were placed. They got Devon to his feet. Skye looked at Devon and walked over to him with Officer Bennett behind him taking out his handcuffs, getting ready to handcuff Devon. The look of contempt on her face said it all. With as much umph as she could muster, she slapped Devon hard across the face, knocking him against a chair.

"You bastard!" Skye's voice was raised and she was shaking, and turned to walk back toward Talia and Jason. Devon started to go after her, but both officers grabbed him, and then Devon yelled at them to arrest her for assault as they put the handcuffs on him, reading him his Miranda Rights.

"I didn't see anything, did you, Officer Bennett?" Officer Lockner asked.

Officer Bennett shook his head no. "I don't know what he's talking about."

Officer Lockner saw Jason's paramedic backpack sitting on the floor, giving a little nod. He looked at Jason and then Officer Bennett and said, "I have a good one to tell you when we get back to the station." Jason walked toward the officer's, and they all shook hands. They told Skye she wouldn't have any more trouble from Mr. Potts, and then the officers left, with Devon cursing under his breath.

Chapter 31

Skye was shaking as she plunked down near the end of the dark brown loveseat sofa, turning on the lamp. Talia came and sat down next to her, watching the tears streaming down Skye's cheeks as she grabbed a Kleenex from the box sitting on the end table. Talia leaned over, hugging her friend while Jason sat down in the swivel rocking chair that matched the sofa's dark brown color.

"Skye, I'm good a listener," Talia said. "I only have a vague idea of what you've been going through. I didn't lose friends and become isolated because of someone like Devon. What Tim did to me was bad enough. I know you're angry about this, and that fear of looking over your shoulder all the time wondering what's going to happen or where he would show up next, I can't even imagine."

"I just want to forget about it." Skye looked at Talia and then Jason. "I need to get you back to your hotel, if you're ready to go."

Talia looked at Jason with a shake of her head.

"Skye, I think we should stay here with you tonight," Jason said. "Devon's been arrested. I got Officer Lockner's cell phone number, so I'll call him in the morning and see what's happened. But he won't be bothering you anymore." She looked at him with tears still coming down. "We just don't think you should be alone, OK?" She nodded.

"Do you want to try to eat anything?" Talia asked.

"No. I lost my appetite after all of this. Today, the drink that was served, the black flower under my windshield, and then those tracking things on my car. There have been other things, and I thought I was losing it," Skye said. Talia took hold of her hand.

Jason said, "You're not losing it. That was probably his plan all along. He was playing on your emotions, probably belittling you, intimidating and putting fear into you. We've had a few discussions like this back at my station where a victim had been isolated. Friends leave or are afraid to help or get involved. It's sad, but it happens."

"It just makes me so angry," Skye said, looking at the floor and wiping her tears away.

"Hey, we've got the rest of this evening and all day tomorrow and tomorrow night," Talia said. "I told you I want to spend it with you. We can talk about whatever you want. And if there's something you'd like to show us tomorrow, that would be great."

"Well, I don't know about you ladies, but I'm going to have a bite or two of those delicious looking desserts we bought," Jason said, smiling as he stood up and headed toward the dining room table. Talia watched him, smiling as he took them out of their little individual yellow bags with the Piroshky Piroshky name on the outside. He laid them on a plate and cut them into halves to share with Talia, and then he sat down.

"You're so lucky, Talia," Skye said softly as she looked at Jason and then back to Talia.

"I know I am. Jason is the love of my life. I don't know what I would do without him, and I don't ever want to find out. Our love runs pretty deep," Talia said.

"I'd like to hear more about the two of you. But I think right now, I'd like to show you where you'll be sleeping. As I said, Marti, short for Margaret, left yesterday to spend a week with her parents. I think she's making arrangements to move back home. She lost her job and can't afford to stay here." Skye stood up and headed for Marti's room, with Talia following. Jason turned to watch them walk down the hallway. After preparing the bed with clean sheets and an extra blanket, they came out with Skye, showing Talia the bathroom. It was a bit smaller than Talia's, but it was bright and clean.

"I have a long nightshirt if you want to borrow it. I can't help your husband, though," Skye said.

"It's OK," Talia said with a slight grin. "When we're not at home, he has a pair of light sweatpants. Otherwise, it's nothing. I think he'll be fine for tonight."

"I'll get that shirt for you," Skye said, and headed to her bedroom. After retrieving it, she took it to Marti's room and laid it on the end of the bed. She headed to the dining room where her two guests were seated and sat down herself.

"I want to thank both of you for being here with me. And Jason, thank you for capturing Mr. Dumb Potts on your cell phone camera—"

Talia broke out in laughter now, with tears running down her cheeks. She couldn't stop laughing at what Skye just called Devon. "Mr. Dumb Potts," Talia said out loud, then had Skye and Jason both laughing. It was so funny.

"You know, I think I will have part of my dessert. Maybe just having the two of you here makes things better," Skye said.

After having some of their dessert, they did feel better. The rest they would leave until morning. Talia helped Skye clean up, and then headed back to the living room. Jason was sitting on the right side of the loveseat sofa. He told Talia he called the hotel to let them know they would not be back tonight. She sat down beside him, and he put his arm around her and kissed the side of her head. There was a light, soft throw blanket behind her in various black, off-white, and turquoise stripes, and she brought it around and placed it over her lap.

"So how did the two of you finally get together, again?" Skye asked as she started to rock in her chair, and then pulled another beautiful throw blanket over her lap.

Talia and Jason took turns talking about the way they met up in Basel. Talia spoke about why she went overseas, for herself, and the opportunity to shop for new fabrics. It took her a year to plan and save for the trip, and then six months before she left, her dad died. And it was her birthday when she landed in Basel.

Skye told Talia she was sorry to hear about her dad's passing, but said she always liked her parents. They were fun, from what she remembered.

Jason talked about Kurt telling him where to find Talia months before going to Germany. That trip had been planned for two years. He had a week in between his first and second, waiting for his other comrades to head over. So, he took the train from Stuttgart to Basel, hoping to find her at one of the hotels Kurt told him about.

He didn't have a plan if he couldn't find her, and if he did find her, well, he really hoped that she wasn't involved with anyone and that she would be willing to spend it with him. So the entire week, they did the tourist thing from Basel, to Bern, to Villars, and Ollon. They talked about hiking up in the mountains, the rainstorm, and Jéan-Paul's cabin, leaving out the best part. Skye saw how they looked at each other, with Jason giving a wink to Talia. Skye had a grin on her face imagining what really happened that night.

She listened to this almost fairy tale they were telling her, feeling envious at the wonderful journey these two had been on, especially how Jason found Talia, on a footbridge in a botanical garden in Switzerland. She wondered if she would ever have such a beautiful experience, and it made her long for it that much more.

Her life wasn't going the way she hoped it would. It hadn't for a very long time, and any relationships she had were the worst. She just wanted that someone special in her life, to fall in love, to have that soft place to fall, and to share what Talia and Jason have.

"Your proposal must have been wonderful and romantic," Skye said. "All those people got to see and hear it, and then you all danced with the Rhine River behind you. I don't know if you would hear of people around here dancing like that after someone proposed with music playing, but maybe they would."

"We'll have to show you the video. We brought our digital picture frame with us, but it's back in our room," Talia said. "That was a gift given to us by our two hotel desk friends in Switzerland."

"I'd love to see it," Skye said with a smile.

"Well, there's a lot to see," Jason said, smiling. "So, maybe later tomorrow afternoon or evening, when you take us back to the hotel, you come up with us and we'll all watch."

Talia continued. "I had a car accident right after Thanksgiving, during a winter storm. My car rolled down an embankment. I was hospitalized and put on a breathing machine."

"Oh, no," Skye said. "I'm sorry to hear that. That had to be scary for you."

"Well, I was unconscious. But this beautiful man never left my side, I was told." Talia looked at Jason, and he kissed her.

"I needed to be with her, and I promised her at the scene that I wouldn't leave her. I couldn't bear the thought of losing her. That was a good possibility, as well as our unborn baby," Jason said. He saw the look on Skye's face and explained that his fire station got the call and he was on duty that day. "You know, when we were young and first met, for me, it was love at first sight. But at that age, I didn't know what love was or what it was supposed to feel like. But every time I saw her on those vacations, I just wanted to be near her and hold her and look at her. I don't know how to explain that kind of feeling." Skye only had to look at the two of them and saw it. She wanted that so much.

"Our wedding was pretty amazing," Jason said. They both talked a little about it.

"Your wedding sounded beautiful, and at the Des Moines Botanical Garden," Skye said, smiling.

"When my mom came into the dressing room and saw me, she had tears in her eyes, and she said to me, '*Vous étes belle.*' I told her, '*Merci, Maman.*'"

"Aw, that had to be a special moment between you and your mom," Skye said.

"I'm really going to have to learn French and Italian," Jason said, looking at Skye and then Talia. "I hadn't heard about that. What does '*Vous étes belle*' mean?"

Talia looked at Skye with a smile to see if she remembered any more French, and Skye told Jason, "Her mom said, 'You look beautiful.' Talia replied to her mom with, 'Thank you, Mom.'"

Jason looked into Talia's eyes. "I would have totally agreed with your mom that you looked beautiful, and even more so today." He kissed her again.

"And the last thing is, it was the middle of January when I received an invitation to participate in a fashion designer contest," Talia said, looking at Jason and back to Skye. "I submitted my application with the requirements, and that's what brought us here to Seattle."

"Wow. That's why you're here," Skye said, and Talia nodded her head. "I don't remember when we were little that you ever talked about clothes or anything like that. Where was this held? How many designers were there? Where were they from? How did you do?" Skye asked, throwing out the questions to Talia with her eyes wide.

Grinning, Talia responded. "It was at the Meydenbauer Convention Center. And there were ten of us designers from ten different states. I was totally shocked and blown away when Norm Shetler announced my name as the first prize winner, along with an interview by *Rising Fashion Magazine*." Skye all but squealed with joy.

"Oh my god, that is so exciting, and then to be interviewed by a fashion magazine. That is so cool!" Skye beamed at Talia. "I'm so proud of you. Wow."

"Thank you," Talia replied. "You know what, I want to hear what's going on with you. But I'm getting tired, and the baby's been doing some light moving around." She looked at Skye, and then Jason. "Can you get your stethoscope?"

"I can do that," Jason said with a smile, getting his bag and sitting back down. Talia lifted her top over her belly while Jason took out his stethoscope, putting it around his neck first, and then placed his hand where Talia's was. He felt the slight brush of the baby move under his palm, and motioned for Skye to feel the movement. She looked at Talia, who smiled, nodding her head. Skye moved to the floor near Talia's feet and placed her hand softly where Jason indicated. She waited several moments, and then her eyes got big, feeling a slight brush against her palm. She looked up at Talia, her eyes misting over.

Jason then listened for the heartbeat. Once he found it, he had Talia listen. She closed her eyes, and a big smile appeared. Talia then had Skye listen. She closed her eyes for a moment, wanting to hold on to that memory of hearing this tiny heartbeat. She knew she wouldn't be around for the birth of this baby, at least not that she was aware of.

It was after 10:00 p.m. Jason put his stethoscope back in his bag. Talia got up, telling Jason that Skye had laid out a nightshirt for her. She showed him the bathroom and then went to Marti's room, finding the soft, dark blue nightshirt on the bed and putting it on.

Talia came out and sat back down on the loveseat sofa. Both girls were quiet before Skye spoke. "Thank you for staying here with me. I wish today had turned out differently."

"It's OK. I'm just so happy that we were here with you, when you know who came to your door, and that you were the one to pick us up this afternoon and take us to a few other places. Being with you has made me miss you all over again," Talia said. "I miss my best friend. I know you live here, but I wish there were a way that you might at some point consider coming back to either visit or maybe transition yourself back toward the center of the country?" She gave Skye a goofy look. Jason walked out and leaned against the wall. He'd taken off his shoes and pullover sweater, leaving his jeans on momentarily and his chest bare, looking at Talia. Skye glanced up at him, noticing his very nice body, and then averted her eyes quickly back to Talia, who stood up.

"Yup, there's that bare chest again," Talia said with a sigh and a giggle. "I'm going to the bathroom and head to bed. Skye, we'll see you in the morning."

Skye nodded and said, "Good night. Sleep well." She waited until she heard the bedroom door close before going to the bathroom, and then headed to bed.

Chapter 32

Our last full day here, Jason thought as he lay in bed. He heard the toilet flush and then the sound of the shower. Before heading to bed, Jason had opened the bedroom curtain just a little ways, letting in a little light from a street lamp. Turning his head toward Talia, he saw she was still sleeping peacefully. He looked at his watch and saw that it was after 6:30 a.m. His phone buzzed. It was Jim texting him.

Jim: *Morning, partner. I know it's early. I hope all is OK. Had Cole over for a late dinner last night. He was somewhat talkative but kept looking at his phone.*

Jason: *Morning, Jim. We're doing well. It's our last day today. We'll be flying home tomorrow. So what was so interesting on his phone?* Jason knew exactly what it was.

Jim: *Well, there is a picture of a very pretty lady he couldn't stop looking at. You wouldn't know anything about that, would you?* ☺

Jason: *Oh, I might know something about it.*

Jim: *I'm going to come right out and ask. Who is she? I caught Cole looking at her photo again this morning. Glad he doesn't have driving privileges with the truck yet.*

Jason: *Lol. That pretty lady was, is, best friends with Talia. Her name is Skye Chaundler. We'll explain when we get home.*

Jim: *We have the midwife coming this afternoon for training. Heard about the pregnant woman on the plane. What are your plans for today?*

Jason: *Not sure right now, but it does include Skye. Talia is waking up. Tell Cole to keep his phone in his pocket.*

Jim: *Oh gee, why didn't I think of that. Lol. Have a good one.*

Talia opened her eyes, looking at Jason. "Who were you texting already this morning?" she asked, then yawned.

"Jim." He turned and looked at her. "I sent a photo of Skye to Cole when we were driving here yesterday. Then Jim and Nadine had him over for a late dinner last night, and apparently, he looked at his phone several times. And then this morning, he was looking at her photo again. Jim said he was glad Cole wasn't driving the truck." He grinned.

"So why did you do that?" Talia asked.

"Cole is the one that Skye emailed with information for us. If it weren't for the fact that you know her and she's the one that met us at Acres of Clams, I wouldn't have sent her photo to him. But I thought he might like to see what she looked like."

"And?" Talia asked, sitting up and raising her eyebrows. "What did he say?"

Jason showed Talia the text he had with Cole. He noted the big grin on her face.

Moments later, she said, "I know we know little about Cole and what brought him to Iowa, or at least I don't know. He seems like a very decent guy and quite nice looking. And he is a travel agent like Skye. She is very pretty."

"Oh, hold on there," Jason said, sitting more upright. "Where do you think you're going with those thoughts of yours, huh?"

"Nowhere in particular," she said with a nonchalant shrug.

"Uh-huh. He recently moved from Ohio, and she lives here in Seattle. I don't know if he has a girlfriend or had one, or anything." Jason was thinking she's going to try to play cupid long distance.

"I'm just thinking, wouldn't it be nice if the two of them could meet somehow," Talia said with a silly look on her face. "And if he's looking at her photo that much, maybe he's also wondering. You know what we could do—" She stopped mid-sentence when Jason laid her back down kissing her.

"It's time we get up. Skye's been up for a while now. I heard her in the bathroom earlier." Still looking at her, he said, "You let this go."

With a pouty look, she changed back into her clothes and then said, "I'm going to the bathroom and then head out to the other room." She left the bedroom door ajar. Jason sat on the edge of the bed for a few moments, looking out the window at the bare trees, then stood up and put his pullover sweater on. If he was real honest about it, his train of thought was on the same track as Talia's, which put a grin on his face, but he couldn't let Talia know this. He headed for the bathroom.

It was about 7:15 a.m., Skye was in the kitchen and had made some coffee. She turned partially around, hearing someone behind her, and saw Talia.

"Good morning. Did the two of you sleep alright?" Skye asked.

"We did. That coffee smells good." Skye reached up into the cupboard and brought out three pretty mugs, setting them down on the counter. She started pouring coffee into them, and moments later, Jason walked toward the kitchen.

"Morning, Jason," Skye said.

"Good morning. And how did you sleep?" Jason asked, looking at Skye, hoping that she slept a little more peacefully knowing, as she put it, 'Mr. Dumb Potts' had been arrested and wouldn't be stalking her anymore.

"For the most part, much better. Maybe having you two stay here with me helped."

"Good. As I said yesterday, I have Officer Lockner's phone number, and I'll call him after bit and see what's going on." Skye nodded and said thank you.

"Either of you use cream or sugar?" Skye asked.

"No, black for me," Jason said.

"Me too," Talia replied.

"Are you ready for a little breakfast?" Both nodded. After having some really good scrambled eggs and bacon and toast, and finishing up their desserts from last night, Talia helped Skye clean up and joined Jason in the living room.

"There are a couple parks I'd like to show you today, and one other food place, if that's alright?" Skye asked. "I thought maybe just being out in the open, fresh air, and doing a little walking, even if it is February."

"That would be nice, a perfect way to wind down our time here after all the things we've seen and eaten," Talia said with a big smile. But before they went anywhere, she wanted to find out what happened to Skye's sister, if she was willing to talk about it.

"Skye, I wanted to ask you what happened to Jules." Talia looked at her, and saw the sad look return to Skye's face as she stared at the floor. Skye lowered her head and closed her eyes. Pictures were coming up in her mind's eye from seeing the photos the Coast Guard showed them, and she pursed her lips together with a slight shake of her head. Talia looked at Jason and then back to Skye. When she opened her eyes, there were tears.

"Jules died in a bad boating accident on the Columbia River. It's long. It's huge, and deep, and feeds into the Pacific Ocean. There's a four-mile-long bridge called the Astoria-Megler Bridge that connects Oregon to Washington. It was because of Jules' so-called boyfriend, L.J. His family are boating people, and they gave their irresponsible, arrogant, show-off of a son a speed boat. According to the Coast Guard and other rescuers, the day it happened was a Friday. It was a foggy and murky morning. L.J. decided to go for a joy-ride in his boat, and talked three others into going with him, or intimidated them, which included Jules. She was afraid of deep water, and I still can't believe she went out with them." Tears started down Skye's cheeks, and Talia couldn't help but have tears seeing her best friend in pain like this.

"No one knew they were going out on the river. Before lunchtime, the weather had pretty much cleared, and a couple other boaters were out and not too far from the bridge, saw parts of a speedboat, and called the Coast Guard. They heard someone yelling and found a kid hanging onto a buoy. It wasn't Jules. The kid recounted to authorities what happened, that L.J. was trying to turn the boat at a higher speed than he should have and didn't know what direction they were going. The bridge is held by huge concrete piers, and L.J. crashed into one of them, killing him. Jules and the other girl hit the corner of a pier and drowned. The surviving young man was badly injured, barely holding onto a buoy until he was rescued." The tears came steadily.

"I wish I could have stopped her. I wish she would have talked to me. That she would have had the courage, and told me something, anything. I could have helped. She'd be safe and here." More tears fell down her cheeks. Talia got up and moved next to Skye, kneeling, putting her arms around her, tears of her own falling. Skye continued,

"Jules kept a couple diaries relaying how she met L.J. and his family. She wrote about his family being quite wealthy, self-centered and worldly, how L.J. treated her, the filthy and dirty names he called her. She was too scared to tell anyone what he was doing to her, and didn't know how to make him stop. He intimidated her. Mom barely made it through the first diary, and got sick to her stomach. All she could say was she was glad the little bastard was dead."

Talia wrapped her arms around Skye and held her saying, "I'm sorry, Skye. I'm so sorry." Jason moved over on the sofa. Talia knew Jason felt that pain and more, and how it haunted him for a very long time, and he's never forgotten. It's always there. It was very plain to see that Skye was still suffering from her sister's death. That's something you just don't let go of. More than likely, she didn't have anyone to talk to especially not her parents or siblings, about how she was feeling. Jason wondered if any of the rest of them read Jules' diaries and what they were feeling or how they coped or who they could talk to.

Skye continued, "No one knows what I'm feeling. They haven't been in my shoes." She saw the looks on Talia and Jason's faces. "I know you've lost a parent, grandparents or aunts and uncles, but to lose a sibling, you have no idea how that feels.

"I'm just so angry, pissed, hurt, scared, and tired. I'd go to the grocery store or a mall and stand there and look at the people walking past me, going on about their merry way, not even looking at me. They're talking or laughing, and they don't see my tears or my pain. No one asks me if I'm alright. It's like no one cares. Why don't they get it? They shop for crap they don't need or talk about people behind their backs. Don't they know I lost my sister? That I'm feeling lost and so alone." More tears run down her cheeks.

Skye's voice became angrier. "We buried her down in the cold ground in a damn coffin." Her voice then became louder. "She shouldn't be there. She had a life and family. She was my sister. We had a trip planned together. She should be here, safe." She took more Kleenex wiping her tears.

Jason knew all those feelings of hurt and anger and grief. He felt he needed to say something here, to let her know he did understand and knew where she was coming from, that he gets it, and before he knew it, out of his mouth came, "I'm all too aware of how that feels Skye." He said it in a quiet voice.

"I felt guilty for most of my life, thinking it was my fault. I will never see my baby sister again." Skye looked at him. "I had a sister once. She died. I shoved that guilt so far down, thinking I was to blame for her death. I didn't think I deserved to have love in my life because I didn't protect the one I did love until about five months ago when it rose for the last time."

Jason looked at Talia and back to Skye. "She was five years old. She was taken as I sat next to her, only three feet away. Someone grabbed her and started running. My parents and I went running after him. He had her under his arm, and went between two parked vehicles trying to cross the road. They never saw the truck that hit them, and they both went flying into the air. It was only then that my sister Amy's screams stopped, only to be followed by the screams of my mother." Jason's eyes misted over.

"It was deafening. I can't get that out of my head. I was seven years old! That was the first time I experienced someone dying, my baby sister and I saw it. That has left a scar on me." Skye's eyes became wide, and more tears fell; not for her, but for Jason.

"Then, it was a crew I worked with in Colorado, helping at the scene of a nasty accident in the mountains. A semi and a car tangled, with the car up against a concrete barrier. We knew whoever was in that car died. We broke through the front windshield, and who do I see but my best friend and her parents, dead. Talia's dad died almost a year ago. I almost lost the love of my life and our baby this past December due to a snowstorm. It was my fire station that got the call. How do you think I felt, arriving and finding out it was Talia?

"I'm a paramedic and firefighter, I see death and dying all the time. People die right in front of me or in my arms. We risk our lives going into burning buildings. I've had friends go to war and come home in the back of a large military aircraft with an American flag draped over their coffin.

"People die, and sometimes there's not a damn thing we can do about it. Families everywhere feel that pain, that hurt, and anger and they're still grieving. They'll never see their loved ones again. There is no time frame here in healing, and letting go of the pain and sorrow."

His voice softened. "I know you feel like you're the only one. But I also know that you know you aren't the only one. I'm so sorry for all of your pain and the loss of your sister." Jason stood up and motioned for the girls to stand up while putting his arms around them. Skye let her tears fall. Jason kissed the top of Talia's head, holding her a bit tighter as her tears fell.

Chapter 33

Skye headed to the bathroom, leaving Talia and Jason to sit on the sofa. Jason had his arm around Talia as she leaned against him, and he held her hand. Looking at her, he said, "I didn't mean for all of that to come out of my mouth. I don't know what possessed me to tell her that. I wasn't trying to make her feel worse than she already did."

"I know you didn't," Talia said, speaking softly. "She's had this bottled up inside of her since Jules's death, not being able to tell anyone and have anyone listen." She looked into Jason's eyes with a sad look. "There are so many that can't talk about it or confide in to anyone. Skye was my best friend, and I don't want to leave her feeling even more alone.

"I wish there were a way I could get her to at least consider moving, but I don't know that she'll go for it. This is her home. I don't know how many friends she had and then left because of Devon, no family close by or that's willing to communicate with each other, maybe just her co-worker. I can see why she feels alone."

"I'm going to call Officer Lockner. I'll step out on the balcony," Jason said, kissing her on the forehead.

❧

Skye came into the living room, sitting down in the rocking chair. She looked at the two of them. Her eyes were still slightly red from crying. She looked a little tired but also seemed relieved. Maybe now, having had the opportunity to talk about her sister and having someone actually listen to her and validate her feelings and emotions, she might be able to envision a little brighter future for herself.

"Skye, are you OK?" Talia asked. She nodded yes.

"I want to apologize to you for going off the way I did," Jason said, shaking his head. "I didn't mean to make you feel worse or more guilty or angry that you couldn't help her. I just wanted you to know that I know how it all feels and where you were coming from, and I am so sorry for what happened to your sister."

"Thank you," Skye said, taking a deep breath. "You know, I was thinking while in the bathroom that when I was to meet you at Acres of Clams, I told myself that 'help is on the way,' meaning I was going to be there to help you. And I'm wondering now if that 'help is on the way' wasn't meant for me. And here you are, helping me when I needed it most. Talk about serendipity."

It was almost eerie what she said, and then Jason and Talia looked at one another, remembering when Grandma Jean spoke directly to Talia that very same message before walking through the airport sliding door yesterday morning.

"Skye, I called Officer Lockner. He wouldn't go into detail, but Mr. Potts won't be bothering you or anyone else for quite some time," Jason said. Skye nodded and let out a sigh of relief.

Talia asked Skye, "With Marti moving, was she going to find a roommate for you, or will you have to find one?"

"I honestly don't know," Skye said, taking a moment looking toward the far wall. "I'm not sure what I'm going to do or the right thing to do. No family around to help if I was to lose my job, and I've lost the few friends I did have. I have no one else here, and it feels pretty lonesome. Even though I enjoy living in Seattle, and there's so much here, it's also expensive."

Her phone rang, and she got up, walking over to the small cabinet where it lay on top still plugged in. Anisha let her know her clients called and asked if they could stop in this morning and pick up the map and booklets if she found them. Skye told Anisha to tell them, yes, and she'd be in soon.

"That was Anisha from my office," Skye said. "So you heard, I have clients stopping by. I didn't think they'd come until later in the week. But I'm thinking after that, we could head over to one of the parks."

☙

It was lightly raining when they left Skye's apartment. Arriving at Mélaton Travel Agency, Skye wanted Talia and Jason to come in with her to meet Anisha once she finished up with her clients. After they left, happy to have their little treasures, Skye had Talia and Jason come into her office and then had Anisha join them.

"Anisha, I'd like you to meet my childhood best friend Talia Rose-Porter, a fashion designer, and her husband, Jason Porter, a paramedic and firefighter. They're from Iowa, where I spent my first fourteen years before moving with my family to Oregon," Skye said.

"Oh, so you're the fashion designer," Anisha said, smiling at her. "It's very nice to meet you." She reached out to Talia and shook her hand, then did the same with Jason and stated, "So it was your grandmother who got to be in the show. That had to be interesting."

"It was pretty amazing and fun. I'm very proud of her, as I am of my lovely wife," Jason said, looking at Talia and taking hold of her hand.

"Well, it's nice to meet the both of you. I hope you've been able to enjoy some of the wonders that Seattle has to offer while you've been here. I hope some of the suggestions we made for sightseeing were helpful," Anisha said. Talia and Jason nodded, saying thank you and that they have many great memories to share when they get back home. Anisha looked at Skye and headed out of her office, with Skye following.

In a whispered voice, Anisha said. "Whoa, he is good-looking. Where can I get one like him?" Her eyes were wide as she smiled.

"I know. Wouldn't that be nice, having someone like him. It's quite the love story these two have. Guess I'll have to keep dreaming for that special someone to come into my life. I at least get to spend the rest of the day with them. They leave tomorrow morning." Skye also spoke in a quiet voice.

"Hang in there, Skye," Anisha said, laying a hand on Skye's arm. "Good stuff is bound to happen soon. You deserve happiness, more than anyone I know. I'm putting it out there for your highest good to come to you."

Skye turned and headed back to her office. Her phone rang, it was Robert. He and Lynne won't be able to come home until tomorrow evening. She told him not to worry about his two new favorite people. She'd get them to the airport on time. She put her coat on and picked up her handbag as Talia and Jason also stood. On their way out, Skye told Anisha she'd be in after taking them to the airport tomorrow morning. Anisha nodded, telling them to enjoy the rest of their day and have a safe flight home.

It was impressive, standing in front of The Volunteer Park Conservatory. Talia knew her dad would have enjoyed this building.

The Historic Victorian-style greenhouse was modeled after London's Crystal Palace. There were tons of glass window panes. The rain let up as they stood at the end of the sidewalk. Skye took a few photos of Jason and Talia with her phone and Talia's. Then Jason said he wanted to get a picture of both girls. Someone was heading for the main door, and Talia asked if they could take a photo of the three of them, which they were happy to do.

They took their time walking through the five distinct temperate houses where the Conservatory showcased a large variety of tropical and subtropical plant life. Each being so unique and beautiful. Talia really appreciated seeing everything in English underneath the long name most people can't pronounce, like *Dionaea muscipula* (Venus flytraps), *Crassula argentea* (Jade tree), or *Strelitzia* (Bird of Paradise), or how about the *Amorphophallus titanum* (Corpse flower). That plant blooms two or three times in its forty-year life span. Two of the oldest plants were the Sago Palm (*Cycas revoluta*) and the Jade Tree (*Crassula argentea*), both over 100 years old.

They learned that there were over 3400 panes of glass, and that the oldest part of the building was the lunette or peacock window over the main entry. It is the only original wood still remaining from 1912. There was some wonderful history associated with this park.

Having enjoyed their time at the conservatory, Skye asked who was hungry as her stomach talked to her. Both Talia and Jason concurred that food was a priority.

"I think this next place will be almost as delicious as Piroshky Piroshky, but with an English flare," Skye said smiling. They chatted on the way down to Pike Place Market. Finding a parking place, they got out of the jeep and followed Skye across the street and up around the corner. When she came to the shop, she stopped in front and let Jason and Talia look up at the sign. It read: The Crumpet Shop.

"Was this another one of your favorite places?" Talia asked, smiling as she looked in the window and then back to Skye.

"Ya. I would come down here to the Pike Place Market and walk all around. That's how I found this place, Metsker Maps, and Piroshky, plus many others, including the fish market where they throw the fish," Skye said. "Talia, give me your phone. I'll take a photo of you both with the sign above your heads." Skye took a photo or two of Jason and Talia, and then one of them making a funny face.

"OK, my turn. Skye, stand next to Talia," Jason said, smiling, and then his thoughts took over, *Here's another photo I might send off. But of course, the day isn't done yet. Nuts, now my brain is doing what Talia's was this morning. Can't have two cupids in the same family, or can we? I don't even know how this would work.* Fate always has a way of working things out.

Walking inside, there were several people in line. Here they could smell the wonderful aroma of baked goods. They watched one of the baker's filling the little crumpet tins with batter, directly on top of a large griddle. This also gave the three of them a moment to look at the menu board.

"OK, Skye, what do you recommend here?" Jason asked, looking at the board.

"Now I realize this isn't your everyday lunch, but it will fill you up. And I don't know that you've had anything like this," Skye said. "There are a variety of things you can put on a crumpet, and they have scones. Some of my favorites are the egg, cheese, and ham on a crumpet, the fresh ricotta, and lemon curd, also put this on a scone. The pesto, tomato, cheese one is good. Anything like the strawberry, raspberry, or orange marmalade spreads are good. Oh, and a favorite is the honey walnut with ricotta cheese or the Vermont, which is the ricotta, maple butter, and walnuts. Sometimes, it's hard to choose.

Every time I come in, I try a few different things. They're all delicious, as are their cappuccinos and teas."

"Well, I'm pretty hungry," Jason said. "I already know what I'm going to get, which includes the smoked salmon spread. Sweetheart, what looks good to you?" He looked at Talia.

"Oh boy, I also see several things I want to try. Maybe between the two of us, we can split several things?" Talia looked at Jason with a grin. "I'm also going to try the Crumpet Shop Blend Tea."

After ordering and finding a table to sit at, Talia took her phone out and snapped several photos of the different crumpets and scones to show everyone back home. Jason then looked at Talia with a grin and asked, "You're going to eat all that?" She nodded. When they had finished eating, there wasn't anything left on their plates.

"Skye, thank you for bringing us here. Again, this was something new and different, and it was wonderful. I'm not hungry anymore, but give me several hours and I know I'll be ready to eat something else," Talia said, smiling and rubbing her tummy.

"You're welcome. If the two of you are ready, I think first thing's first; the restrooms, and then we can head out," Skye said.

℈

Getting into Skye's jeep, they left the Pike Place Market. She told them this next place was another favorite of hers, and it was just down the road a piece. She saw the look on Jason's face in the rearview mirror.

"Yup, I've heard that phrase many times before," Jason said. "I would ask my parents where we were going, and they would reply, 'oh, down the road a piece' or 'you'll see when we get there.'" The girls laughed, and Jason looked out his window. It started drizzling again, and Skye hoped that it would ease up or just plain quit by the time they got to where they were going.

Talia looked at Skye and asked, "As a travel agent, people talk to you about a trip they want to take, and you either plan it or provide them with wonderful books and maps. Is that the scope of what you do?"

"Yes. It was six months ago when the owners finally agreed to let me also do more travel research writing for groups and then set up tours. I even tried to do some fun quirky tours, but that didn't go over very well." Skye glanced over at Talia. "There's been a few times when I thought, I need a change. I need to kick start my life, but then I get back into the same rut and nothing changes. I get scared and feel like there's no one to help me or encourage me.

"They're more than willing to give me their long-winded opinion about what they would do or what I should do, to stop dreaming or fantasizing. So, I stay stuck, and then it's fear and feeling safe. OK, I take that part back after the crap with Devon. And I have a distrust of people."

"I want to tell you something," Talia said as she looked out the front window. "I almost wasn't going to enter this contest, even after my loving husband back there tried telling me to remember what my grandfather told me, which was to design my dream. I'd been afraid to get out of my comfort zone because I felt safe in my little world. However, I did take a trip across the ocean where the love of my life found me. We think that was fate." She looked back at Jason with a loving smile, and then looked out the front window toward Skye. "Both of these loving men believed in me, so it boiled down to me believing in myself and getting out of my own way.

"I was scared that I wasn't good enough to compete with anyone else. But seeing my grandfather's face, he smiled at me and nodded.

I decided, what have I got to lose? And here we are. I still find it hard to believe that I won first prize. That wouldn't have happened had I not changed my thought pattern. And then the five of us got to see so many wonderful things. Jason and I wouldn't have enjoyed a wonderful ferry ride." Talia looks at Skye and states, "Who would have thought that my past would meet me head-on." Skye glanced at Talia and then back to the road, not saying anything.

"And I've been thinking, ever since you picked us up at Acres of Clams, and spending this time with you, I realized how much I miss my best friend," Talia said. "I feel like that might have been fate for both of us. You were part of our family, and then you were gone for good. Being here with you now has made me miss you all over again." Talia's eyes misted over, and when she looked at Skye, hers were a little misty as well. "I know you have a life here, but I'm just going to say it. I want you to think about the possibility of coming home."

Chapter 34

Arriving at the Kubota Garden, the rain had let up. It was perfect timing. They sat in the jeep for several moments. Jason watched Skye look at Talia, and then Skye said, "You have given me a lot to think about. I realized after seeing you and spending time with you that I also missed my best friend, and you feel like home."

Getting out of her jeep, Skye stood near the front. She waited as Jason helped Talia out, then giving her a hug and a kiss. Skye watched and felt another ping of envy and thought to herself, *When will I have that in my life? Would someone come find me, the way Jason found Talia and love me like that, and I could love him back? I'm not even sure I know what love is at this point because I've never experienced it.*

It was early afternoon as they headed toward the entrance to the garden. Skye walked over to the self-help kiosk and picked up some pamphlets for the self-guided tour. They opened them up and saw the map. All the features were numbered to easily find which path you wanted to walk, and it gave descriptions. There would be many photo opportunities here, starting at number three—the Entry Gate and Ornamental Wall. It read that you cross the threshold from the everyday world to a sacred space. It already felt peaceful walking through.

They approached the bell and drinking fountain. Not that they felt silly about doing it, but the description said to ring the bell with your knuckle and let the spirits know you are in the garden, and then take a refreshing sip of water. As they continued following the paths, it felt so serene. There was much to look at. The ponds with koi fish and turtles, the trees and foliage, the rock formations, gardens, benches, and stepping-stones. As they were getting ready to cross the Heart Bridge, Skye stood back as Jason and Talia walked almost to the center of it, looking out over the large pond. Talia leaned against the red railing, and Jason stood behind her, wrapping his arms around her chest.

Skye was quick to capture that embrace, and then Jason leaned around as Talia turned and looked up at him with her beautiful eyes. He kissed her deeply, forgetting for a moment where they were. Again, Skye captured that moment. She was truly happy for Talia but also desired that kind of passion in her life, bringing a tear to her eye.

Skye walked toward them and Talia asked her if she would take Jason's phone and take a picture of the two of them. It was nice having someone help with photos like that. And then Jason did a selfie, having longer arms, with the three of them with the pond and trees behind. Skye didn't want to tell them that she had taken two beautiful photos of them and would do something special with those later on.

Continuing, they saw the waterfall at Mountainside. There's something about watching and listening to water as it gently flows down and over rocks. There's a peace about it.

And then there was one more bridge, called the Moon Bridge. It was a physical representation of life's trials, both difficult to walk up and down. Skye walked up the three steps, holding onto the railing, and before walking up any further, she stared out over the pond below. Her face showed a longing for someone special to wrap his arms around her as she rubbed one of her arms up and down. Jason was in the perfect position to snap a picture of Skye, unbeknownst to her.

Soon Talia was walking up behind Skye, and Jason called to them to look his way, taking a photo. Following the path around, he joined them. Here were a couple more photo opportunities. Knowing that Talia was going to upload all of their pictures onto the digital picture frame later, Jason didn't want the single photo of Skye in with the rest of them. Taking that brief moment, he sent the picture of both girls and then Skye alone to Cole, simply texting they were enjoying the day with her. He then moved that picture to his email and deleted it off of his phone.

He didn't know who had been in Cole's life before. It was a week or two ago, but there was the start of a conversation that had been interrupted by the fire bell. It was how Cole left his answer, and the look on his face, but Jason knew there was a story there, just maybe not a good one.

They worked their way back toward the entrance and then headed for the parking lot. Once inside Skye's jeep, they sat for several minutes, letting that wave of calm continue.

"This was an absolute treasure, Skye. Thank you," Talia said.

"That goes double for me as well. This was amazing," Jason said.

"You're welcome. I came here last fall, and I was blown away by what I saw. I spent several hours wandering and sitting and looking," Skye said, smiling. "I did come away feeling more peaceful." Then Skye thought to herself, *Maybe today there was a little more clarity about what I want for my life.*

◌

Talia's phone buzzed, and she looked at the message. It was a text message from Grandma Jean that read, *Change is inevitable.*

Talia handed her phone back to Jason so he could see.

"Is everything alright?" Skye asked.

"Yes, it's fine. It was my grandmother," Jason said, handing Talia back her phone.

They headed north on Interstate 5. There was one last stop Skye wanted to make before the end of the day, something she knew Talia and Jason would have never seen before. Skye had been to it several times and was awestruck by the black steel sculpture and what it possibly meant to the one who designed it. It was called *Changing Form*. It sits in the middle of a small public park called Kerry Park. The vantage point is on the south slope of Queen Ann Hill.

Anytime Skye had gone to the park, there were families and kids, and always lots of people taking photos of the incredible view of the entire Seattle skyline. You can see as far as Mount Rainier, Elliott Bay, Pudget Sound, and of course, you couldn't miss the iconic Space Needle. Skye herself captured different views either in the early morning when there was fog or late afternoon and evening sunsets, even after a rain shower. She smiled to herself, thinking this would be another unforgettable memory of Seattle for Talia and Jason. She hoped not too many people were around, as she just had an idea pop into her head.

As she drove to Kerry Park, she was able to parallel park allowing Talia and Jason to look right out their windows. Then, Skye opened her door, getting out, and Jason and Talia followed. There were only a handful of people now taking pictures as the three of them started walking toward the center of the park, where the structure stood tall. They saw several benches and large flower pots, but the structure itself was kind of weird, unusual, and yet amazing to look at. The brick that lay from the street to the scenic wall was in shades of rose gold with gray tiles here and there. The structure lay dead center, with six brick steps half encircling it to the top on the north and south sides and three brick steps on the east and west sides. It was stunning to see.

They first walked to the brick wall, looking at the marvelous view while taking photos of the city skyline and each other. Talia and Jason took turns looking through one of the two coin-op telescopes. Then Skye asked Talia and Jason if they would stand inside the form for a few pictures. She was inspired by something she saw not too awful long ago and wanted to try her hand at the image in her mind.

Positioning herself so that the Space Needle was to the left of the *Changing Form*, she had Jason and Talia face one another, with arms wrapped around each other and look toward the ocean, and then one of Jason kissing the top of Talia's head as the sun was setting on the horizon. After taking another picture or two, someone then passed by, and Skye asked if they would take a photo of the three of them.

When they were ready to leave, heading past this anomaly and toward Skye's jeep, Jason looked back and saw the nameplate on the north side of the structure near the ground. He walked back to the base of the steps and took a photo to remember it. It said *Changing Form*, Doris Chase, 1969.

Talia and Skye stood close to him. Jason said, "I think it was quite appropriate that we stopped here now. We've all had changes happen in our lives, good and bad. I don't think things happen by accident." He looked specifically at Talia with a loving smile and then kissed her. Then he looked at Skye and said, "Maybe this whole trip will have turned out to be a win–win." And he left it at that.

⁂

Arriving at their hotel, the three headed up to Talia and Jason's room. Putting the lights on, Talia got the digital picture frame out, along with the cord. She wanted to upload her and Jason's photos, but food first. They decided on something fairly simple, so they called Panera Bread, which was close to the hotel. After uploading their photos, they started showing Skye from the beginning. Their only interruption was when their food came, and they ate their dinner while looking at the pictures.

Skye asked questions about their Europe trip and said many "wow's." They could see it in her eyes, wanting to experience something like that. She loved Jason's proposal and the wedding pictures and everything that followed. There were so many fun and wonderful photos of Talia and Jason, his grandmother, and the girls. And then Talia got a little embarrassed, as there were several pictures that Jason took of her pregnant belly from side to side when she pulled her top up over her stomach, showing the slight protruding roundness. Jason smiled at her, kissed her, and told her how beautiful she was.

When they finished with the last photos, they sat back as it started on a loop. It was now after nine o'clock.

"I should go so you two can pack," Skye said. "What time does your flight leave?"

"We have a United Airlines flight, and it leaves at 10:10a.m., so we need to be at the airport no later than 8:45 a.m.," Jason said.

"What if I pick you up at about 8:00? That way, we have plenty of driving time to the airport. I'm not sure what traffic will be like."

"Sounds good," Talia said. She stood up and hugged Skye. Jason did the same. They exchanged phone numbers. "You text me when you get home, so we know you're safe." Talia already had the mom thing down pat. Walking Skye to the door, they said good night, and she left.

Laying their luggage on the bed, they both did some repacking. The digital frame was left plugged in and would be put in Talia's shoulder bag in the morning, as she wanted to look through the pictures again on the plane. Jason's medic backpack lay on the table and was ready to go as well. When Skye left, it didn't seem that long, but she texted almost forty minutes later that she was home safe and was heading to bed. She'd text them in the morning when she was leaving to pick them up.

☙

Skye texted Talia that she was on her way. Jason and Talia were ready to go and decided to check out, then have some breakfast and wait for Skye in the lobby. Minutes before Skye was to show up, Jason looked at Talia with a guilty look on his face.

"What?" Talia asked.

"I think parts of you are rubbing off on me," Jason said, with a silly grin on his face.

"Why?" Talia asked.

"I took two photos at the Moon Bridge. One with Skye, and then one with you and Skye. Before we left there, I sent Cole both photos. I texted him that we had another wonderful day with her," Jason said.

"That was it," Talia said. "Nothing else—"

"Morning, you two," Skye said, noting the weird look on both of their faces.

"Morning, Skye," Talia said, standing up, as did Jason.

"So, are you ready to head to the airport?" Skye asked.

"We are. It would be nice to stay longer, but it's time to go home," Jason said.

"OK then," Skye smiled at them and turned, walking back out the door ahead of them. She didn't want them to see the sadness in her eyes. She felt like she was getting left behind, and she couldn't do anything about it.

◌

Heading down Interstate 405, there wasn't a lot of talking. Skye wasn't real familiar once getting to the airport in finding the right expressway to the United Airlines drop-off. She followed a few other cars that stopped by the United Airlines doors, and she did too. The girls stepped out onto the unloading curb as Jason pulled the luggage from the back and closed the jeep door. Skye thought, *This is it. They're leaving.* She tried not to show her tears and wiped them away.

Talia looked at Skye and said, "I'll text you when we board and when we get home, so you know we're safe. For now, this is our connection to each other. You call me or text me anytime you want."

Skye said, "And you do the same. I'm so grateful that you were here and that we got to spend this time together. I can't believe how much I missed you." She gave Talia a long hug. Both girls had tears. She turned toward Jason and gave him a hug, telling him thank you for helping her and to take good care of her best friend and that baby.

"Believe me, I will. They are both very precious to me, and I love them more than you will ever know," Jason said. Talia then kissed Skye on the cheek, gave one last hug, then pulled up the handle on her luggage and walked toward the door. Jason also gave a last hug.

Before walking through the sliding doors, Talia turned to Skye and said, "Hey best friend, I love you." And through the doors, she went.

Jason turned back to Skye and told her that maybe her next trip should be a permanent one going east. He smiled at her, and then he was gone as well.

ৎৎ   ೮ఠ

What events will take place in the lives of

Talia, Jason, Cole and Skye?

Sneak Peek of what's to come...

There are decisions that you make of your own accord, and sometimes decisions are made for you.

Have you ever wondered what your life would have been like had you taken that leap of faith and gone down a different path? We all wish we had a guidebook to follow step by step and then be allowed to accept what will be or change it freely.

Based on a single decision, like Talia after entering a contest where it took her to the west coast, and then having someone from her past come out of nowhere. Will we learn that Talia isn't the only one whose past has to be crossed? Life can be funny, or not, and it can change without notice. Sometimes, change is exactly what we need, whether we agree that it is for our highest good or takes us down a road that will challenge us to our very core.

Will Skye decide to leave behind what she's known for over half of her life, and look forward to something wonderful, even if she doesn't know what that looks like?

As for Cole, the volunteer firefighter and travel agent, after seeing a couple of photos of Skye, will he wonder if it's safe to have love in his life, someone who doesn't know his past, or will that safe place be found and turn deadly? The old saying, "Hell hath no fury, like a…" Could there be any hope that these two might be destined to be together? Is change really inevitable?

And Jason, this loving and devoted man who seems to have it all, is there someone from his past that will try and sever that love he has for his wife and unborn baby? Will his love stay strong, or waver and be tested? Can this unborn child be the tie that binds.

 Cß

If you would like to know when this third book will make its appearance and want to keep updated, you can email the author at *trishtitus.dyd@gmail.com*.

References, Resources, and Permission granted to use people and business names:

Memoirs from Korea, Grade, Louis.

Personal interview by Elyse Titus

SA – midwife from northern Utah

Anisha Moten, Carroll, Iowa

James Todd – Seattle, Washington

Ivar's Acres of Clams

1001 Alaskan Way, Pier 54
Seattle, WA 98104
(206) 624-6852

https://www.ivars.com/acres

Metsker Maps of Seattle

1511 First Ave.

Seattle, WA 98101

(800) 727-4430

www.metskers.com

Museum of History & Industry (MOHAI)

860 Terry Ave N,

Seattle, WA 98109

(206) 324-1126

https://mohai.org

Piroshky Piroshky

1908 Pike Place
Seattle, WA 98101
(206) 764-1000

www.piroshkybakery.com

The Crumpet Shop

1503 1st Ave
Seattle, WA 98101

http://thecrumpetshop.com

Theo Chocolate Factory

3400 Phinney Ave N
Seattle, WA 98103

www.TheoChocolate.com

Other interesting sights visited:

Argosy Cruises

**Changing Form – sculpture by Doris Chase, 1969
   (Kerry Park, Seattle, WA)**

Chihuly Garden and Glass

Fallen Firefighters Memorial

Garden of Remembrance

Kubota Garden

The Space Needle

The Tropical Butterfly House

Volunteer Conservatory Park

About The Author

Trish Titus was born and raised in the city of Carroll, in west central Iowa. Each year, her family went on vacation traveling throughout the US. It was her mom that had started her reading romance books back in high school, letting her imagination take over with dreams of love and adventure, and maybe one day writing a romance book herself. Writing seemed an impossibility during the next 44 years of working and raising a child on her own. The travel bug never let up, though, and neither did her desire to write her own romance stories.

Her first book was a non-fiction book, titled *DELILAH and Others Like Her.* There are nineteen beautiful stories shared about loving and losing a beloved pet, along with photos and lessons learned from many contributors, including this author's beloved cat, Delilah. She is currently working on a second pet loss book.

Trish loves writing about romance. She says she's still waiting for hers, maybe one day soon. People love romance novels because they take you on a journey of finding that perfect mate, your one true love, no matter where you are, or what obstacles have to be overcome. The question she asks is, how many of us have made a long list of the qualities we're looking for, just to name a few: a strong healthy body, beautiful eyes, a great smile, a sense of humor, kind and caring, understanding, respectful, well educated, enjoys life and animals, and it doesn't hurt to be well off financially. But always on that list is finding the one that will love us for who we are and that we can love them back.

With her first novel, *A Miracle or Two for Christmas*, she took her readers on a journey abroad where fate finally brought two people together after twenty years, and it was true love.

Her latest novel, *A Win - Win*, introduces a few new characters who may or may not eventually find this same type of love from two different places. Is fate on the move again?

She felt that taking her travel experiences and illuminating them would help others dream of the day when they could go on a journey, and perhaps someone special would come into their lives.

Throughout her writing of these first two romance novels, she conveys that she wants people to design their dream for the life they want, and with whom, and be open to all possibilities. Here's to love.

www.ingramcontent.com/pod-product-compliance
Lightning Source LLC
Chambersburg PA
CBHW072053190726
48294CB00005B/1487